By the same author:

Kate Gallagher and the Bexus Prophecy

Kate Gallagher AND
THE HORNSHURST TALISMAN

ALAN CUMMING

PARTRIDGE
A Penguin Random House Company

To order additional copies of this book, contact
Toll Free 800 101 2657 (Singapore)
Toll Free 1 800 81 7340 (Malaysia)
orders.singapore@partridgepublishing.com

www.partridgepublishing.com/singapore

*For Keegan, Cameron
and Brayden*

CONTENTS

PROLOGUE

June 13, 1991.

lood leaked from a hole in Charlie Hughes's back and settled in a pool beneath his body as he stared up at the ceiling and wondered what had gone wrong. A voice inside his head that had started singing *Happy Deathday, dear Charlie, Happy Deathday to you!* didn't help matters either. He squeezed his eyes against the growing pain in his chest and tried to concentrate.

Charlie had begun his life of crime as a gofer for a local bookie who ran numbers for the Gökhan family. This was a Turkish gang who had colonised an immigrant sector in the East End of London. The Gökhans were recent arrivals to England, but were exceedingly ambitious, and this required a degree of vicious ruthlessness that splintered the existing gang territories, and created the sort of temporary vacuum at the top that they were only too delighted to fill. None of this came cheaply, so anyone built like a brick wall, and who lacked morals and conscience, and who was looking for work could virtually name his price.

Charlie clearly fitted that bill and named his price. The Gökhans looked at him and laughed, but they hired him and promised to review his salary package subject to his performance. In the years that followed, he rose to the rank of chief enforcer within the family and the only thing that outstripped his salary was his fearsome reputation. If the Gökhans wanted you gone, Charlie would be the last person to bid you farewell.

When Ecebay Gökhan wanted his brother and partner-in-crime, Nazim, to disappear as well, Charlie's loyalty was tested but not strained. Nazim ended up in tiny pieces spread across Britain, and as a result, Charlie finally got a slice of the action he'd been hoping for. Ecebay sanctioned armed robbery as long as it was off the Gökhan turf because local businesses paid exorbitant protection fees. Ecebay was a thug, but he was a good businessman too.

Charlie assembled a gang with three of his childhood friends. These were men he could trust and who were still a little in awe of him—men from the meaner streets of Hackney. Over a period of twelve months, they held up seventeen jewellery stores across London and made off with goods valued by insurance companies at more than five million pounds. When the gang turned its attention to banks, the police set up a special investigative squad at Scotland Yard, and when one robbery turned violent and resulted in the death of a cashier, armed response teams in the form of SCO19 Police Firearms Unit, and the SFO Specialist Firearms Officers, were called in to assist.

Detectives in Scotland Yard called in more than a few favours. Snitches and touts were pushed to their limits, but one scrap of information after another tied into other snippets, rumours and conjectures, and the whole patchy picture pointed to Benny Hardcastle and his recent good fortune. The police pulled Benny in to 'help them with their inquiries'. Benny, naturally, was reluctant at first but, in the end, the power of persuasion helped change his mind.

It takes a thief to catch a thief, according to collective wisdom. The day the West Dulwich branch of NatWest bank was to be hit, Benny Hardcastle phoned in with a broken wrist, so he was unable to drive the motor. The heist was too late to postpone; months of meticulous planning had gone in, so Charlie called in Pimples, his back up driver.

Charlie and his mob hit the bank at ten minutes past ten. They burst through the doors brandishing sawn-off shotguns and a couple of Glock semi-automatic handguns. Even as Charlie was screaming, "Everybody down on the floor! Now! Get down! Get down!" the little voice in the back of his head was remarking on how the bank seemed busier than expected for this time in the morning, and how there didn't seem to be too many women amongst the customers. But Charlie had more urgent things to worry about than these anomalies, so he fired a shotgun blast into the ceiling for good measure and strode towards the manager's closed door, intending to request the combination of the safe.

His back was turned, so he didn't register the movement behind him, although he did hear the click of an opening door. He was unable to ignore the cry of, "Police! Freeze! Throw down your weapons!" just as he reached for the door handle to the manager's office. He spun immediately and saw the stream of uniformed, black helmeted, armed police rushing into the room waving stubby semi-automatic weapons. He also noticed the stunned, wide-eyed shock of the other two masked gunmen who dropped their weapons and raised their hands in surrender. Some of the customers were picking themselves off the floor, and reaching beneath their jackets for pistols.

Goddam! We've been stitched up! was Charlie's first thought. *Hardcastle!* was his second.

He whipped up the shotgun and pulled the trigger. The noise was deafening, but almost immediately, one of the customers was blown off his feet as the front of his jacket was shredded by the peppered blast. He skidded across the tiled floor on his back, but then tried to rise again unsteadily. *He was wearing body armour!* Charlie swore, ditched the shotgun, and turned back to the door, twisted the handle, and shouldered it open. He expected the door to be pocked and splintered with returning fire as he dove through the gap, but the police were restrained, almost subdued. He immediately discovered why.

Cowering down behind a large desk was a small bespectacled man with a terrible ginger comb-over. Squatting beside him was a taller woman whose greying hair had been pulled back tightly into a bun at the back of her head. The woman screamed and dropped out of sight behind the desk while the man beside her raised both his hands above the desk and squeaked, "Don't shoot! Don't shoot!"

Charlie Hughes smiled and tugged the handgun from his waist belt. There was one chance, after all. He strode around to the back of the desk and grabbed the terrified manager by the back of his jacket. He placed the short, cold barrel against the man's right temple and stood him up.

"I've got hostages!" he screamed through the partially open door. "Anyone comes near the door, I shoot! I see any movement out there, I shoot!"

He jammed the pistol hard against the man's skull and hissed, "Tell them!"

"He's right!" the manager croaked, and he began to cry. "Don't shoot! Please!" Tears streamed down his cheeks.

"Easy! Easy!" came the muffled reply. "Nobody is going to try anything. Just calm down and we can try to talk this through without anybody getting hurt."

"Back off, and get me someone I can negotiate with. Someone with the authority to make things happen quickly!" Charlie called. "Else someone is going to have to explain away the bodies left behind."

"Okay. We're working on it, but calm down! Don't do anything rash!"

Charlie sneered. He wasn't afraid. He had two hostages to work with. He could shoot one of them in the leg, and show the cops he meant business. He knew about hostage negotiations:

knew that the negotiators stalled for time and that they would try to wear him down, all the while getting the assault squad ready to rush him. Well, he wasn't about to wait that long. A car to the airport, a small plane with one pilot on standby, maybe a parachute or two—he'd have a little time to figure things out.

He dragged the manager backwards, over towards the window. He glanced out and saw several police cars and an armoured vehicle parked in a line while his own getaway vehicle sat abandoned with no sign of Pimples. Nevertheless, he relaxed slightly. He knew the cops. Nobody was going to try anything yet.

The grey-haired secretary slugged him from behind with a paperweight, so hard she cracked his skull. He almost passed out as he let go of the manager and brought his left hand up to feel where she'd hit him. His palm came away bloody and matted with a few black hairs. Lights were flashing behind his eyes as he staggered around and saw her standing, holding the brass weight in one hand with her other hand covering her mouth in horror. She'd made him truly angry. She shouldn't have done that! He raised his gun and pointed it towards her face.

The gunshot wasn't so loud, but it took a millisecond longer for him to realise it had been fired from outside the room. The window glass shattered inwards in a thousand sparkling shards, and the bullet passed through his chest and embedded itself in the opposite wall. The gun flew from Charlie's outstretched hand and clattered noisily onto the floor tiles as he lurched forward from the impact, dropped to his knees, and then slithered all the way down to the cold floor.

He managed to roll on to his back, felt the pain grow, heard a strange gurgling sound as blood began to fill his lungs, and listened while the little voice he'd previously ignored sang *Happy Deathday* to him. The ceiling was made of white acoustic tiles, the ones with little holes drilled through them. The holes fascinated him, and he was annoyed when first one dark shape, then more, crowded his vision. Faces—blurred faces—stared down at him. He tried to laugh, but blood spat from his lips and the laugh turned into a grizzled, choking cough and a struggle to breathe.

"Someone get the paramedics, quick!" he heard someone yell in the distance.

"Too late," were the last words that he heard as the room grew dimmer. Then someone turned out the lights altogether.

Charlie Hughes opened his eyes and stared up at a bright blue sky. His head pounded for some reason, and he felt light-headed and nauseous. He tried to sit up, but his world seemed to spin, and he leaned to one side to be sick. He dry-retched; nothing came up. He lay down very gingerly and closed his eyes and planted his palms in the dirt to try and stop the weird, spinning sensation.

Charlie's senses returned as the feeling of nausea slowly subsided. One arm brushed against his body and felt the smooth hard skin of his belly. But, where before there was a mass of black, wiry hair, now there was nothing but skin. Skin! He lifted his head and looked down on his naked frame.

Where was he? He tried sitting once again, keeping his head between his legs just in case. When he felt well enough to risk another glance, he looked around.

He was sitting at the side of a dirt road, resting on a patch of grass. He tried to remember how he had gotten there, what had happened to him. There was a dull ache and constant throbbing at the back of his head that was strangely familiar, but that was it. He checked the rest of his body for bruises and got the shock of his life.

His skin was glowing. It was patchy brown mostly, black in some places across his chest and belly and down his legs. But he was giving off a dull light that could be seen even under the brilliant glare of the sun. His skin seemed to be pulsing with this strange light as if connected to a faulty resistor in an electrical circuit: sometimes brighter, sometimes no glow whatsoever. There was an angry redness to the glow as well that seemed to turn the dun skin to a copper colour at its brightest.

My name is Charlie Hughes, he recalled in a moment of clarity. He tried to recall other events in his life, but his throbbing head made it impossible to concentrate. In the end, he gave up. He stood slowly, and although he felt shaky and unsteady, he was able to move about. He checked the area for his clothing. He must have dropped it somewhere nearby.

He peered under the low-lying bush that skirted the edge of the dirt road. Nothing. Not a stitch! He racked his memory to think of the reason for his predicament. Drunk! He had to have been drunk beyond belief. It was all some sort of joke. His friends had undressed him and dumped him out in the 'sticks' and left him to find his own way home. That would explain the headache: a hangover of giant proportions. He felt the rage within him rise. Some friends! They would live to regret it, humiliating Charlie Hughes in this way! They wouldn't be laughing at him for much longer!

Something else clicked for him. The barely suppressed rage that burned a hole in his gut was familiar also, like spotting a single friend in amongst a sea of strangers. He revelled in the thrill of this powerful sensation. Yes, he was a hard man, one to be feared; he remembered this.

He noticed the sun again. It was larger than normal, and bright orange. He'd never seen that before and it startled him. It made him uneasy once more, and he needed to do something to keep his mind occupied.

First things first! he thought. He had to find some clothing—if someone else happened to be wearing it, then too bad. Then, find his way home again. Home? He tried to concentrate, heard a tiny voice in the back of his mind. Lumdum . . . Lungtun . . . London! Yes, London, that was it! His memory was coming back slowly.

He looked up and down the road, which was deserted. Right or left? He chose right and began walking down the middle of it. He stumbled on a couple of sharp stones but oddly enough, the pain was fleeting and when he stopped to examine the soles of his feet, there was no bruising; just dust from the road.

He hadn't been walking long before he came to a path that led into the bush at the side of the road. He stopped because he'd heard the distant murmur of voices. Someone was coming along that path, somebody fully clothed. Well, he'd see about that.

He ducked along the path about ten feet from the road, to a point where the track passed to one side of a dense head-high shrub. He concealed himself behind it and waited for the voices to draw nearer.

His timing was perfect. He stepped out into the path, blocking it, and came face to face with two men; both dressed in some kind of black uniform with a strange red insignia above the chest, containing the letter 'V'. Both carried short sticks, like walking canes, thickened at one bulbous end and tapering to a blunt point at the other. One of the men also wore a short sword, sheathed in a leather scabbard on his belt. The good news was that one of the men was about the same size as Charlie.

He smiled, keeping his hands loose at his sides, and said, "I'm very sorry, but I'm going to need those clothes. Would you mind?"

The smaller of the two men was quickest to react. He swung his little stick up and tried to point it at Charlie. It was like waving a ring of garlic at a vampire—next to useless. Charlie snatched the staff out of his hands in one swift movement, then reversed the tug and turned it into a powerful thrust that thumped butt first into the man's chest and sent him sprawling backwards along the path. He turned the thrust into a sideways swing in one smooth movement and caught the second soldier in the side of the head. The man promptly sank like a stone and collapsed into the bush beside the path.

Charlie dropped the stick he was holding and grabbed the man by the boots, pulling him out of the bush. He tried to sit up, but Charlie pushed him back with his heel.

"Sorry, me old China," he said by way of an apology, "but I need these more than you," and he began to undo the man's tunic. He caught a movement from the corner of his eye, and turned to face the smaller soldier who had scrambled to his feet again.

"Don't make me hurt you," warned Charlie, still squatting above the prostrate soldier in the dust. The little soldier didn't seem too fazed by this threat, however. He even flashed Charlie a crooked grin.

Charlie paused and frowned. *Strange,* he thought. That was when he heard a low, wicked growl behind him that sent a chill shooting up his back. His neck suddenly felt terribly exposed.

Charlie turned ever so slowly until he was staring at a massive hairy beast, the size of a lioness. It looked a bit like a dog, but unlike any dog Charlie had seen before. It had a broad, elongated snout like that of an alligator, and the gaping jaws exposed rows of inwardly curving pointed teeth. The head lolled from side to side as if the effort to keep it upright was just too much to bear.

Two red eyes glared out from deep recesses concealed by hair either side of the snout, and they were looking directly at him. The beast's ears were folded back along its head, twitching and quivering, and it took one step forward. Charlie saw the curved claws, yellowed with decay; he heard the *clack!* as they scraped over a rock buried in the road. The back of the beast was arched in a hump, made larger by the ridge of bristled black hair standing fully erect. A pink tongue flapped briefly, licking at the ribbons of streaky saliva that swayed from the lower jaw. It gave another menacing, throaty growl as it stalked to within a foot of Charlie's lowered head. Charlie could smell the putrescent breath in his face. He slumped his shoulders in defeat.

Once the larger soldier had recovered, he picked up his fallen staff and brought it down in a vicious chop on to the back of

Charlie's head, right at the spot that seemed to be the source of his original headache. When Charlie came to for a second time that day, he was bound at the wrists by a strange glowing cord that looked like a rope of blue electrical energy. Another of these cords was looped around his neck, originating from the end of the long stick that one of the soldiers carried. The noose was tight and uncomfortable, and when he tried to hook his fingers between the binding and his neck, there was a sudden hiss, and a shock, like a heavy static electrical jolt, and the cord tightened immediately. The two soldiers laughed while the beast stared malevolently up at him, growling softly all the while.

Charlie Hughes began his first day on Bexus as a trussed and beaten prisoner.

It only took a week for Charlie to discover he was dead, and the shock of that news served to keep him docile and manageable. He was placed in a work gang, shackled alongside others, and he used steel hammers and wedges to carve out large stone blocks from a quarry, day in and day out. Over the next two months, he steadily regained memories from his time on Earth, and he grew increasingly belligerent and aggressive. Only after he'd attacked a work overseer—a brute named Petrovius—was he hauled before a disciplinary committee. He remained defiant, insubordinate and argumentative despite the threat of execution that hung over his head, and in the end, the committee favoured mercy, reasoning that these characteristics could be better exploited. He was summarily withdrawn from the work detail and inducted into that branch of the army from which prospective bodyguards were occasionally pulled.

Lord Varak ruled almost all of Bexus. He was a dictator who ruled with an iron fist, and who seemed to have cracked the code for immortality. He'd conquered much of the planet in the four or so hundred years of his recorded history, having amassed immense armies and crushed all opposition in his path. He was a despot entirely without mercy, and he was skilled in the application of fear. His reputation alone kept any thoughts of rebellion totally repressed, and he trusted no one.

Charlie sighed. He was back to being a gofer once more. In his mind, this guy Varak wasn't too different from Ecebay Gökhan; it was just a question of scale. Varak had acquired a much larger territory than the few square miles in the East End of London. However, he figured that the ladder to success would be the same, and he set about hauling himself up, hand over hand, one rung at a time.

It wasn't that long before Charlie's penchant for gratuitous violence came to Varak's notice. He was cautiously inducted into the inner cadre of personal bodyguards, but he remained aloof and he isolated himself from the others. He wasn't there to make friends. He made it abundantly clear where his only loyalty lay and never questioned orders.

It had taken Charlie a further fourteen years before he was once again top of the pops within a brutally repressive organisation. After an incident in which a lone woman assassin managed to penetrate Varak's first security cordon and almost made it as far as the inner chamber of the castle, the current Head of Security was held accountable and publicly executed in one of Varak's many manic fits. The vacancy fell to Charlie Hughes, who inwardly smiled as the new badges of office were pinned and stitched to his uniform.

Charlie became a made man once again.

CHAPTER 1

Six Months Previously

C harlie Hughes wiped his hands clean with a towel. He had finished the interrogation, and there had been nothing more to learn. There had been talk of restlessness and unruliness in the northwest provinces. The city state of Hornshurst was like a pot of porridge on the stove, a slow moving mass that seethed beneath the surface, occasionally bursting before settling back to a simmer. Three times in the past fourteen years, Varak had sent his army out to quell the disturbances, and parts of the city had been literally decimated; one in ten of its citizens arbitrarily executed.

Each time, the populace had been cowed into submission and after most of the invading army had withdrawn, isolated garrisons were left behind to monitor the situation. Charlie received regular reports from these outposts, and had established a covert network of spies to infiltrate the underground resistance movement. He heard about any attempt by the resistance to organise an uprising against the puppet government of city administrators well beforehand, and these enemies of the state would be whisked away in the early hours of morning. Charlie was back in the

1

disappearance game; he had been nicknamed 'The Magician' by the people of Hornshurst because of this ability to cause people to vanish. It was a name he was proud of.

He placed the tip of his staff against the neck of the prisoner hanging from electrical bindings against the wall and mumbled *Exstinguere!* in the same tone as he would have said, *So long* or, *I've really gotta go.* A shaft of blue light sparked briefly from the tip, and the prisoner jerked spasmodically. His eyes flew open, and his mouth formed a perfect silent scream. Then he disappeared; the only traces left behind were outward arcing plumes of dull blue smoke and the remains of his ragged clothing fluttering to the floor. The Magician had performed another trick.

Charlie began the laborious climb from the dungeons to the main floors of the castle. He passed through several large rooms and crossed the cavernous central chamber with Varak's throne at one end, looming like a brooding sentinel in the flickering gloom, painted by the weak light of burning torches lining the walls. The noise of his boots echoed in the vast space as he hurried across the smooth marbled flagstones. Sentries at each exit saw him coming and snapped to attention as he passed. Charlie still privately revelled in the military protocols; the Gökhan Empire could have benefitted from a similar structure.

He climbed another set of stairs and turned left along a short corridor, coming to a halt outside a pair of massive timber doors, inset with a delicate filigree of silver. Two guards stood to either side of the doors, eyes focused straight ahead but fully aware of Charlie in their periphery. Charlie paused and took a deep breath to steady himself. This was the only time he genuinely felt nervous and ill at ease. He coughed quietly to clear his throat, then stepped up and rapped sharply on the door. He waited, heard the muffled command to enter, and then twisted the ornate brass lever and passed on through.

An immense four-poster bed dominated Varak's chamber, sitting on a raised step that bisected the room. At one end, a roaring fire blazed inside a stone fireplace tall enough for Charlie to walk beneath without needing to bend. Logs crackled and hissed, and sparks flew out and spluttered on the brick hearth. The fire was the only source of light, but Charlie could still make out the hulking form of the paranoid dictator, slumped and brooding in an armchair pulled near the fire.

Varak was staring into the flames, lost in thought. He was becoming more preoccupied with one remaining outpost of rebellion, the impregnable, walled city of Hogarth, to the west. The way to Hogarth lay across a vast arid desert that supported little life beyond that which struggled to survive in the rancid pools of slime; tiny oases of decay that punctuated the shifting sands and razor-sharp rocks. The desert ended abruptly at the outer edge of a belt of thick vegetation and towering trees, known as the Great Forest.

This forest had proved impregnable and was peppered with wetlands and mires. Dangerous creatures, both plant and animal, lived beneath the canopy in a constant battle to survive. Most travellers who ventured beyond the verdant edges never returned. The forest was a natural barrier that had foiled Varak's earlier attempts to subdue the city, which stood out like a painful boil on the skin of Varak's military campaigns.

The only way through was to be a full frontal assault on the forest: send companies of marauding scouts to map a path through, then follow up with engineers and woodsmen who would flatten the path into a road wide enough to cater for an army on the march. Already, most of Varak's vast army had been ordered to march across the desert and set up camp at the edge of the forest to wait for him to join it.

This campaign was uppermost in Varak's mind for one further reason. Located in the hills behind Hogarth was a cave, a truly unique cave. Imprinted on one of the walls in the church-like inner chamber was a succession of images, which documented Varak's successful crusades over the previous five centuries. What made them unique was the fact that each image *pre-empted* each victory, like a prophecy that had come to pass. But during Charlie's time, a new image had suddenly appeared. It was a golden girl, and it signalled a barrier to Varak's march towards total domination.

Varak had dispatched spies into the town, and news had returned of a disturbing development. A golden girl had indeed been located and brought safely into the city. Even now, her battle skills were being honed in preparation for the day that she would be expected to face Varak. If this were another prophecy about to come true, it spelled the end for the dictator. Charlie Hughes's job was to make certain it didn't happen.

"Excuse me, my Lord," Charlie said as he tipped his head in deference.

Varak looked up at him. He was an immense man, once broad and strong, who seemed to have slipped and wilted with age. His features were puffy, and his eyes burned from two holes that pierced the flesh of his face. He looked like a man who had sought refuge in hard drugs, and displayed the addict's same erratic mood swings that made him as unpredictable. However, he looked subdued and withdrawn.

"What is it?" he snapped.

"The Hornshurst prisoner, m'Lud. The rumours are false as we'd expected. There will be no outbreaks of resistance within the city."

"You're sure of that?" Varak asked. His questions were always loaded; he didn't like to hear bad news, and Charlie knew he'd be held accountable for his answer.

"Yes, sire," he replied. "In the end the prisoner was—" he searched for the right term, "—entirely cooperative." Charlie appreciated the irony of understatement. He continued, "I have to say I'm still a little concerned."

"Why?"

"Hornshurst is a big place. If the people there could just get organised enough, they could field an army to match our own, maybe even larger. I'm worried they might take advantage of the fact our own army is headed west, towards Hogarth. We can't afford to fight a battle on two fronts. We'd be stretched too thinly."

"Are you questioning my military strategy, Mr. Hughes?"

"I'm concerned for your own safety and success, my Lord. I would be remiss in my duties if I neglected to mention this."

Varak smiled at him for the first time that evening.

"Such honesty is refreshing, Mr. Hughes. But let me show you something."

He reached down and picked up an object sitting on the floor beside his chair. It had been covered with a dark purple velvet cloth and had been so unobtrusive that Charlie hadn't spotted it. Varak sat the object on his knee and carefully removed the cloth.

He was nursing a small, stumpy figurine that glinted in the reflected firelight. Charlie first thought it had been cast from pure gold, but when he looked more closely, he could see that it was made of a different kind of metal, like burnished pewter. It was moulded in the shape of a man wearing a highly ornate kind of headdress that appeared to be constructed from a collection of animal effigies: spiders, monkeys, jackal-like dogs, snakes and lizards, all intertwined, that sat perched on the figure's head and cascaded down either side of his protruding ears. His eyes were wide hollow orbits, stuffed with two enormous emeralds, and his open mouth lent him an eternal look of mild surprise. Coils of wire hung beneath the headpiece, draping down like dreadlocks, and came to rest above a semicircular block necklace made from chunks of embedded lapis.

He appeared to be holding a rectangular box against his chest. His arms were crooked, and each hand was curved up in a delicate gesture of thumb touching forefinger, resembling the Buddhist Mudra, the *cincihna*. The arms pressed the box against his chest. In the space between the two hands, there was a red ruby in the shape of a heart inset into the shining metal.

The remainder of the figure was ornately detailed, down to the flowing robes and the sandals covering his feet. It looked pretty. It looked as if it had been pulled from the tomb of a Mayan emperor. It looked downright harmless.

"What is it?" Charlie asked. He wondered how this metallic doll bore any relation to the possible threat of invasion. Perhaps the appearance of this Hogarth golden girl was affecting Varak after all.

"This is the Hornshurst *Toki-Moai*," Varak said, and his eyes greedily caressed the icon.

"I don't understand."

"*Toki-Moai*. It is the name given to any object that can attract unseen forces, universal powers that are responsible for the direction your future will take—forces dictating your health, your success, your path forward—and possession of it will place you in command of these powers. This is Hornshurst's talisman." Varak whispered this last sentence reverently while his fingers gently caressed the idol's headgear.

"Which you now have."

"Which I now have."

"But . . . surely they can just make another one. They must have kept the mould."

"Aah, but they can't, you see. This is one of a kind. The elders and alchemists of Hornshurst discovered a way to ensnare all the wisdom and knowledge of its citizens. Those memories, stretching thousands of years back, have all been stored somehow within this figure. Memories which made their city the most powerful in its heyday were able to be tapped and used by a select few elder druids. This is my ace-in-the-hole. As long as I hold this, the armies of Hornshurst won't dare rise against me, for fear of losing it entirely. So, no, Mr. Hughes, we need not fear an attack against our flanks."

Charlie licked his dry lips and hesitated before asking the next question.

"Have you thought about using it for yourself? You would be truly unstoppable."

Varak turned his gaze to his security chief and stared at him between hooded lids, searching for any signs of sublime treachery. The silence between the two grew, and Charlie had to resist the urge to look away.

Finally, Varak said, "The talisman is protected by a series of three locks. All those who know the combination have been long hidden away from my grasp, and, believe me, I *have* tried to find them." He smiled again. "But, really, it's only a matter of time."

He reached forward and grasped one of the folded arms between his fingers. Pulled gently. The arm swung away from the body, pivoting at the shoulder.

"One," said Varak.

He repeated the action on the other arm, which swung open as well. The figure looked as if it were waiting for an embrace.

"Two," said Varak. He looked at Charlie. "One to go."

Charlie watched as the tiny arms were folded back in place across the chest, and the velvet covering replaced. He wondered what Varak did with the talisman and glanced about the room while Varak was bending to stand the doll beside his chair once again. He noticed one of the rugs in the far corner of the room was slightly skewed, and one corner was folded underneath as if the whole thing had recently been moved. He quickly looked away again before Varak sat back upright.

"Anything else, Mr. Hughes?"

"The arrangements for the Hogarth campaign. I have assigned ten of the palace guards to accompany you at all time. Their instructions are never to leave your side unless by your expressed orders. To get at you, the girl will first have to pass through them."

Varak grunted his satisfaction. He favoured the human shield approach.

"One more thing. The girl is mine. She is to be taken alive, if possible. Disarmed, certainly. But mine to dispose of."

"Are you certain you want to take that risk, my Lord?" Charlie asked. "If the prophecy is true, she will triumph. Why run the risk?"

Again Varak smiled. "I have a spy in their inner circle. There have been new developments. The girl's image on the wall is being overshadowed by one of me. She is growing weaker while I grow stronger. The prophecy is changing. This is why we are making the move now. By the time we are camped outside their city, she'll be gone from the wall. I feel it. I know it! I *will* destroy her!"

Charlie nodded. He wouldn't want to be in her shoes, come the day.

"Then, that's all, my Lord" he said.

"Good. See to it that the men will be ready by first light. I leave tomorrow." He stood, facing Charlie, and placed one oversized paw on Charlie's shoulder. "Chamberlain MacNeill will be coming with me. I will leave the city in your care, Mr. Hughes. Look after it while I'm gone." The hand momentarily squeezed Charlie's shoulder in a vice-like grip, and then relaxed again. He had been warned.

"Thank you, my Lord. Safe travels," Charlie said, then bowed and turned and left the bedchamber. He pulled the door closed behind him, then leaned against it and blew out his breath. Neither of the two guards reacted.

He made his way towards his own bedroom at the other end of the corridor. He was surprised that Varak had chosen to show him the talisman. Still, Charlie firmly believed there was never such a thing as too much information, and so he stored that fragment in the back of his head.

The following morning, he stood wrapped in a woollen cape which warded off the chill from the cold desert night, and looked down from the ramparts on the small, armed column with Varak at its head, riding on gigantic lizard-like beasts the size of a horse.

The red and black insignia fluttered on pennants as the column filed through the gates and began a steady loping run out into the desert, kicking up a cloud of powdery, yellow dust in its wake. He continued to watch until the tiny figures could no longer be seen, then made his way indoors to hunker beside the blazing fire once more. He had no idea that this was to be the last time he would lay eyes on the cruel despot.

CHAPTER 2

The Present.

The news of Varak's demise and the defeat of his army without a battle having taken place spread across Bexus like a wildfire. The first of Varak's retreating troops to leave the Great Forest on the return trip home had barely left the shelter of the majestic towering trees before messengers were collapsing with exhaustion inside the gates of Hornshurst.

A cohort of Varak's soldiers policing the town dragged the first of these runners from the square, but as more arrived bearing the same news, the occupying forces quickly retreated to safety behind their garrison walls.

It was as if a lid had been blown from a pressure cooker. At first, groups of dazed looking citizens crept from their houses into the streets, normally bustling with black uniformed troops. The pavements and street corners were deserted; not a soldier in sight. As the realization dawned on the populace, a mood of relief and jubilation swept like a fever through the city, to be followed by one of growing outrage and bitterness towards the occupying forces. The crowd found voices to fan the fires of hatred, and they moved like an incoming tide, grabbing whatever weapons they could lay hands on as they surged through the streets towards the section of the city that had been walled apart and which served as the garrison for Varak's troops.

The reinforced gates were barred shut, and lines of helmeted heads looked down from the battlements across the sea of angry citizens screaming obscenities and threats at the soldiers. These soldiers were heavily outnumbered, but also heavily armed and well fortified. A few enraged people had already tried to charge the gates and had been blasted into oblivion, empty piles of clothing the only evidence of their foolhardiness. The situation quickly became a stalemate with tensions rising to breaking point, and was about to turn into a horrific massacre.

There was some jostling amongst the crowd, easily seen from the top of the walls. The defending soldiers scanned the disturbance, expecting the spark that would ignite the crowd, fearful in those final few moments before the onslaught. The crowd appeared to be parting reluctantly as a small group pushed their way to the front and burst through to the open killing field in front of the walls.

At their head was a woman. She was tall and slim, and her auburn hair was pulled tight in a thick braid that ran beyond the nape of her neck. She appeared to be supremely athletic. She was wearing a sleeveless top, and her bare arms were brown and sinewy, suggesting strength beyond their size. A black leather vest that wrapped about her torso was laced tight at the back. She wore a short, pleated leather skirt that fell midway along her thighs, and her legs were encased in black tights and high boots made of supple black leather. She was every inch a warrior and was instantly recognised by the crowd whose frenzied cries died away to harsh muttering, then to a reluctant silence.

She strode out into the middle of the clearing and kicked at the loose piles of scattered clothing in the dust. The soldiers along the wall trained their staffs on her, but if she were aware of this fact, she showed no interest, no fear.

"Is this what you want?" she addressed the crowd, "because if so, here is where it will end for you."

Someone in the crowd jeered. "Are you here to fight or here to talk, Siobhan?"

The woman named Siobhan lifted her chin and scanned the crowd of faces.

"That's the voice of Torsten Fassbinder. I'd know that nasal whine anywhere. Torsten! Where are you? My god, man! Is that you way at the back? That's not where the fighting is done. Come forward, man! Let him through please."

Her voice was pleasant, familiar, and some of the crowd tittered, but there was also an element of steel beneath it, and the crowd parted, clearing a path backwards. It stopped at a heavyset man with a bulging paunch and a look of surprise plastered across his ruddy face. Someone gave him a shove from behind, and he stumbled forward a pace. Once he was moving, he stepped reluctantly along the open avenue that had appeared in front of him, occasionally glancing in silent appeal at the faces he passed by.

Fassbinder had been one of the rousers, stirring up the enmity of the crowd, urging them forward. Now exposed at the front of the crowd, he no longer seemed so willing to race into battle.

Siobhan looked at him. "What? A butcher with no knife? Someone kindly hand him a weapon."

A flat blade with a wooden handle—a farmer's machete—was thrust into his hand. He almost dropped it, and his ruddy complexion paled as he stared across the gap to the fortified walls beyond. Siobhan stepped forward and took hold of his free wrist, raising it in the air as a kind of salute before the crowd.

"Together, Torsten," she cried. "You and me together, right at the front. Let's show them what we're made of—you and me."

She raised her staff and took a stride forward. Along the battlements, every staff was pointed down at her, waiting. Fassbinder had also noticed the vast array of weapons aimed at him, and he remained rooted to the spot. Siobhan was jerked backwards by his inertia, and she exaggerated the stumble. This time, there was general laughter behind them, and Siobhan sensed an easing of the tension. She turned to Fassbinder and put her hands on her hips and cocked her head to one side, appraising him.

"Torsten," she admonished him gently, "we've already died once. Why were you so eager to insist that others of us do it all again?"

He couldn't look her in the eye, and the machete made a kind of *flumpf* sound as it dropped into the dust at his feet. She gazed out at the crowd.

"Torsten wants to know if I'm here to fight or to talk. Well, he's not here to fight, and neither am I. There have been too many lives lost already. Nothing, at this point, can justify losing more. If we have to fight, then let us choose our battles, and let us come more prepared than—" she kicked at the dusty machete, "—this. But, if anyone disagrees, then don't let me stand in your way. Step on up front, and go do your best."

She waited, silently. Nobody moved.

"Very well," she said. She considered the garrison for a moment, then walked deliberately up to the gate and stood directly beneath the wall.

"Who is in command?" she called up.

One of the soldiers removed his helmet and shook his head, freeing the thick tangle of curls that were plastered to his head with the heat. He was a swarthy, solid man with heavy eyebrows and a simian jaw.

"I am Generalissimo Moreti," he answered. He glared down at her suspiciously. "Who are you?"

"Who I am shouldn't matter to you. Your master has fallen, General, and his army is in full retreat. You no longer have an allegiance to pledge. You must now consider your own situation. You are safe and secure behind those walls, but you are also trapped there. You cannot stay there forever, and when you decide to come out, we will be waiting for you.

Your other choice is to surrender. I guarantee no harm will come to you or your men if you choose this path. You understand we cannot allow you to return home until we negotiate a treaty with your city, and until everything that has been stolen from us has been restored to us. Those are our terms. We will withdraw and give you time to decide."

She saw his jaw clench, and smiled. He just needed more time. She turned her back on the soldiers and walked calmly back to the crowd who were decidedly subdued, but watchful.

Members of the group who had also pushed through the crowd now came forward to confer with her. One, a grey haired man with a face lined from stress and worry was the city's previous mayor who had been toppled and replaced after Varak's victory over Hornshurst. That he had survived at all was due to the ability of the resistance movement to protect their most valued citizens from capture, imprisonment and likely execution. He was accompanied by an elder druid who was the only survivor versed in the mysteries of the *Toki-Moai*. The last member was a young man, tall with dark skin and fine, noble features, who looked as if he'd been carved from a trunk of mahogany. He carried a staff loosely at his side, and his tunic was crossed with a bandolier containing a number of *hira-shuriken*, or bladed throwing knives, constructed from copper-tungsten alloy that could cut by shorting out the energy field it passed through. His eyes were constantly alert, searching faces in the crowd in the manner of competent security agents everywhere. He was Siobhan's bodyguard, and his name was Kareem El-Amin

"Will they do it?" whispered the mayor.

"Before the day is out," Siobhan replied. "There's no point holding out for a lost cause. Even if the General insists on fighting, his soldiers won't be quite as enthusiastic. I think he knows that already."

"What now, General?" The old seer addressed Siobhan by her military rank.

"We need to strike back immediately. I suggest we leave a small force here to contain the soldiers as prisoners within the garrison. Remember, there must be no retribution; I have given my word. We mobilise our army once more, take whatever arms are within the garrison and whatever weapons we've managed to store or hide, and march on Varak's city of Cherath. We can intercept the retreating forces, disarm them, and then lay siege to the city until the *Toki-Moai* is returned to us."

"Varak was no fool," said the elder. "He would have hidden it far from prying eyes. No one will know where it is."

"Then we will take the city apart, brick by brick, until we find it," she replied grimly. "Timing is everything. We must move before it is too late to do anything."

"And if Hogarth intercedes?" asked the mayor.

"Our fight is not with Hogarth, but they will not prevent us from claiming back what is rightfully ours, I promise you that!"

The druid spoke again. He had been eyeing the crowd who were straining to overhear the whispered conversation.

"Can you even raise such an army?" he asked dubiously. "All these brave souls were slavering over the prospect of a massacre, yet none was quite so willing to rush the walls. I remember a saying: to get to heaven, you first have to die. Have we been cowed for so long we have forgotten how to fight?"

Siobhan glanced at the faces, at the crestfallen figure of Torsten Fassbinder. There was still some work to do.

"On the day, they'll be ready!" she guaranteed.

Once Moreti had capitulated, the garrison was looted of all its armaments—the weaponry, the armour and the clothing. The resistance movement had stockpiled weapons as well, and these were quickly distributed. Officers were inducted and battalions reformed, and although there were gaps in the ranks from Varak's violent excesses, the citizens of Hornshurst turned out with pride and passion in the quest to recover their treasured *Toki-Moai*.

Within three days, the van of the army, led by General Siobhan and her aide, Captain El-Amin, left the city gates and began the long trek towards Cherath. Watchers along the road were astonished by the immense size of the army and word of another impending battle between city states spread far more rapidly than the dogged tread of the foot-soldiers.

Inevitably, word filtered west, across the arched bridge and through the gates of Hogarth.

CHAPTER 3

*K*ate Gallagher was sitting alone in the attic room of one of the corner towers. The tall tower stood at the eastern edge of the imposing wall that fortified the city of Hogarth. She had opened the doorway that led out onto the wide balcony, which swept around the circumference of the tower. The view from the balcony was extraordinarily beautiful.

Below, the drop was sheer all the way to the river hundreds of feet beneath. At the river's edge, the water tore through a series of rapids and waterfalls and the noise was deafening, but from this height, it looked more like a light blue crayon had melted in a thin line across a page. The ravine itself was soon lost from sight as it twisted and carved a slit through the Great Forest that stretched to the horizon. All that could be seen was the dense canopy, which soared above the ground and threw the forest floor into perpetual deep shadow.

Kate had arrived on Bexus, barely more than one year previously, and although the experience had been harrowing and had created so much personal sorrow, she had come to view the place as home. The encounters leading up to the final defeat of Varak had taken a heavy toll on her soul, and the once brilliant golden skinned girl was now a kind of patchy, mottled brown.

There were places visible on her arms and legs that still retained the golden quality, which marked her as unique on Bexus, and during times of stress, her hand would absently caress those unblemished areas for reassurance.

Lord Varak's power had been centred in a crystal that sucked the life force from his victims and transformed it into a form of dark energy that magnified his own powers and kept him from aging. Kate had stolen the crystal, and turned it against Varak to defeat him. Suddenly, she was the invincible one, the one who held sway over those around her, feared by her enemies. What nobody knew was that Kate had stood at the balcony of this same tower and had tossed the crystal far out into the ravine, willing it lost forever.

It was because others coveted the stone. In the days following Varak's defeat, more and more pressure had been brought to bear by the Council of Hogarth, made up of a good number of self-serving businessmen who administered the city. This group had served as a war council during Varak's campaign, though many of its members would have capitulated had it not been for the tireless efforts of Kate's mentor, Mirayam, one of the city elders and one of the few women ever to advise the Council. The leader of the Council, Commander Elward Carter, had been a close ally of Mirayam, and had been part of the learned few who'd believed Kate's purity of being would have been enough to counter and defeat the negative energy of Varak's distorted soul through a process known as annihilation. The theory had never been tested, but Kate's possession of the source of Varak's extreme powers had tempted Carter beyond reason, and he yearned to be the one to wield its staggering potential.

At the last Council meeting two days previously, Carter had issued an insistent decree for the crystal to be retained by the Council. Kate had refused outright: she had run from the council chamber and left it to Mirayam to argue her case. More of the councillors were siding with Carter. They believed that Kate was too young and too inexperienced to claim ownership. Most saw economic benefits that would multiply in a city-state that would become invulnerable and invincible.

Kate refused to divulge the fact she had thrown the crystal away. The knowledge that she possessed it was a deterrent. Too many of Varak's defeated forces still roamed between Hogarth and Cherath, and the thought of a swift retribution was the only thing that prevented widespread lawlessness and looting. Varak's army had witnessed the cold manner of his destruction, and his soldiers believed they had merely swapped one despot for another. They took the opportunity to retreat with their lives intact in what they perceived was a moment of weakness on Kate's part. Who knew the consequences if word leaked that the crystal was no longer in her possession?

She sighed to herself and leaned on the balustrade, letting the gentle breeze tug at her hair. She had seen the pining avarice in Carter's eyes and knew him to be a weak leader of others. She had two options: tell Mirayam the truth, and have her relay it to Carter to make him back off, or do what she seemed to have always been doing since she'd arrived, and that was just run away. It was likely Carter wouldn't believe Mirayam, and that he would think it was another strategy to prevent him laying his hands on the stone. The other problem was that it was unlikely the news she no longer had it could be kept secret for long.

The second solution seemed even more appropriate that evening after Mirayam arrived back from an extended session with the Council. She was tired, and her shoulders had slumped forward in defeat. Kate feared the worst.

"It's final," Mirayam admitted after lowering herself into one of the chairs in the quiet courtyard of their home. "The Council has issued an ultimatum: either hand the stone over by noon tomorrow, or else a squad of soldiers will arrive and take it from you."

"That's not fair!" came a cry from one of the doorways deep in shadow.

Sigrid Rasmussen burst from the darkened alcove, followed by the other students who were Kate's closest friends. They had worked and trained for battle alongside Kate, and had been ready to make the final stand united against Varak.

"I'm so pleased this conversation isn't private," Mirayam remarked dryly.

"But Sigrid's right!" exclaimed Mia. "It was even prophesied. Kate is the rightful heir to the stone!"

"The prophecy was always ambiguous at the best of times," said Mirayam, "and it never indicated the existence of any such stone."

"I'm not handing it to Carter," said Kate with an air of finality.

"You go, girl!" Olivia's Australian accent had survived the light years and one lifetime of travel.

"We'll barricade the doors," added Jackson. "They'll have to get by us first."

Kate pictured a brawl between her friends and the unwelcome soldiers. She was suddenly struck with a misgiving.

"Will Hawklight be involved?" she asked.

Mirayam smiled. "No, Captain Hawklight is still out on patrol somewhere in the Great Forest. No one knows when he is expected back. We can be thankful for that, or the Council would have assigned him to the squad."

"He wouldn't have done it!" said Ethan. "He said as much himself."

There was a sudden, sharp series of raps on the outer door that made Kate jump in alarm. Olivia, who was nearest the door, ran across and tapped the pentangle-shaped key that opened it. A familiar, tall, mop-haired figure bent as he passed through the doorway, and Kate felt a moment of thrill at seeing her protector once more.

"Nathaniel!" she cried and leaped out of the chair and ran to him. His face softened briefly when he saw her, but fell back into its default setting of seriousness as he strode forward into the light.

"Mirayam, I'm sorry to intrude," he apologised, "but I've just returned, and have been sent to accompany both you and Kate to an emergency meeting of the Council."

"I've only just finished with them," Mirayam grumbled. "I wish they'd make up their minds."

"I believe this is something different," said Hawklight, "but it is urgent."

"Very well, then," she said. "Are you ready, Kate?"

Kate nodded and gave her friends the briefest glance. The students had discovered a disused cellar where the ceiling vents opened out through grilled enclosures at floor level of the council chamber, and it was used to eavesdrop during closed sessions. Hawklight also noticed the look she gave because he said, "And try to keep the noise down. The acoustics aren't that great to begin with."

Kate laughed out loud. She had long suspected that Hawklight knew of their clandestine activity. The others looked a little embarrassed and hid their smirks by turning away.

On the way along narrow, twisting alleys, Mirayam asked, "What's this about? Do you know?"

Hawklight nodded. "Hornshurst is marching against Cherath. There's going to be carnage now that Cherath's army is in disarray. We may be the only ones capable of negotiating a truce."

"I say we leave them to sort it out by themselves!" shouted one councillor. "They brought this on themselves in the first place!"

"That's not entirely true," interrupted Mirayam, ever the voice of reason. "Varak ruled most of them through fear alone. Most of them had no choice, as would we, had Varak triumphed, or are your memories so short that you cannot remember?"

"It's not our fight!" another councillor added. "What happens beyond our borders is not our concern!"

"Are we a city so bereft of morals?" Mirayam countered angrily. "According to history, before Varak, the three cities were closely allied in trade and in friendship. And if we are to learn only one thing from our recent past, it ought to be that we cannot ever sit by idly again just so matters can run their course. We have the moral imperative to intervene and try to prevent more bloodshed. We have the power of the crystal at our disposal and we must use it wisely."

Kate shifted nervously in her seat, and she was aware that she had attracted Hawklight's keen interest. He had the ability to see past her charades, and she wondered what he suspected now. She settled, and then raised her eyes, looking around in a bored fashion, hoping to cover her discomfort. Her eyes flitted past Hawklight, and she was relieved to note he appeared to have relaxed once more, and he was watching the proceedings with interest.

"Mirayam is correct, of course." Elward Carter's bass voice cut through the clamour. "With the power of the stone behind us, we can force the others into some kind of negotiated truce."

"That won't be that easy, Commander," said Hawklight from the back of the room. All eyes turned towards him, and Kate saw the briefest flicker of a shadow behind one of the ventilation grilles beside his boots. "Varak stole the Hornshurst *Toki-Moai,* and the city is willing to risk everything to get it back. If it can't be found, my guess is the army of Hornshurst will ransack the city, stone or no stone. In that case, would we intervene?"

"Then we must implore the citizens of Cherath to hand it over, and bring whatever pressure we can apply to encourage them to do so," replied Carter. He turned his gaze to Kate. "We still need the stone, Miss Gallagher. You will hand it over to me now!"

Kate was cornered. There was nowhere to run, no time to hide. She had to brazen it out, and began by returning Carter's ominous stare.

"You cannot wield the stone," she said. "People will wonder what right you have to wear it. They will not trust you, and, frankly, neither would I. I defeated Varak. I have earned the right to wear it. I also showed mercy where Varak didn't, so I think I have earned their trust. If the stone is to go to Cherath to prevent a war, then I must be the one to take it there. I'm prepared to do this. I am not prepared to hand over the stone." She folded her arms across her chest as if to show that this was the final word on the matter.

Carter began to bluster but was interrupted by Mirayam.

"Everything the girl says is true. You haven't yet earned the right, Elward, certainly not in the eyes of those we would hope to impress. Equally, we can't afford not to take a stand on this matter. If we succeed, we could rekindle the old alliances and live in peace for the first time in more than five hundred years."

Kate cringed inwardly. Perhaps she ought to have confessed to tossing the stone away. She'd just managed to argue her way to the head of another army when she thought she had finished with all of that. Mirayam certainly believed in her; had done since the beginning, and Kate felt she was betraying that trust once again. But it was too late to backtrack now, too late to recall the words.

In the end, the Council sided with Mirayam, and Kate was conscripted into the Hogarth army with Captain Hawklight at her side. She felt sure her friends would not want to miss out on this adventure either.

Great! she thought to herself. *Me and my big mouth!*

It took a further three days to mobilize enough troops for the march on Cherath. Most of them had been preparing for battle for months, ready to repel Varak's invading force and Kate felt relieved to be surrounded by such fierce warriors. The other students would not be dissuaded from going.

"Why should you have all the fun?" Olivia commented as she assembled her battle dress. Only Mirayam opted to stay behind. The long trip down Varak's hewn road through the Great Forest and the subsequent march across the lifeless flat oven of a desert would be too taxing for her as she had grown progressively frailer in the year that Kate had known her. The only disconcerting note was that Elward Carter would lead the column in his capacity as Commander-in-Chief, and Kate privately thought he wanted to be nearer to the stone so ultimately he could lay claim to it. *Well, he was in for a bit of a surprise,* she thought. *He wouldn't be a happy man that day!*

The column filed beneath the portcullis and out through the gates and over the arched stone bridge that spanned the ravine. Many of the soldiers sat astride *Hon'chai,* animals that resembled large red deer, with a single prong of horn where the antlers ought to be. Their coats glistened in the sunlight, and their hair was surprisingly thick and soft along their backs so that hard saddles were not required. Kate had never ridden a horse before, let alone one of these strange animals, but they seemed docile and responded to the lightest touch. An hour into the journey, riding three abreast in the shade beneath the towering canopy of the forest, she felt as if she'd been doing this all her life. Her sleeping roll, a waterproof cape, and her staff, Rhyanon, were strapped to the animal's flanks behind her. Jackson and Mia rode either side of her, and Hawklight took up his unassuming role as bodyguard directly behind her.

She heard Sigrid's soft voice rise in lilting song and smiled. With luck, this wouldn't be such a big deal after all.

CHAPTER 4

harlie Hughes sat in his bedroom at the end of the hall with his head in his hands. He'd hung the first of the returning soldiers by their wrists, and zapped them a few times with an instrument which did to a soul what a halfway decent taser did to the human body. He reflected that he wasn't so different from Varak in that respect: he hated bad news.

But their stories didn't differ and as more of the vanquished troops passed through the gates of Cherath with the same news, Charlie had to face the fact that his career had nose-dived yet again. He cursed the years of investment he'd made climbing the ladder, and he'd been certain Varak hadn't suspected anything, didn't know of Charlie's carefully hidden plans for a coup. He wondered if he could salvage something anyway; maybe reorganize the structure with him at the top before anyone else came up with the same idea. He drew up a list of potential competitors to eliminate, but that was as far as he got.

Varak, Chamberlain MacNeill, and General Titus were gone. The rest of Cherath had figured there was no one else to fill the vacuum, no one left to fear. Their murmurs of discontent grew into a rumble, then a roar as more of the citizens of Cherath streamed out of their homes and into the streets, searching to beat upon anyone associated with the old regime. The palace guard had bolted the doors to Varak's castle, but the hired help—the butlers, footmen, maids and the slaves—had slunk out the back doors. Charlie and a small contingent of the personal guard were trapped as the crowd gathered and began assaulting the gates. Worse still, they began chanting his name, and it wasn't an encore they were after.

He had to get away but for what purpose? Even if he managed to escape Cherath, he'd have to go where nobody knew his name, or what he did. He had nothing. He was just a bully; he could survive by preying on the weak, but what sort of life was that? If things had worked out the way Charlie had planned, he'd have been king of the world. Anything less was fair to say, a bit of a disappointment.

Varak had amassed wealth in the form of gold, diamonds and precious stones; his real drug had been absolute power. Besides, Charlie wasn't going to get far with his pockets laden with gold bars, despite what his inner voice was telling him. It hadn't actually made the transition away from lusting after material wealth during his time with the Gökhans. He, too, craved power. He needed something small that would get him back on his feet once again, and that could be easily carried in case he got into a foot race with a mean crowd bent on revenge. Then it struck him! He needed the *Toki-Moai* of Hornshurst!

He raced down the hall to Varak's chamber. The towering, filigreed doors were double locked, but Charlie had a key and knew the code. He wasn't the Head of Security for nothing! The guards beside the doors had long since gone to beef up the detail defending the inner courtyard, so there was no one to prevent him from pushing the doors aside and entering the dark chamber.

He knew where to look. The expansive mat was tucked back in place against the corner of the room. Charlie grabbed one end and pulled it away from the wall, exposing the wooden floor beneath. He dropped the rug in an untidy heap and bent to examine the floor. He ran his eye along the boards, looking for any anomalies: planks cut short, gaps between boards, scuff marks, dents in the wood where a knife might be inserted to lever up a trapdoor. He saw nothing!

He faltered. He knew the rug had been moved the night he'd witnessed Varak caressing the *Toki-Moai*. It had to be here somewhere!

He stood and quickly searched the rest of the bedroom, checking for hidden vaults behind hanging canvases, looking under the bed, feeling the stonework of the immense fireplace for any sign of weakness. He came up empty-handed again.

He heard a distant crashing sound, the sound a sturdy wooden gate might make as it splintered beneath the ceaseless attack of an intensely angry mob. The tearing, wrenching sounds were accompanied by shouts of anger, shouts of pain. Time was running out for Charlie Hughes.

He shut his eyes and took a deep breath to try and block out the pitched battle that had unfolded in the outer courtyard, and to calm himself. *Think!* His first instinct was to return to the wooden floor. He knew the talisman was hidden there, somewhere. Varak would never have let it out of his sight. If he were in Varak's boots, what would he have done?

Magic! Varak had used his magic. That was it! The talisman was beneath the floor, protected by a charm. And out of reach of Charlie Hughes, unless . . .

A great axe, crossed with a serrated-edged broadsword hung above the fireplace. He ran to the fireplace and gripped the handle of the axe and tore it from the wall. The broadsword clattered to the floor beside him, nearly decapitating him in the process, but Charlie was too preoccupied to have worried about that. The baying noise of the distant crowd was drawing closer.

He began to walk a grid across the floor, starting from the back corner and working in measured steps. After each step, he let the handle of the axe slide between his palms so that the heavy iron head came crashing down onto the floor planks with a dull *thuunk!* Another step. *Thuunk!* And another. *Thuunk!*

Charlie strained to hear any change in pitch, a hollow echo of sound that might indicate a cavity beneath the boards. And twenty paces later, he heard it.

He took a step back and raised the fearsome weapon above his head, then swung it with all his impressive strength. The boards splintered as the steel wedge was driven through them and their backs were broken. Charlie levered the embedded axe sideways, and the boards squealed their protest when they were torn from the nails that had anchored them.

Charlie pulled the axe head free, then kneeled and continued to tear at the hole with his hands. He tossed the loose chunks of wood aside and peered into the hole that had formed in the floor. A small, rounded shape carefully wrapped in a purple velvet cloth lay nestled in the space like a rabbit in its burrow.

Ka-chiing!

Charlie could picture in his mind the spinning images on a slot machine coming to rest on the same three fruits. He was winning big time, baby! He allowed the luxury of a smile to cross his face as he lifted the bundle from its cubbyhole and deposited it in the knapsack he'd carried with him into the room.

The sound of running feet brought him to his senses. The crowd had overrun the guards and had begun leaking like a blocked bathtub throughout the castle in search of him. There was no more time to waste, but he had one more ace up his sleeve.

He raced to the door and dropped the steel bar into the brackets either side of the door. The bar wouldn't keep the crowd out, but it would sure slow them down some!

He picked up the bag and slung it across his shoulder as he hurried across to the bed that dominated the room. He ran his fingers down the wooden post on the left hand side at the head of the bed, feeling for the lever that had been fitted into the wood. His fingers traced the faint outline of the lever, so cleverly engineered into the frame it was almost undetectable. Almost. He pried it loose and pressed down and felt the slight *snick!* as the lever engaged the hidden lock, and part of the fireplace swung outwards. Another smile. Every good castle had a whole raft of hidden passageways, and this one was no exception. Charlie knew about it; it was his job to know, after all, and where better to have a bolthole than in the bedroom of the one most likely to use it.

Charlie squeezed through the narrow opening and found a pile of torches—wicker frames wrapped in cloth soaked in oil at one end—just inside the entrance. He lit one and pulled the entranceway shut just as the first of the rioters arrived outside the bedroom and hacked at the imposing wooden doors. His timing was impeccable.

A flight of stairs led to a sloping passageway that ran beneath the castle walls and below the city streets. The air was damp and smelled of mushrooms, no doubt laden with the spores of a hundred different fungi. Charlie held a cloth over his mouth as he skittered along the slippery cobblestones. Three times the path divided, and each time Charlie chose the left hand fork that led him on a slow outward curving path away from the castle.

It took the better part of an hour before Charlie hit the end. The passage stopped against a wall of dark brick, which had a set of rusted iron handrails bolted into it. Charlie peered upwards into the gloom, but the chamber dissolved into blackness beyond the weakening flicker from his torch. He couldn't very well retrace his steps, so he had to climb. He dumped the torch in the dirt and started hand over hand up the ladder.

He must have climbed sixty feet or so before his head struck a cast iron plate covering the hole. It had a grille, so he was able to slot his fingers between the gaps and heave upwards. At first, the cover refused to budge, and Charlie experienced a moment of panic as he pictured being trapped by the mob at the top of this underground chimney. He imagined them stacking piles of wood at its base for fuel in order to roast him slowly, and the thought was enough to motivate him to shove harder. The cover shook loose, and with one final heave, he was able to pop it free and slide it to one side.

He felt the fresh air about his face and scrambled out of the hole. He discovered he was standing in a small, windowless shed with a concrete floor. The gaping hole took up most of the floor space, and he had to edge his way round it to the door. The door itself was locked, but it was a flimsy affair and it smashed open the moment he put his shoulder to it.

He burst out onto a narrow alley behind a row of houses and discovered it was night-time. Light from a distant street lamp reflected off the wet cobbles in taffeta patterns where slicks of oil had dribbled, and a light mist brushed his face. He glanced left and right and saw no one. Left had served him best during his escape, and he saw no reason to change now. He turned left and ran to the end of the alley and into the adjoining street where he collided with a family group who were just about to step off the pavement.

Charlie tripped over the first body and landed hard on the uneven ground. The knapsack slipped from his shoulder and flipped end over end. The straps came loose and the purple bundle protruded from the opening. One end of the cloth had folded back, partly revealing the gleaming silvery statue. He rolled to his knees and cradled the elbow that had taken the brunt of the tumble. He looked about. A woman was standing with her back against the fence of the corner building, and a hand over her mouth in shock. Two men sat up groggily, and a there were a couple of kids as well. One of them started to cry.

The man closest to Charlie began to abuse him.

"Why don't you watch where you're go—?" he shouted, but then he saw whom he was shouting at and the words caught in his throat.

Charlie heard the woman gasp.

"It's The Magician!" she whispered, and her eyes widened in fear.

There was a moment when nobody moved; when all time seemed to stand still and then reluctantly moved on, tired of waiting for something to happen. Charlie was first to react. He reached across and grabbed a staff that had fallen to the ground and come to rest against his legs; at the same time he grabbed one of the smaller bodies, a spindly-looking youth with a strange aura that appeared green under the lamplight. He stood and hauled the youth to his feet, wrapped one arm about his neck, and pressed the bulbous tip of the staff under his chin. The youth whimpered and stared at the staff in Charlie's grip.

"The boy and I are going to take our leave now," he growled. "Hand me the bag!" he said to the woman. She remained where she was, still in a state of shock.

"*Now!*" he screamed at her.

She was jolted back to reality. She bent down and picked up the canvas bag. The statue almost fell out the top, and she had to catch it before stuffing it down inside.

"Do it up!" he snarled, and he willed her shaking fingers to secure the buckle. She reached out and passed the bag to him.

"Give it to the boy to carry!"

The youth grabbed the bag and almost dropped it again.

"Both hands," Charlie whispered into the boy's ear. "Don't let go of it."

They backed away. One of the men tried to stumble after them, so Charlie stopped and brandished the staff, pushing the end harder under the boy's chin until he began to choke.

"One more step and The Magician will perform his first trick!" he warned. The man stopped and was then held back by the others. Charlie nodded and smiled.

"That's better," he said. "If we're followed, I'll kill him."

He took another step backwards, and this time the family members stayed rooted to the spot. Charlie half dragged, half carried the boy to the end of the street, all the while watching the helpless family staring back at him. He turned the corner and was lost from sight. He let go of the youth, and then belted him hard with the thick handle of the staff. The boy dropped like a sack of sand, and a few sparks fizzed from his scalp where Charlie had whacked him. He'd be nursing his head with ice water when he came to, but that was the least of Charlie's worries at that point. He pulled the bag from the boy's loose grasp and swung it across his shoulder once more.

He heard cries for help and the sounds of running feet. He turned and disappeared into the night.

CHAPTER 5

The dust cloud was visible two days out from Cherath. By now, everyone knew that Hornshurst had mobilised its army and was seeking retribution for the centuries of repression under Varak. The outer gates were winched shut and the rag-tag army that had marched to Hogarth and back again nervously paced the walls, gazing out at the dust, searching for alternatives to the despair that overwhelmed them.

A day out, and they felt the vibrations of the ground beneath their feet from thousands upon thousands of pairs of marching boots.

Whoommpf! Whoommpf! Whoommpf!

Like the ticking hands of a clock drumming an incessant beat.

Scouting parties were sent out to track the progress of the invading party; some never returned, and those that did were barely gone more than a few hours. Most of the citizens hiding behind the city walls believed that any resistance would be pointless, and they didn't want to end up as statistical footnotes in the final battle. However, since no one knew what to expect, they all stayed hidden away.

Mid-way through the second day, the desert horizon became peppered with black dots as the leading edge of the army strode into view through the swirling heat haze. The dots grew bigger and morphed into a blanketed mass of soldiers as numerous as seed heads in a wheat field. They were led by Siobhan, sitting astride her dusty mount, accompanied by the young Kareem El-Amin who was walking beside his own, harnessed beast.

The army pulled up two hundred yards short of the city's walls, and the soldiers streamed outwards like two powerful arms to encircle them and lay siege. By nightfall, the trap had snapped shut. There were no campfires to illuminate the extent of the siege. The only light seeped from the city, which bathed the low hung clouds in a dull orange wash. Beyond it, the desert was smothered in an air of dark menace, and the expectation of an imminent battle grew steadily as the hours ticked by.

Early the next morning, before the sun had shaken off the chill of the cold desert night, Siobhan and Kareem crossed the ribbon of open ground separating the two sides. They walked casually, unhurriedly as if they were there for the sake of exercise and a quiet time away from the troops. Before they were halfway across the gap, every eye was upon them, and a collective breath was being drawn in readiness.

Siobhan carried a white flag of truce, and she stopped in front of the gates to the city and let it trail at her feet in the dust. She squinted up at the wall above the gates. The cloud had disappeared and already the sky was a brilliant blue although the ground still remained in shadow. The figures above the wall were silhouetted against the sky in their black uniforms, watching and waiting.

"I come in truce," she called up to the wall. "Who is in command here?"

"Speak your mind, woman!" The reply was sharp, the officer unidentified.

"Very well. The city of Cherath possesses an item that belongs to Hornshurst. It was stolen from our city and has been held hostage by Lord Varak ever since. We want it back."

There was no reply from the wall.

"If it is returned to us intact, we can negotiate a settlement between our two cities and return home.

"How can we trust you?"

"You have my word, provided we can agree on a satisfactory settlement. But that which is rightfully ours must first be returned to us."

More silence. The first rays of the sun caught the top of the city walls, illuminating the blood red brick from which they were made. The faces of the soldiers on the battlements could be clearly seen now, and Siobhan was able to make out the decorative uniform and helmet of one of Varak's generals. Their eyes met, and he called down to her.

"And if this item is not returned?"

"See for yourself, General. The city is completely surrounded. There will be no escape. If our talisman is not given over to us, then we will have to find it by ourselves, even if it means tearing the city apart, brick by brick. And believe me, General, we *will* find it! If it comes to that, then there will be no settlement, and we will take no prisoners."

The threat hung over the battlements.

"We need more time!"

"Very well. You have until midday!" And with that, Siobhan turned her back on her enemy and she and Kareem walked back to the safety of their own lines.

Kareem found Siobhan meeting with some of her field officers an hour before the deadline.

"We've just received word that the city of Hogarth assembled an army to intercede. They're just days away," he reported.

Siobhan's face turned grim. She stared at the imposing walls two hundred yards away. The tops bristled with defenders. Both sides would lose many soldiers in an attack, and Siobhan had planned to lay siege to the city and wear down the inhabitants. If the army of Hogarth arrived, she would face a battle on two fronts and knew her troops lacked the experience needed to succeed. If the talisman weren't returned, then battle would be inevitable.

"Let's hear their answer," she said to Kareem. "Keep your eyes peeled for any signs of trouble," she murmured as they walked out into the open space for the second time that day.

"You're an hour early!" the grizzled general called down to her.

"We're anxious to resolve the matter!" she replied. "One hour will make no difference in the end."

Siobhan returned the general's stare, and saw him squint the way an unlucky gambler might signal if he'd just been dealt a losing hand. He was weighing up the same odds of survival, reaching the same conclusion that the price to pay would be too high. He shut his eyes and shook his head as if the weight of the world had just been placed on his shoulders.

"We don't have it," he admitted.

"General, there is a difference between 'don't have it' and 'can't find it'. It will be hidden away. Are you telling me that you are prepared to sacrifice your city because of a poorly organised search?"

"We don't have it! We discovered where Lord Varak had hidden it within his bed chamber, but the talisman was gone."

Siobhan felt an icy chill slide down her back. She tried to keep her voice even.

"In that case, we will need to search for it ourselves. You understand the consequ—"

She was knocked aside brutally as Kareem cannoned into her side, and she fell heavily in the dirt. There was a brief pulse of light from the top of the wall, and a short, sharp sound like an insect frying on an electric bug zapper before the ground beneath where she had just been standing erupted in an explosion of dirt and debris. She saw Kareem roll smoothly away, then push upward and onto his feet again. She saw him reach across his chest for one of his *shuriken* knives. His arm extended out in one fluid movement, and the blade caught a glint of sunlight as it whistled upwards at the wall. She heard a brief shriek and saw a tiny shower of sparks as the knife blade sliced across the skull of a soldier, then watched as he tumbled from the wall and crumpled as a pile of empty clothing at its base.

What followed was a moment of madness as blasts of energy from both sides ruptured the air. Siobhan scrambled to her feet and dived sideways as another explosion rocked the ground beside her. She heard Kareem cry out and twisted in his direction, afraid that he had been hit by one of the shots raining down from the top of the wall, but he had retrieved her staff and was screaming for her to catch it as he tossed it towards her. She snatched it one-handed and brought the narrow end to bear on the spot where she'd last seen the general.

She was about to launch a counter curse when she was distantly aware of his voice shouting above the din.

"Cease-fire! Cease-fire! That is an order!"

A blast from one of her own troops hit the wall where he was standing, and rocks and shards of flying stone were blown outwards. The general barely reacted as he fought to regain control of the wall.

"Cease-fire!"

The shooting stopped abruptly. The ionised air quivered with static as the dust settled.

Siobhan lowered her staff and waited.

"That was not supposed to happen," the general apologised. "The price has been paid." He nodded in the direction of the empty uniform at the foot of the wall.

"The talisman, General," Siobhan prompted.

She heard a muffled discussion as the general turned away from the wall. Moments later, he reappeared with a woman beside him.

"You must believe me when I say we don't have it," he said. "Listen to the woman's story."

The face of the woman peered down at Siobhan, and her knuckles gripped the edge of the stonework as though she was deathly afraid of heights.

"I have seen your statue," she began nervously. "It was silver in colour. It looked like a little man wearing a fancy hat made of animals and his arms were folded across his chest. He had big ears, and there were green stones in his eyes. That's all I remember."

Siobhan took a silent breath and held it. The woman had seen the talisman. It had to be within the walls of the city. She heard the woman continue.

"The Magician had it. He carried it in a bag."

The Magician? Siobhan recalled the rumours about Varak's vicious Head of Security and knew of the many purges he'd instigated against Hornshurst's leading citizens from time to time. It was he, rather than Varak, who had been the man most feared by the resistance movement.

"The Magician, where is he now?" she asked.

"Gone," replied the general. "He escaped the castle via a secret tunnel that led from the main bed chamber. We found the hole in the floor where he had broken through to discover the hiding place of your talisman. This woman's family encountered him near the gates in the wall the other side of the city. He hasn't been seen since."

"When was this?" Siobhan asked again.

"Six nights ago," came the reply.

"I want guaranteed safe passage," Siobhan called. "I need to see for myself."

The general nodded. He understood. He quit the wall in search of suitable hostages who would be exchanged into safekeeping when Siobhan entered the city.

Siobhan and Kareem were unarmed. The general from the wall escorted them, and a group of elite troops accompanied them in a protective phalanx through the streets and into Varak's castle.

The castle was in ruins. Doors had been smashed and burned; furniture had been broken into splintered slabs and ruined empty uniforms lay scattered in retreating lines, which marked the passage of the swift retribution meted out to the palace guards by the angry crowd. Siobhan held no sympathy for the victims as she was marched through the lower levels and up the stairs to Varak's quarters.

They entered the room tentatively as if Varak's spirit still pervaded the space. Siobhan could see across the room to where the enormous rug had been pulled aside, and the floorboards smashed. A battleaxe had been carelessly discarded beside the ruined floor. She exchanged a fleeting glance with Kareem, and noted with silent satisfaction that his eyes constantly roved the room, drinking in the details.

They stood above the hole in the floor and gazed into it. It was the right size for the talisman. Siobhan even felt the slight vibrations where it had disturbed the air within the hole as if it were leaving a scent to follow. It had been kept there; she knew that now.

She looked across to the general who appeared lost in his own private thoughts. The question was: did she trust him? The story about The Magician could have been an elaborate ruse to keep possession of the talisman himself. The temptation would have been almost too powerful to resist. He was inscrutable, and she couldn't make up her mind about him.

"Thank you, General," she said and her words seemed to shift him from his reverie. "You have been most helpful, but I'm afraid we must return and discuss this new development with our own advisors. I'm afraid there are no guarantees."

The general nodded. The fate of his city still hung in the balance, and he was a pragmatist; he didn't like their chances. However, the woman and her bodyguard had seen the chaos and carnage within the castle. It was evident that the citizens had set about righting the wrongs of the previous centuries, and he believed the woman would ultimately speak out in their favour. He smiled at her, and although she looked long and hard at him, he didn't flinch.

They had averted the threat of battle for now. What they had instead was a stalemate, a standoff between two armed camps. There were those who demanded a swift retribution, who wished nothing less than the destruction of Cherath and the enslavement of its citizens, but in the end, wiser heads prevailed.

"We cannot lose the talisman!" Siobhan argued. "That is our priority here. The people of Cherath will have to atone for the crimes of their leaders, but that will keep for now."

"What do you suggest, General?" asked one of her captains.

"Kareem and I will pick up the trail of this Magician. We'll hunt him down, and we will retrieve the talisman. The army will stay in place and will lay siege to the city. No one moves in or out." There was a severe chill in her voice. "If we fail to return, then wipe it from the face of Bexus."

"How will we know?"

"The Magician has a week's head start. We have Kareem El-Amin. If we are not back within ten weeks, torch the city! And while you're waiting, give them something to think about."

There was no dissent. Siobhan scrutinized the faces of the councillors, and she saw a grim resolve in each. Satisfied, she left the tent to prepare for the next stage of her journey.

The following morning, she and Kareem met with the family who had collided with Charlie a week previously. They took the two of them to the corner, and while they explained what had happened to Siobhan, Kareem began a careful grid examination of the street surface. He seemed to find what he was looking for because he smiled and nodded at Siobhan and began to track away down the street towards the gates that led through the wall and out into the desert beyond.

CHAPTER 6

A yellow smudge of dust blotted the view of the horizon from the walls of Cherath for the second time within a week. Nervous eyes turned westward as news of a second army converging on the city filtered past the siege and into the city.

The general impassively watched the swirling dust clouds through a spyglass although his mind was seething with troubled thoughts. He'd read the woman correctly; he had felt that he could trust her after he had shown her the ravaged bedchamber, and he'd bought a little more precious time for the city. He was under no illusion that Cherath and its citizens would be spared if she failed to return, but he planned to use the time he'd won to prepare the city's defences against the attack when it came.

The dust cloud changed everything. The army of Hogarth was arriving at his doorstep, no doubt led by the child soldier who had defeated Varak in open combat. He had heard how she had usurped his powers. He presumed she was leading the charge for swift and decisive retribution and knew she would be impossible to resist. If Hogarth allied with the army of Hornshurst already camped outside his gates, his city was about to be crushed like a bug beneath a boot.

Kate arched her back as she reined in her mount and gazed at the splendid city in the distance. She was constantly amazed by how much the soul remembered of its time trapped inside a body. The memory was the glue that kept the form long after the soul had departed, although some of that glue consisted of the memories of stretched and strained muscles that no longer existed. She had to remind herself that the pain and stiffness from a couple of weeks of riding were all in the mind.

She dismounted and began to walk, leading the *Hon'chai* by the reins. The others had also dismounted in order to rest the animals before the final ride up to the city gates. Kate fell into step beside Sigrid, with Hawklight to her right.

"Oh god! That feels better!" she moaned as the stiffness in her lower back eased. Hawklight smiled down at her.

"How much further?" she asked him.

He shrugged. "The way you're walking? A week, maybe."

Sigrid laughed, and Kate smiled. Her initial relationship with Hawklight had not gone well, and the dislike and resentment at having to spend time in each other's company had been mutual. But multiple near-death experiences had altered those perceptions, and they had been replaced by trust, respect and friendship. Kate felt safe in his presence, and she missed him when he was not around.

She looked at the distant towers shimmering in the heat haze above a mirage that looked like a silver lake. She squinted against the glare and spat out the pebble she had been sucking.

"Do we have a plan?" she asked Hawklight.

"Carter wants a show of strength. He wants you to use the crystal to deliver the kind of thunderclap you made when you were standing on the bridge. It'll keep their heads down and let them know we mean business. Are you up for that?"

Kate knew she wasn't. She had thrown the stone from the balcony of the tower into the ravine below the city. She decided to come clean.

"Uh—Nathaniel, there's something—"

She was interrupted by a shout from behind and a clatter of hooves across an outcrop of rock. She turned to meet Elward Carter cantering up to them.

"Mount up!" he ordered. "We can be there well before nightfall." He eyed Kate with some disdain. "You'd better be ready."

He jerked at the reins and galloped back along the line of soldiers, full of bluster and encouragement. Kate watched him as he bobbed awkwardly up and down and thought that his best days as a soldier were past.

"What were you saying?" Hawklight asked as he hauled himself up on to the back of his mount.

"Oh? Ah—it was nothing," she replied and kept her head down as she gripped the fur on the back of the *Hon'chai* and swung her leg up and over. When she glanced at Hawklight, he was looking at her suspiciously. Damn the man! He could read her like a book.

"What?" she asked, and she raised her chin and tried to stare him down, but he said nothing, just gazed back with that stupid, inscrutable look of his, and she turned away first.

As they rode closer, they could make out other details through the haze, and the shimmering desert slowly transformed into a sea of tents swarming with men. Hornshurst had arrived ahead of them, but so far, the city was still intact.

They could see other activity outside the walls as the soldiers of Hornshurst prepared for their arrival. The ring around the city was broken as they peeled back to form two sweeping arms like the horns on a bull. The horns pointed away from the city, towards the incoming tide of men from the west, and flanked an avenue that led directly to the main gates of Cherath. Any army riding into the gap would be crushed in a pincer movement.

Commander Carter raised his arm and halted his advancing army five hundred yards from the tips of the horns and just shy of a mile from the gates of Cherath. Division commanders were consulted, and the men were formed up into a triangular wedge facing the gap with flanks radiating outwards diagonally left and right of the main body. It was a classic standoff needing a catalyst and both sides were anxious not to provide one just yet.

Carter rode up alongside Kate and nodded curtly.

"Hit them with your thunderbolt! Lay them flat!" he demanded.

Kate glared back at him. She reached behind and pulled Rhyanon from the sheath that was strapped to the back of the *Hon'chai* and dug the animal in the ribs with her heels. Her mount jumped forward, then settled into a steady walk as she peeled away from the triangular wedge and crossed into the gap between the two opposing armies.

Her hands were shaking so hard she had to grip the reins tightly against the animal's neck to hold them steady. She heard Carter's surprised exclamation followed by a series of curses as she urged her mount forward. She suddenly felt small and insignificant as she came abreast of the tips of the horns to either side and knew that thousands of staffs were pointed in her direction.

A noise from behind startled her, like a stone being thrown at her feet, and she turned quickly. She could have wept. Hawklight was riding quietly ten feet behind her, his eyes sweeping left to right, showing no fear. He had her back! He gave her a brief *Are you out of your mind?* look before she turned and faced forward once more.

They continued on, unhurried, down the throat of Hornshurst's army and out into the clear space beyond which lay in the shadow of the city walls. She dismounted and stood, gently stroking the nose of the *Hon'chai*. Hawklight reined in beside her but stayed mounted and watchful.

"What are you doing?" he muttered like a ventriloquist.

"I'll explain later," she whispered as she stepped away from her mount.

She cleared her throat to ease the constricting fingers of fear that were wrapped around it.

"My name is Kate Gallagher," she called, and her voice rang true and clear and echoed off the massive brick walls. "I am the girl who defeated Varak. The powers that were his are now mine to control. Many of you know this. Many of you have witnessed it. With these powers and an army at my back, I am invincible. You know this also.

But I am not Varak. I prefer to seek peaceful solutions to problems. But before this can happen, you must first put your weapons down. That is your choice."

She waited. No one made a move, from either side.

"What are you waiting for?" Hawklight whispered. "Use the stone!"

Kate tried again. "Open the gates."

Hawklight blinked in frustration, but nothing else moved. Kate needed to move the bluff one step closer to the edge. She faced the wall and raised her staff, pointing it directly at the massive iron gates set into the wall.

"I'm getting tired of waiting for someone to do something sensible," she called.

Finally, she heard the sentence she was hoping to hear.

"Open the gates!"

Chains clattered noisily in their runners and the gates groaned as they inched outwards.

"Wait!"

The voice cut the air keenly and the squealing of metal ceased. All heads turned upwards to the top of the wall. Kate's heart sank: she recognised the nasal whine.

"Let's see what she can do," Copely called again. "Go ahead! Blow the gates apart! You ought to be able to manage that!"

"Seize that man!" cried the general. He looked panic-stricken. He was being offered a way out, and the fool was about to slam that door in his face.

Several soldiers started towards Copely who backed away, then leapt on to one of the battlements.

"The girl is bluffing!" he screamed. "She has no power. If she had, I wouldn't have this!" He thrust his hand into a pocket, then drew his arm back and tossed something out through the air towards her. It appeared to separate in two, and the twin objects bounced in the dirt and rolled to a stop near her feet. Kate looked down at the two halves of the shattered crystal that had split when it had hit the rocks at the base of the ravine. *How did Copely find it?*

The blue stone was chipped and lifeless. Kate bent and picked up the two pieces and brought them together at the splintered face. It was a perfect fit, but the energy with which it had buzzed and hummed in her hand was gone. She looked up at Hawklight.

"I was going to tell you about it. Honestly," she apologised. "Carter would have turned out just like Varak," she added, to justify her actions.

"We're standing in a patch of desert, totally surrounded by tens of thousands of enemy troops who are just beginning to realise you are no longer any real threat, and *this* is the time you choose to let me know these things?" Hawklight asked her.

Kate turned petulant. "How was I to know Copely would find it?" she asked. "What was he doing down there anyway?"

Hawklight shook his head. That question was the least of his worries at that moment. They both gazed up at Copely who was laughing maniacally as he was dragged down from the wall by a group of soldiers.

All eyes turned back to the two of them, isolated in the narrow ribbon of No Man's Land.

The soldiers in the ranks of the Hornshurst army had begun a low, ominous muttering, which slowly withered away into silence. No one was prepared to make the first move.

Kate cleared her throat once again. If anything, the fingers of fear had squeezed tighter.

"As you can see, Mr. Copely is perfectly correct. This was the crystal that held Varak's power. It's broken—useless now. I threw it away because I believe that nobody should hold that much power over others ever again. I don't regret doing it, not for a second." She held out her hand and let the two halves of the blue stone drop back into the dust, and ground them into the dirt with her boot while she paused to gather her thoughts.

"I thought I had good reasons for misleading you all, but I misled you anyway, and I apologise. Not for lying to you, but because I was trying to bully you, and that makes me no better than Varak.

I knew I didn't have the crystal, but I came out here just the same. I guess Captain Hawklight can't help himself, so he came too. And if you even suspected that I didn't have the crystal, you wouldn't have listened to me.

My message hasn't changed. Too many lives have been lost already. Our army is here to help keep the peace, and we will guarantee your safety while you negotiate what you need to negotiate and then we can all go home."

She waited. Nobody responded. It was more awkward than trying to make conversation with a great-auntie who bought you socks for your birthday.

"Please . . ." she implored.

She turned towards the sudden clanking of rattling chains that broke the stillness, and watched and waited as the imposing iron gates swung open and a stout, muscular, balding general stepped out into the sunlight waving a white flag of truce.

By the time evening fell, Kate and the others had learned of The Magician and his disappearing act with the Hornshurst talisman. They learned that two trackers were actively pursuing him and that the fate of the city hung on the outcome.

The negotiating teams from both Hornshurst and Cherath postured and jockeyed for position, but beneath it all, it became clear that neither side wanted a war and that neither side trusted the other enough not to start one.

Carter was furious when he learned that Kate had destroyed the crystal, but his position as mediator had thrust him into the spotlight and his ambition quickly discovered an alternative pathway as the elder statesman. By mutual agreement between the two opposing factions, he manoeuvred his army between them, where it sat—a brooding but effective buffer to conflict.

The details of the negotiations looked set to stretch into weeks, and Kate would have happily sat out the time in the company of her friends now that the immediate threat of war had been averted, but for one thing. As an indicator of his own good faith, Carter had volunteered to send his own trackers out to assist in locating The Magician.

Hawklight was his best and was nominated and asked to choose another scout to accompany him. But before he could reply, the old general interrupted.

"Commander Carter, I'm sure your intentions are indeed honourable," he began, "but I am a suspicious and cautious man by nature. What happens to our city will be determined by the success of this mission to recover the talisman. I have no doubt that Captain Hawklight is an honest man, but . . ." He paused delicately and chose his words to avoid giving offence, ". . . we have twice witnessed the integrity of young Miss Gallagher, and it is this city's wish that she accompanies the captain on the mission. We would feel . . . comfortable . . . with that option."

Carter secretly bristled. The girl was fast becoming the bane of his life. On the positive side, it was possible something could happen to her. He could but hope.

Outwardly, he smiled. "Yes, of course, an excellent suggestion. If Hornshurst is in agreement, we can organise for them to leave as soon as possible." He checked the gentlemen sitting to his left, and they nodded their assent.

"Excellent!" he exclaimed. He rubbed his hands together then rested his elbows on the table and clasped his hands together and began to flap his fingers up and down as he glanced at the sheet of paper in front of him.

"Let's move to the next item on the agenda, shall we?"

Early the following morning, Kate leaned against the rough stone wall beside the back gates of the city, shivering with the cold and yawning, watching the horizon giving birth to another day. Sigrid, Mia and Jackson had accompanied her this far and were trying to convince Hawklight to let them come too.

Hawklight was inside the gates talking to the family who were once again pointing out the direction in which The Magician had fled. Hawklight was interested in the two pursuers, and was asking more details as he cast his eye about searching for clues only his practised eye could spot.

When he was satisfied he'd found as much as he could hope to find, he thanked the family and rejoined the others outside the gates.

"Please, Hawklight, pleea . . . ase let us come with you," Sigrid moaned. "We can help! You know we can!"

"Yeah," Jackson joined in. "Safety in numbers. Many hands make light work. All of that."

Hawklight smiled at them but shook his head. "I'm a soldier, not a schoolteacher," he replied. "Class is dismissed." He turned to Kate. "Are you ready?" he asked.

She sighed and yawned again and pulled herself to her feet.

"The sooner we leave, the sooner we can return, I guess," she said.

"That's the spirit!" he replied. "Look and learn," he said. "Look and learn." And with that, he nodded to the others and mounted his *Hon'chai* and rode out into the desert.

The three students gathered around Kate and embraced her, then watched her leap astride her mount and trot out into the glowing dawn to catch up with Hawklight.

CHAPTER 7

harlie Hughes lay spread-eagled in the shallow ditch that ran parallel to one side of the animal enclosure no more than sixty feet from where he was concealed. He had been in the desert for three days and was totally lost. He had a feeling he was tracking in a wide arc to the left and experienced enough moments of déjà vu to wonder if he were walking in circles.

The terrain looked the same: rocks and sand and clumps of needle sharp salt crystals stretching to the horizon and beyond. There were occasional dunes of sand, which he climbed early into the journey in order to have some vantage point high enough to see where he had come from and where he was going. The view from the tops of these dunes was disheartening. All he saw was heat and sand and sameness—three hundred and sixty degrees of it. He gave up climbing to conserve his energy and tried to keep some direction by noting the position of the sun, which drew him left in its implacable journey across the sky.

On the third night, he stumbled into the ditch exhausted and wrapped his coat tightly about his body to ward off the desert chill. He lay shivering in the hollow, watching each of the three moons rising out of the east, behind him to his right. He fell asleep while making a mental note to adjust his direction the next day.

He woke to the sounds of shouting and felt the ground trembling beneath his body. He cautiously peeked above the rim of the ditch and saw he had lain up near some kind of farm. A group of hardened sun-baked men were sitting on poles that formed a fence for an animal pen. Inside the enclosure was a gigantic reptile that resembled a frilled lizard with a spiky, armour-plated tail. The tail had been lashed to a peg driven deep into the dirt, and ropes pulled taut by two pairs of men tethered one front leg and one back leg.

He watched, fascinated, as another wrangler tossed a lasso that looped over the head and slid behind the bony arches of the animal's jaw. The leather frills snapped erect the way an elephant flares its ears moments before it charges, and the beast hissed and tried to lunge at the man who skipped back out of reach and yanked the rope tight.

The powerful lizard was pinioned. Charlie saw another man step out into the sunlight from a nearby barn. He was shorter than the others, but broad across the chest, with thick muscular arms and a narrow waist. He was dressed in a tight-fitting suit made of toughened fish leather. Charlie could see some of the shallow elliptical cavities where the scales had been removed, but the suit was worn and dusty and pliant and fitted the man like a glove. He carried a fistful of leather straps and a wide steel bar hung down and gleamed in the sun. Charlie recognised it as a harness; he had seen the same contraption on the animals that Varak rode into battle.

Charlie couldn't move. If he stood, the men would spot him instantly, and he didn't know if he would be recognised, nor if the word had filtered this far out that he was a fugitive on the run.

The man in the leather suit crawled between the palings of the fence and cautiously approached the lizard. The animal's eyes swivelled towards him, and it tried to rear its head, but the rope was too tight. The jaws opened to reveal twin rows of gleaming triangular teeth and the reptile hissed again in warning.

ALAN CUMMING

"Hold that rope tighter!" he called as he edged behind the head and tucked himself in close to the erect frill. He held the steel bit loosely in one hand, and Charlie could see that its surface was toothed like a file.

The lizard knew he was there, and the whites of its eyes showed as it tried to roll its eyes back and down. The frills flapped, but he stayed tucked tight against the neck behind the jawline.

The beast hissed again, and it was the moment he'd been waiting for. He stepped out away from the head and brought the bit up and slid it into the gaping mouth. The lizard was quicker, and the man on the end of the rope was caught by surprise. The colossal head jerked sideways and tore enough slack from the rope to clamp the gaping jaws hard down on the man's arm. He was caught like a rag doll and tossed into the air and flung against the heavy wooden gate that opened into the pen.

He lay against it, stunned, and a few sparks fizzled from his arm as all around him, the watchers burst into laughter. He stood unsteadily and brushed the dust from his clothing, shook his head, and stormed over to the wrangler holding the head rope. The guy watched as he approached and was still straining against the rope with both hands when the little cowboy landed a roundhouse punch that dropped him where he stood.

"When I say hold the rope tighter, I mean *hold it tighter!*" he screamed as the rope handler struggled back to his feet holding his hand against his mouth as if he were checking for signs of bleeding. The others fell about laughing once more, and Charlie smiled at the entertainment. He might as well enjoy the show.

The second attempt to place the bit in the animal's mouth was successful. The noseband of the bridle was secured, and the headpiece tightened. The reins were passed back over the animal's head. The guy in the suit, the head wrangler, clambered up onto the animal's back and wedged his legs behind the frills either side of the neck.

That was the easy part. When the others let go the ropes, the animal reared up on its hind legs and twisted its head in an attempt to reach behind and snag the rider who was pulling savagely on the reins to turn the head back while trying to keep his seat.

The lizard bucked and twisted like a demented radius defining a circle as it strained against the rope that tethered its tail to the peg hammered into the ground. It hissed and squealed like fingernails scraped down a blackboard, and the rider was constantly thrown from its back. Each time, the trailing ropes about its body were retrieved and tightened, and the animal would be immobilized long enough for the rider to remount. It was like watching a rodeo and Charlie privately marvelled at the skills of the rider and the gutsiness required to break the beast's resolve.

Once it had been beaten, the animal seemed to accept its fate. It waited docilely to be saddled and harnessed and accepted different riders with an air of indifference. Charlie wondered if horses had reacted in the same way. The tail tether was the last to be removed before the lizard was put through its paces within the enclosure.

He'd watched the wranglers breaking in two more of the beasts throughout the afternoon. In between, he rolled onto his back and slept.

The men quit half an hour before the sun painted the sky in pastels as it dropped towards the horizon. They herded the three lizards into the pen and corralled them for the night.

Charlie was a 'motor' man. He enjoyed the comfort and leather luxury of his Audi a7 humming down the M1, nestled snugly in the driver's seat with the stereo turned up loud. He wasn't a 'horse' man if you didn't count the hours he spent at the track studying form and placing bets. It never occurred to him to want to ride one then, and he wasn't too fussed on the idea now, particularly given that the mount was armour plated and likely to make a meal of him.

But he was a desperate man, and desperate men fixate on the positive. He made his move after the sun had set but before any of the moons had risen and when the raucous noise from the bunkhouse was in full swing.

He crept from his ditch and snuck up to the paling fence. The lizards were just dark, humped shapes, their bodies lethargic and cooling in the crisp desert air. He heard the stertorous breathing, like queer little gasping sighs, and his inner voice remembered scenes from the *Jurassic Park* movie franchise and warned him to move slow and steady.

His hand brushed a bridle contraption slung across the top pole of the fence, and he gathered it in and spread it on the ground, untangling the reins and trying to remember how all the bits were arranged about the animal's head. He knew where the bit went and he wasn't looking forward to putting it there.

He sidled up to one of the beasts and put his hand out to brush against its scaly hide. The muscle quivered beneath his hand, and the animal snorted and twisted its neck to look back at him.

"There, there," he purred and stroked the animal's side, feeling the bony ribs against the skin. "E-e-eeasy, boy. Easy. It's just old Charlie, coming to say hello,"

He stepped closer. The frill fanned slightly and quivered, the way a dog shakes water from its fur, and the beast snorted. *Slowly! Steady!* said his little voice.

He was stroking the neck, now the head. The animal watched him with curiosity, snuffling and snorting air through slit-like nostrils. Its mouth remained closed, and Charlie was stuck holding the bit with nowhere to put it.

"Open your mouth, you bugger," he whispered. The reptile continued to snort at him.

He gave it a good whack on the head with the palm of his hand, the head reared up, and the lizard hissed at him. He thrust the steel bit into its jaws and pulled back to avoid being clamped by the serrated teeth.

The beast tried to dislodge the metal bar, but Charlie yanked back hard on the rein and it seated firmly in place at the back of the mouth. He fumbled with the straps, first twisting the noseband so that it sat comfortably across the animal's snout and then buckling the headpiece tight.

He didn't think the apparatus quite looked the way he'd seen it worn earlier in the day, but it felt secure enough not to tear loose. Charlie checked around and noted with satisfaction the hoots and laughter were as loud as ever. He stepped in front of the beast and gave a sharp tug on the reins. He felt the resistance in the heavy, inert body slacken as the animal rose up on its splayed legs and followed him to the gate. He eased the latch back and swung the gate outwards, then led the animal out beyond the pen and into the desert gloom.

Charlie picked out the east since the first of the moons was thrusting the crown of its bald white head into the sky. Anything in that direction was going to be further from Cherath, and that was where he wanted to be. He made sure his knapsack was secure against his back; that was one package he couldn't afford to lose. The staff he'd taken from the family in Cherath was also lashed across the top.

He passed the reins back across the animal's head and stepped in close behind one of the flapping frills. There, the lizard's skin was surprisingly smooth, and he slid back twice before he managed to hoist himself in an ungainly manner on to its neck. He wedged his legs in tight and his feet found hollow pockets of skin, which he used as stirrups.

"Giddayup!" he ordered and slapped the reins. The animal stayed slumped with its belly against the stony ground. He tried digging his heels into the sides of its neck but his legs were wedged too tightly. Finally, he leaned forward and slapped the lizard hard on the top of its head, and he nearly tumbled backwards as it rose up and skittered sinuously into the night.

It took a little time for Charlie to fine tune the controls, and he was pleased he had a flat expanse of desert free of thorny vegetation and eroded cliffs in which to experiment. The ride was surprisingly comfortable—the animal slithered its body in a snake-like fashion, but it kept its head and neck steady, and Charlie was spared the motion sickness he was prone to back when he was alive on Earth. It didn't handle as smoothly as the Audi, but it was a whole lot cheaper to run. When Charlie eventually dismounted to stretch his legs and massage his numb backside, he had put many miles between him and the farm. What's more, it was in an easterly direction.

Charlie travelled across the desert in intermittent bursts throughout the following two days. He didn't know what food the animal ate; judging by its impressive array of teeth, it was more likely to be animal in origin rather than plant. He kept a wary eye on the creature in case he caught it eyeing him up and licking its lips, but it didn't seem to grow hungry and remained docile when he hauled it in to rest. He'd have to congratulate the little cowboy on a job well done if he ever ran across him again.

He maintained a constant vigil behind him also. His little voice often took keen delight in wandering through fields of paranoia and bathing in streams of doubt. It was only logical and reasonable that someone should try to follow him; if someone had stolen from him, he would have hounded them to the ends of the universe. Ergo, a smart man is a cautious man.

He sat astride the lizard on the top of a shallow rise and examined the path he'd just taken. He saw no one behind him. The footprints of the lizard were clearly visible, but even as he watched, the sultry desert zephyrs breathed across them and slowly filled them with sand. He laughed to himself. Good luck to anyone who followed *those* tracks.

As a result, he was totally surprised the same evening when two men materialised out of the dark night and into the warm glow of his campfire.

"Evenin', Squire," said the first man. "Mind if we join you?"

Charlie's eyes flicked sideways to his staff strapped to his knapsack, just out of reach at the other end of a fallen log he was resting against. He smiled.

"Please. Be my guests." He waved vaguely at the flames and shuffled across on his bottom towards his pack as if making more room around the fire.

His guests were hollow-eyed and nervous as if they'd spent way too long in the desert. Their clothing was dirty and shabby. They had made a crude attempt to disguise it, but Charlie was able to make out the familiar uniform of Varak's foot soldiers. He could even make out the darker patches that looked like stains but were, in fact, part of the uniform that had been covered with the red and black insignias that had been torn away. They looked like deserters.

One of them stuck out his hand. "I'm Pavel Soucek," he said. "My friend, here, is Albert Lachapelle." He pronounced it the French way—*Al-bear*—and the other man nodded and stared morosely into the flames.

Charlie shook Pavel's hand. "George Canning. Pleased to meet you both," he said.

They sat in silence for a few minutes. Charlie wondered how he could edge nearer his knapsack without arousing suspicion, since each time he moved, he drew a sharp look from the Frenchman.

"The desert is a lonely place for a traveller," said Pavel, breaking the silence at last. "Are you headed far?"

"Aye," Charlie answered. "Goose Bay."

Charlie had no idea why it had been named Goose Bay. There were no geese on Bexus, and the port city sat at the mouth of the mighty Kampala River and not in a bay. The river emptied out into a lake more than two hundred and fifty miles long and seventy miles wide. Ships and ferries and all sizes of trading vessels plied the waters in brisk trade between neighbouring city-states. Charlie was aiming to get lost among the busy docks and find a boat that would take him to the other shore. He wanted a bolthole far enough from Cherath where he could relax and begin work on breaking the final lock of the *Toki-Moai*.

He caught the end of a knowing glance that passed between the two men and understood that he was in for some trouble. He'd seen that look too many times in the past; usually he'd instigated it—sort of a *Ready, Set, Go!* signal to coordinate his next moves with his accomplices. He was still too far from his staff.

"And you?" he asked. "You're from Cherath, aren't you? You headed back there?"

Pavel appeared startled as if he hadn't expected Charlie to recognise the tattered uniforms. He opened his mouth to reply, and that's when Charlie made his move.

Only, Albert was quicker. Charlie had barely taken two steps and was still hunkered in a half-crouch when Albert tackled him with a low body block. The two men crashed over the log to the ground in a tumbling ball of flailing fists and snarling grunts. Charlie attempted to lock one of his massive forearms across Albert's throat, but the wiry Frenchman was slippery as a snake and he ducked and rolled away.

A fireball exploded in the dirt next to Charlie's head, sending a geyser of stones and sand raining down on him. He was deafened by the blast and slightly concussed, and the fight went out of him. He raised his head gingerly and saw Pavel smiling down at him, standing five or six feet away with his staff levelled.

Charlie shook his head to clear the ringing in his ears, and then slowly rose up on to his hands and knees. His right hand brushed against a rock the size of a baseball, and he closed his paw around it to conceal it. He could see Pavel's lips moving but couldn't hear what he was saying.

Albert was on his feet, unbuckling the knapsack where Charlie had left it. Charlie watched as Albert fished out the cloth-covered statue and unravelled it. The shiny metallic object fell from the cloth and rolled in the sand, stopping up against one of the rocks that ringed the fire. All three pairs of eyes tracked it greedily.

Pavel kept his staff pointed at Charlie while he bent and retrieved the *Toki-Moai*. He blew away some sand that had lodged in the crevices of the carved headdress and admired the craftsmanship.

"Well, now, Mr. Canning, what have we here?" he asked. He hefted it in one hand as if weighing it. "It certainly feels expensive, whatever it is. I'm sure we can find a buyer for it." He tossed it to Albert who caught it and began to wrap it back in the purple cloth.

Charlie took a step forward, and Pavel snapped his staff up and aimed it dead centre at Charlie. Charlie's imposing size caused both men to step backwards involuntarily, despite the fact that they were both armed.

"Steady, Mr. Canning. We don't want any accidents here, do we?"

The statue disappeared back into the knapsack, and Albert refastened the straps. He slung the bag around his shoulders and slipped his arms through the shoulder straps. Both men stepped backwards, both facing Charlie. He took another step forward and raised his arm.

Pavel caught sight of the smooth stone beneath his fingers.

"Uh-uh!" he warned. "Don't be stupid. Throw the stone away!"

Charlie's shoulders slumped. His statue was slipping away. His frustration boiled over. He turned to one side of where the two men stood, drew his arm back and hurled the stone away with all the pent-up anger fuelled behind it.

His aim was good. The stone whistled well away from the two men, but it struck the sleeping lizard on its skull, just behind its eye. Instinctively, it lashed out with its armoured tail that caught the two soldiers in a scything arc just below their waists.

Goodnight nurse! Charlie needed to search to find the spot where they'd landed beyond the glow of the fire. They'd hit a rocky outcrop and bounced across the ground, coming to rest at the base of a large, weathered boulder emerging from the sand. Both were unconscious, fizzing sparks from the wounds where they'd first hit the dirt.

He dragged them back into the firelight, stripped them down to their underwear, then shredded their torn clothing into long strips and bound them together tightly, both hand and foot. Happy with his handiwork, he slumped back against the dead log against which he'd been resting and brushed the *Toki-Moai* clean of all the sand, humming to himself.

Pavel came to just before the dawn. He felt the hot snuffling breath of the large lizard blow across his face. He and Albert were tethered together beside the jaws of the sleeping beast. He whimpered at the sight.

Charlie looked up. "Mr. Soucek! Welcome back to the land of the living. I still don't know what those things eat—" he pointed to the prostrate lizard, "—but whatever it is, it isn't either of you."

He picked up a handful of gravel and flung it at the sleeping reptile. It swung its tail and the frills flared outward. It rose up on its front paws and saw the two men trussed together at its feet. It opened its mouth wide and plunged down to within an inch of Pavel's blanched face before hissing at him as he twisted away and screamed at the top of his lungs. Charlie laughed. He couldn't stop until the beast had settled down again. Pavel was sobbing in the dirt, straining against the ties that bound him against the unconscious Frenchman.

"See what I mean?" he said at last. He stood and brushed the dust from his pants and strolled across to the two men.

"You made me very angry," he said.

Pavel stared up at him. In the growing cold light of dawn something registered; he suddenly recognised the face staring back at him.

"You're not George Canning!" he gasped. "You . . . you're The Magician!"

Charlie smiled at him; gave him that distinctive, knowing smile he reserved for when his victims reached that epiphany of understanding that their fate was well and truly sealed. *Yes, my friend*, it said, *there's no way out!* Pavel began to cry once more.

The man was pathetic, and Charlie had no use for him—no time for him either. He'd already rifled their pockets and broken their staffs. Anything of value was tucked into his knapsack on his back. He slid his leg across the neck of his mount and pulled back gently on the reins, feeling the strain of the bit twist the scaly head towards the east where the horizon glowed brightest.

He dipped his head in mock salute.

"Gentlemen."

The lizard slithered away in the general direction of Goose Bay, leaving the two soldiers immobilized and at the mercy of the desert.

CHAPTER 8

"*How* does he do it?" Siobhan wondered.

Kareem El-Amin had followed The Magician's trail deep into the desert. The chase had begun slowly because of the confusing mass of tracks leading into and out of the gates of Cherath, and they had to backtrack twice after Kareem noticed they were running down false trails.

They took a gamble and headed east and picked up the telltale signs after another half-day of searching for spoor in the desert dust. Siobhan couldn't detect any footprints in the sand. There were some scuff marks, barely smears in the dirt at irregular intervals, but to Kareem's trained eye, they resembled a track decorated with signposts.

Late in the afternoon of the third day, they found the farm. In fact, one of the wranglers found them. He ambushed them. He aimed a pulse from behind an outcrop of rock, which exploded against the side of the wall in the small canyon in which they were tracking. They dived from their mounts and sought cover against the sheer walls. They split up, and Kareem continued to draw the fire while Siobhan circled around and came in on the wrangler from behind.

He may have been accomplished at rough-riding lizards, but he was no soldier. She disarmed him without so much as a struggle and called out to Kareem to join her. They frogmarched him all the way back to the farm.

There was an awkward, somewhat tense moment when the whole gang burst out of the bunkhouse and surrounded them until they discovered they were all seeking the same person. Then it became 'the enemy of my enemy is my friend' kind of deal. Three frilled lizards had escaped the corral after the gate had been left open. One set of riding gear was also gone. It only took a moment for Kareem to verify that the culprit was The Magician and that he had continued eastward with one of the animals in tow.

The wranglers were no friends of Cherath. The Magician had been right to follow his instincts and remain hidden out of sight; otherwise the chase would have ended there. But it was no use considering what might have been, and so Siobhan and Kareem pressed onwards, promising to return the lost animal if they caught up with The Magician.

Kareem judged that they were still four or five days behind him. They needed a break to catch up some of the lost time.

They didn't get it. Further out into the desert, the tracks became fainter and, at one point, Kareem lost them entirely. They had to stop, and Siobhan took the opportunity to rest against her mount, catching what shade she could while Kareem began another patient search for spoor.

By the time he'd returned, the sun had disappeared below the horizon, and the three moons of Bexus were visible. Siobhan had wrapped herself in a cloak and was warming herself by a fire she'd made by gathering the dry, dead branches from half buried trees that had lost the battle against the encroaching sand.

Kareem's eyes reflected the dancing flames, and he smiled in triumph. The Magician had mastered the beast and he was confidently heading due east still, making good time, but taking less care to cover his tracks. He must have been confident that he was no longer being followed, and that was his first mistake.

Kareem used a stick to draw a line in the sand. There was nothing due east until the port of Goose Bay, latched to the mouth of the Kampala River at the shoulder of the great lake. He had to be making for the port; there was no other logical explanation for his behaviour. The question was: should they follow his tracks or should they gamble and head directly for Goose Bay in the hope that they might claw back some lost time? They didn't want to think about the alternative if he managed to elude them and cross the expansive lake.

Siobhan made the decision. They would ride for Goose Bay. She doubted The Magician knew enough to navigate by the stars. By pressing on through the night, they would make up some time. She doused the fire with sand and climbed wearily back onto the *Hon'chai*. Kareem showed no signs of fatigue, and she envied his youth as she followed him across the moonlit rocky landscape.

By the following morning, it was apparent they had made up some of the backlog. Even Siobhan could see the impressions in the sand where the lizard's feet had pressed down and where the heavy tail had dragged a light sinuous furrow through the softer ground. They were closing on him!

Once again their luck changed for the worse. Kareem called a halt to the chase and carefully dismounted, searching the ground about him intently. Siobhan could see the remains of a fire that had been lit close to a fallen log. There were numerous footprints in the sand and some strips of tattered material strewn over the ground. She waited astride her mount until Kareem had completed his close examination, then she slid down from the back of her *Hon'chai* and joined him

"There were three of them." Kareem pointed out the different footprints. "There was a scuffle here—" he indicated a patch beyond the log where the sand appeared to have been kicked violently aside, "—and over here, you can see how the footprints have separated: two sets there, and these are The Magician's. It looks like they got the drop on him, whoever they were."

"Are you saying he was mugged? Here, in the middle of the desert?"

"It looks that way," Kareem replied. "And yet, over here—this is the imprint made by two bodies lying side by side. He may have gotten the drop on them, and yet again, it may just be where they rested up. Here is where he hitched the lizard for the night. You can see the tracks heading off in the direction of Goose Bay. The other two head north, up that way." He pointed towards a row of dunes in the distance. From where they stood, they could see the tracks made by two sets of footprints up and over the dunes.

"Where's the talisman?" she asked.

"If I had to make the call, I'd say it was still with him," replied Kareem, still staring at the dun-coloured dunes. "He rode off, and they walked. But I can't be certain. He may have been robbed and just managed to escape." He looked at her. "It might also be with them," he said.

She thought about what he'd said. In all likelihood, the talisman was still with The Magician, but it was just a feeling. If she were wrong . . .

"We'll split up," she said. "He's headed for Goose Bay. I'll follow him there." She nodded in the direction of the footprints on the dunes. "Find them and relieve them of the talisman if they have it. Then meet me at Goose Bay. If I have to keep going, I'll leave a message at the docks, and you can pick up my trail again from there. But be quick! We're running out of time."

She handed him the reins to his mount. He flashed a broad smile full of white teeth at her and sprung lightly onto the back of the *Hon'chai*.

"Good luck," she said.

"Don't let him get away," he replied as he tugged on the reins and trotted towards the distant dunes. Siobhan watched him as he appeared to melt into the heat haze already radiating upward from the ground before she remounted and squinted as she turned east towards Goose Bay.

"They went thataway!"

Kate immediately burst out laughing, and the squat little head wrangler glared at her from beneath his hat. Hawklight also gave her a queer look.

"What?" she asked. "Nobody speaks like that anymore, not even in the movies. C'mon!"

Hawklight turned to the wrangler. "Thanks," he said and wheeled his mount towards the east. They were following the fresher set of tracks and making better time.

The *Hon'chai* seemed to be able to survive long periods without water, and they showed no signs of tiring. Hawklight rode ahead silently with his eyes to the ground, and Kate was aware she'd embarrassed him by laughing back at the farm. She couldn't help herself; even now it still sounded funny. *He'll just have to get over it,* she thought.

Two hours on, she decided to apologise. She seemed to be trapped in a continual love-hate relationship with Hawklight, and more often than not she'd had to make amends for poor behaviour. She gave the *Hon'chai* a gentle kick in the ribs, and it cantered forward to come abreast of Hawklight.

"Okay," she said. "I get it. It was very rude of me back there."

Hawklight's eyes strayed from scanning the uneven terrain ahead of him, and he looked at her briefly. "It's not me you need to apologise to."

Now he's rubbing it in, she thought. Aloud, she said, "I'm sorry. It was just such a cliché; I mean it was the last thing I expected to hear. Didn't you find it funny?"

"Forget it," he said. "It's no big deal."

"Then why the silent treatment?"

He reined in his mount. "Silent treatment! Is that what you think this is?" He nudged the animal in the ribs, and it resumed the regular gait that was a cross between walking and trotting.

"It isn't? You mean you're not mad at me?"

He smiled. "I was thinking about other things," he said.

They rode together in silence.

Eventually, she couldn't stand it any longer. "Wanna tell me about it?" she asked.

"Do you ever stop asking questions?"

"Nope."

"Look at the tracks. What do you notice about them?"

She peered at the ground in front. The desert reflected the harsh light and her eyes were sore. She looked in vain for some sign that others had also passed this way.

"I don't see any tracks," she admitted.

"Well, they're there. The thing is, there is no deviation, no hesitation. You can tell by the distance between the hoof prints that these two are travelling fast. Whoever is doing the tracking is exceptional; almost as good as me." Hawklight said this without any trace of ego. For him, it was fact, pure and simple.

"There are other problems too," he continued. "They are from Hornshurst, and Hornshurst and Hogarth haven't been the best of friends over the years. We believe they gave in to Varak too easily; they believe we abandoned them to their fate to save ourselves. Both cases are probably true.

The thing is: they don't know we're following them, and they've no reason to trust us. We're going to have to be careful. If they even suspect we're following them, we may never get the chance to explain ourselves first. So keep your eyes peeled."

She nodded, and then pointed to the ground ahead of them.

"They went thataway, right?"

It was his turn to laugh.

Hawklight surveyed the scene keenly. He read the same messages: the two intruders; the fight beyond the log; the standoff; the shallow humps where two bodies had lain side-by-side; the parting of the ways. He noted that the two trackers had also separated company. One was headed in the direction of Goose Bay; that much was certain. But what was the other one doing?

He had to make a decision. He glanced up at Kate who was sitting astride the *Hon'chai*, stroking its neck gently. They couldn't split up. He could point her in the direction of Goose Bay, but she'd wander off course within half a day in the featureless landscape. They needed to stick together.

He looked towards the sand dunes. They had to eliminate that possibility first before the trail grew too cold. He hauled himself up onto his mount.

"This way," he said and nudged the animal forward in the direction of the tracks that already were windblown and only faintly discernible.

Pavel rubbed his wrists. They were sore, felt bruised, although that was impossible since there were no blood vessels to break, no blood to ooze, but the strips of torn uniform had bound him tight nonetheless. They'd pulled even tighter when he wrestled against his bonds in absolute panic as the serrated teeth had lunged down at him. He'd come face-to-face with The Magician and knew he had no right to have survived the encounter. Albert had slept mercifully through the whole affair and had only come around a couple of hours after The Magician had left.

Pavel's fingers had scratched in the dirt, and he'd cut himself on a sharp flake of stone buried between the two of them. He'd gripped the stone between his thumb and forefinger and manoeuvred into a position where he could begin to slice at the reinforced strips of material knotted around Albert's wrists. Albert cursed him and swore each time he was nicked with the sharp edge of the stone, but after another few hours of patient hacking, his bonds were sliced free.

They found some of their clothing. The Magician had ridden off with the rest, scattering it across the desert. Each blamed the other for his predicament, so they started walking ten feet apart, whining and cursing each other from one sandy hillock to the next. When they'd exhausted their formidable vocabulary of obscenities, they trudged along in resentful and sullen silence, with Pavel rubbing his wrists and Albert rubbing the back of his head.

At night, the temperature in the desert plummeted, and the two deserters, dressed only in ragged shirts and underpants, were forced to huddle together to stay warm, so they had to shelve their animosity towards each other temporarily. This was how Kareem found them: cuddled together and still shivering with the cold, despite the pathetic fire they'd managed to light.

Pavel had just finished massaging his wrists when he glimpsed a shadow moving beyond the flickering light. He nudged Albert awake.

"Quoi?" mumbled the drowsy Frenchman.

"He means, 'Don't do anything stupid'," said the young stranger as he stepped into the firelight.

Albert sat up, his wide eyes staring at the staff pointed directly at his chest.

"Who are you? What do you want?" asked Pavel nervously.

The young man uttered two words Pavel had hoped never to hear again.

"The Magician."

"No!" he cried. "He sent you back, didn't he? Please, we meant him no harm, you must believe me!"

The young man's eyes narrowed.

"You have something that belongs to him," he said.

Pavel was confused. "We have someth—? No, wait! Look at us! We have nothing, I swear. He took everything with him. If anything, he has something that belongs to us!"

Kareem cast his eyes about the campsite hoping to see a wrapped bundle lying nearby. There was nothing. The man appeared to be telling the truth. He needed to be certain.

"The statue," he said. "I want the statue."

Pavel was more confused than ever. "The statue?" Then it dawned on him. "You're not with him, are you? Who are you?"

"You saw the statue." This was a statement of fact, not a question.

"I *knew* it! I *knew* it was worth a lot of money! Didn't I say?" he asked Albert whose eyes hadn't moved from the tip of the pointed staff. "We could help you get it back," he suggested, but the young man eyed him coldly and he regretted admitting anything.

Kareem smiled. The Magician still held the talisman, and Siobhan was right behind him. These two idiots only had the clothes they were huddled in. He backed away.

"Wait!" Pavel called. "Have some mercy! Don't leave us! Take us with you!"

Kareem flashed them the same merciless, cold smile Pavel had last seen on The Magician, and Pavel immediately regretted his outburst. He'd sooner face the desert and all she could throw at him. There was a strained moment when Kareem seemed to be weighing his options in favour of a sudden, fatal blast from his staff. In the end, he turned and disappeared back into the darkness.

Pavel felt a wave of relief surge over him, and he slumped back weakly.

"I'm going to have to get a better day job," he whimpered. Albert sat rigid, staring into the void beyond the dwindling fire.

Hawklight hesitated and reined in his mount. It stood quivering and panting in the heat as he searched the ground for clues. Something was wrong!

They'd come across the abandoned campsite. The blackened charcoal was still hot, and the wind that blew stronger after sunrise encouraged some embers to splutter and glow beneath the gossamer of grey ash. Two sets of footprints headed north and a rider had turned towards the east once more. They followed the hoof prints.

The trail led up the side of a shallow ridge and on to a rocky plateau. Years of eroding forces had stripped the softer rock strata away leaving behind sharply defined mounds of hard red rock scattered across the plateau so that it resembled an immense chessboard.

At first, he couldn't make sense of it. The trail had been easy to follow, despite apparent attempts by the rider to mask the trail. Then suddenly the trail ended—nothing, not a sign anywhere! Why would it just disappear without any trace on this exposed wasteland surrounded by—?

"Get down!" he screamed and twisted sideways before lunging across at Kate. He succeeded in knocking her from her mount, but not before the *shuriken* blade had whistled in from nowhere and sliced a deep gash through his raised shoulder where, moments before, his head had been. He hardly felt the cut; it was like being sliced by a razor, but he knew the wound was deep and that he was in trouble. Sparks flew from his shoulder, and he bled energy as the skin of the memories that defined him tore apart.

They crashed heavily to the ground. Hawklight fell across Kate, but even so, he landed awkwardly and was knocked unconscious. They spooked the two *Hon'chai*, which galloped a short distance to safety then turned to watch.

Kareem raised his head tentatively above the rock. He'd chosen the ambush site well; the sun was directly behind his back in the sky. Some sixth sense had warned him that he was being followed.

When he saw the two riders, he'd been impressed by their skills and also had been a little unnerved. He'd failed to notice them before, and couldn't believe how close they'd managed to get without being spotted. He was growing careless. Whoever they were, they were dangerous foes indeed! Who else would be following him?

He needed to take out the big man first and almost succeeded. He knew the blade had struck home from the *snick!* sound it had made, but the man had anticipated the ambush. Had it been enough?

He remained still and watched as the dust slowly settled. There were two bodies lying among the rocks; neither moved. One of the *Hon'chai* slowly wandered back to where they lay. He watched as it lowered its muzzle and nosed the bodies. There was no response. The animal raised its head and snorted.

He waited another ten minutes, straining for any sign of movement. Flies had begun to gather, attracted by the faint fizzing of tiny sparks near the big man's head. Kareem couldn't make out the wound—was it shoulder, neck, or head? It could have been any one of them. With any luck, both would have broken their necks on impact. But they didn't look like soldiers of Cherath, and that troubled him.

He crept out from behind the rock and cautiously approached the two bodies. The tall one was sprawled across the small one. He stepped closer. The small soldier had been wearing a head scarf, like a *keffiyeh* or Arabic headdress, to keep out the sun, and it had fallen aside to reveal a cascade of dark hair that caught the light and reflected a colour back that was almost inky blue. This was a young woman! Kareem had not expected that. She looked familiar somehow, but as he stooped closer something else caught his eye, a flash of sunlight. He glanced away and saw that it was his throwing blade half-buried by sand and so he missed the one moment her eyes fluttered open.

"*Reicitor!*" she cried and brought Rhyanon to bear in one smooth movement. The blast caught Kareem squarely across the chest and blew him off his feet and into a slab of stone twenty feet away. He slipped to the ground unconscious, the way a gob of jelly slides down a glass window.

He drifted back into consciousness slowly, in stages, where he was increasingly aware of growing pain. By the time real images swam into view his entire body seemed to throb incessantly. He tried to sit up and was half throttled by the noose around his neck that then fed down his back to where his hands and ankles were bound together. This was no ordinary rope; it glowed blue and tightened wherever it detected strain against it. Kareem was, literally, spellbound.

He groaned and sank back on to the sand. The young woman, hardly more than a girl, was squatting on the ground across from him, and she glared at him. She stood and sauntered across to where he lay, put her boot against his ribs and rolled him onto his side to check his bindings. He gasped in pain. Satisfied, she let him roll back again.

"You'll live," was all she said before she walked away.

She resumed her position squatting beside the large soldier. She'd stripped his shirt from his body and he was stretched bare-chested in the sand in the shade of a large rock similar to the one Kareem had hidden behind.

She reached into a bag and withdrew a handful of dried-looking green leaves. She placed them on a flat rock and began to pound them into flakes, sprinkling water from a canteen to mix them into a smooth thick paste. When she was done, she dipped two fingers into the paste and applied it to the wound at the warrior's shoulder. He winced as the pulp was worked into the wound, but he stayed silent. The leaking sparks slowed to a trickle then stopped altogether as the pap gummed up the exit.

She pulled a fresh cotton shirt from the bag and set about cutting it into long strips with a knife the soldier had worn. She folded some and applied them as a dressing pad, then bandaged the shoulder tightly using the remainder of the strips knotted together.

"How does that feel?" she asked him.

"Better," he murmured. He managed a grin. "We're back in the business of saving each other again."

She smiled back. "It's where we do our best work." She laid one hand against his forehead, then tore another strip of material and wetted it with water from the canteen and held it against his brow. He closed his eyes and lay still as if he'd just drifted off to sleep.

They stayed that way for most of the afternoon: Kareem trussed up, occasionally shuffling about in the sand to try and get more comfortable, and choking on the noose as it warned him to stay still; Hawklight asleep in the sand, and Kate watching them both while bathing Hawklight with the damp rag.

Hawklight woke again during that part of the day when the sky softens and the air turns hazy and the light strays towards the red end of the spectrum. The gentle wind tugged at Kate's hair tickling her shoulders and the shadows around her face grew more diffuse, highlighting her cheekbones and the angular line of her jaw. Kareem curled on his side and smelled the sweetness in the air and waited for the soldier to wake properly.

Hawklight struggled into a sitting position and tested his shoulder gingerly. The wound had knitted shut as the shafts of surface energy had bonded together in a fibrous lattice across his skin that looked like an ugly scar. Without it, he would have bled energy and withered away to nothing, like air escaping from a balloon. Kate was constantly amazed by how quickly the body repaired itself on Bexus.

"I'm getting too old for this," Hawklight admitted.

"You're looking better," Kate said to him. "You have some colour back in your cheeks."

"I think you'll find it's just the sunset," he replied, "but you're right, it does feel better." He gazed at Kareem. "How's our boy?"

Kate shrugged. She didn't much care. He'd tried to kill them both.

"Did you find the talisman?" he asked her.

Kate was watching Kareem. He'd overheard the conversation, and although he gave no outward sign, Kate detected a change in him; a tension, like the way a child drops a glass and freezes.

"No," she admitted. "Nothing. His saddlebags were empty." Her eyes strayed to the bandolier lying in the dust at her feet, along with a short sword and a beautifully carved staff. She bent and laid the bandolier across her knees and removed one of the curved *shuriken* and examined it.

"These things are razor sharp," she said.

"Tell me about it."

"What are you planning on doing with him?" she asked. "Can't we just leave him here?"

"That's not the Kate I've come to know," Hawklight admonished her gently. He considered Kareem for a long moment. "Perhaps it's time we had a chat. Bring him over but keep him tethered. I won't be much help if he gets loose."

No fear of that! thought Kate as she collected Rhyanon and strode towards Kareem. She stood to one side and pointed her staff at him.

"*Dimittere colligacionis!*" she commanded, and the ropy plasma evaporated. Kareem quickly sized up his situation, but he gave up considering the alternatives when his eyes locked with Kate's icy blue stare. They were unfathomably deep and dark, and Kareem knew she was waiting, daring him to attempt something reckless. He was reckless, but he wasn't foolish, so he massaged his neck where the bonds had squeezed and casually looked beyond her towards Hawklight. Her gaze had captivated him, and it had taken all his will to turn aside.

She beckoned with the tip of her staff, so he slowly stood and walked across to where Hawklight lay with his back against the rock. He saw his weapons arrayed at Hawklight's feet, just as he heard Kate's voice behind him.

"That's far enough, knife boy," she declared. "Sit on your hands!"

Kareem tried to stall, but she tapped his ribs with her staff where he'd hit the rock face, and that was all the encouragement he needed. He placed his hands palms down in the sand and sat his buttocks on top of them. He sat stoically while Hawklight appraised him.

"What's your name, boy?" he asked.

Kareem remained silent. He eyed the soldier, took in the uniform with the blue and green insignia. This was a captain in the army of Hogarth, the rebel city and home of the legendary golden girl who had defeated Varak. He glanced sideways over his shoulder and checked her out again. Her skin was brown, mottled, the colour of honey, gleaming in some places and dull in others. Certainly not the legend! He turned towards Hawklight again and waited.

"We know about the talisman," said Hawklight.

"My name is Captain Kareem El-Amin. And what business of yours is this talisman?"

"Two facing armies, one yours, made it our business, I'm afraid, Captain," replied Hawklight. "We were sent to assist in the recovery of this talisman in order to prevent further bloodshed, so to speak."

"How do I know to trust you?" Kareem spat back.

Hawklight gestured at him, sitting on his hands. "What choice do you have?" he asked.

Kareem shrugged and stole another quick glance at Kate. Her staff had not wavered.

"What now?" he asked.

"Well, since we're both seeking the same thing, we ought to be on each other's side, don't you agree? As a gesture of our good faith, we're giving you your freedom. You'll ride with us."

"Can I have my weapons back?"

"You can trust us, but we still can't trust you, I'm afraid, so the short answer is no," said Hawklight. "And there's no point in trying to escape either since we're headed in the same direction you are."

"You were following me, remember?"

"Yes, and we don't intend to change either. You will ride ahead of us where we can keep an eye on you, but don't worry: we're making for Goose Bay as well."

Kareem couldn't quite mask his surprise, and Hawklight noted the response with satisfaction. He would stay with them until he could determine how much they knew, which wasn't much more than they already had. They needed to keep bluffing. Kareem would lead them to the woman general. Hopefully she was closer to The Magician than they were.

Hawklight leaned forward, grimacing, and swept the litter of weapons into a blanket, which he rolled and strapped into a bundle that could be slung behind him on the *Hon'chai*. He struggled to stand and held out his hand to Kareem.

"Come along, Captain."

He helped Kareem to his feet, then turned his back casually and limped across to his mount where he secured the packed weaponry across its back. Kareem could have jumped him, but he knew the girl was just waiting for any excuse to clip him once again. He made a show of brushing the sand from his pants and tossed a grin in her direction, judging the distance between them. But when his eyes met hers, he felt himself tumbling into the black pits of her resolute stare once again, and a dread chill passed down his back, and the smile slipped from his face.

CHAPTER 9

Siobhan rested on top of the last rise and gazed down at the bustling port. Beyond it, the wide, blue lake seemed to stretch beyond infinity. The desert had thwarted the attempts of any plants to survive its bleak arid rock-infested plains, but they seemed to smell the promise of water and pushed out defiantly as far as the moisture in the air could be held beyond an hour or two each morning and evening. From where Siobhan sat, she could see the healthy green ribbon that grew out from the banks and continued along each side of the silt-laden Kampala River.

The river looked like a curving flat blade reflecting the sunlight in a blinding blaze of silver-white, pocked with tiny black dots that were the vessels that plied their trade along it, and across the magnificent lake. Somewhere down there, The Magician would be attempting to negotiate a fare across the lake to safety. She had to stop him before he succeeded.

Her mount seemed to sense her urgency; more likely, it sensed the sweet air, and the promise of a long thirst-quenching drink at the end of the ride. It snorted and tossed its head, and the famed horn swung in wide circles, so she nudged it forward and it began to pick its way down the slope and across the flat plain towards the road that led through the gates and into the heart of the port city.

She galloped past a long train of desert nomads stretched in a long, languid line as if time held no meaning for them beyond the present. Minutes later, she passed beneath the forbidding semi-circular arches of sandstone that marked one of three entry points to the city. Inside the gates, Goose Bay was like every bustling port of trade ever conceived. Crowds overflowed from the pavements into the streets, and the traffic was fiercely competitive. Hawkers and hustlers vied for business above the noise and the shouts of pedestrians squeezed by the lumbering carts and the litter taxis of the wealthy merchants. Everything was a wild melee of swirling colour and exotic spices that assailed the senses. Normally, Siobhan would have lingered to savour the sensation that some place could be so alive and so robust with activity, but she was impatient and frustrated by the congestion.

A hand from the crowd reached up to snatch the saddlebag slung around the *Hon'chai* and tucked beneath her leg. She swung the hard base of her staff across the outstretched wrist and heard a yelp of pain before the arm was pulled away. She looked for any sign of the would-be thief, but he had melted back into the swirling sea of faces.

The street looked like a logjam in a river, and she needed to find an alternative route through the city quickly. She tucked in behind a large caravan and was able to move to one side where she mounted the pavement and ducked down a narrow alley where the buildings leaned outwards towards each other like an avenue of trees above her head. She pushed past people on foot and collected a number of insults hurled in her direction for her efforts, but the alley emptied out into a maze of lanes and backstreet corridors all pointing in the general direction of the docks, and she was able to move more quickly again.

Nearer the docks, she passed a barn with a number of empty stalls, and she dismounted and led the *Hon'chai* across to a wizened nut-brown man sitting on a bale of straw with his back to the barn.

"Are you the owner?" she demanded.

He looked at her; took in her dusty uniform with the insignia of rank above the left pocket of her coat and noted the easy manner with which she held her fighting staff.

"How much to look after him?" she asked, indicating the snuffling animal standing behind her.

He shrugged. "You from Hornshurst? Used'ta be I'd take five bits per day. What they're minting now ain't worth nothin'."

He was correct. The Hornshurst 'bit' was a squared coin with the corners diagonally trimmed, made mostly of silver with another trace metal added for hardness, traded profitably across most of Bexus until recently, after Varak had annexed most of the silver for his own coffers. These days it was filled with lead: almost worthless. It was something else to be renegotiated with Cherath on her return.

She dug into her saddlebag and extracted a small leather pouch pulled tight with a drawstring. She teased it open and dug around with her fingers, and came up with a delicate ruby the size of her fingernail.

"Will this do instead?" she asked.

The man's eyes widened as the gem sparkled in her palm. He reached out and took it from her and examined it carefully, and then smiled at her.

"I ain't got no spare change," he warned.

"Just look after the animal," Siobhan replied.

"When are you plannin' on returning?"

She watched as he carefully pocketed the ruby. "If I'm not back by the time that runs out, you can sell him." Then she added, "But if I do come back for him, make sure he's still here. You understand?" And with that, she turned and continued towards the docks.

Charlie had had a long and pleasant association with the docklands of his past, and he grinned to himself as he pressed through the crowds seeking passage across the lake. He'd traded the lizard for some new clothing, some coin, a couple of extra sharp blades which he strapped to his ankles, and a long thin shiv that sat inside a narrow leather sheath strapped around his forearm beneath the sleeve of his coat. All three blades were constructed of the same tungsten mix that could shear through a life force with just the flick of a wrist. Now he just looked like any other merchant trader and not like a refugee from Cherath.

He tucked his knapsack tightly under one arm as he walked. The docks were like magnets for the criminally inclined, so there was no sense in tempting fate by being too casual. He scanned the sea of faces checking to see if any looked familiar, or if any were paying him more than just a passing glance. He saw nothing that interested him. *He'd made it!* By the time anyone searched for him here, assuming that he'd survived the desert in the first place, his trail would have long grown cold. Anyhow, once he had accessed the secrets of the talisman, they'd soon find out where he was. And they weren't going to like what they'd found!

He passed by the queues for the ferries. There were too many people waiting to board, increasing the chances that someone would remember his face. In a crowd, he was hard to miss. He continued on, looking for something more private.

He found it moored to the edge of one of the rotting piers at the far end of the docks away from the crowds. It had a wide wooden beam, was green with slime about the waterline, and had been daubed with a paint job so ancient it was difficult to discern the original colour, which might have been blue but was now a wasted, faded grey. The deck held a wheelhouse with a cracked windscreen and a broken wiper. The wheelhouse could be accessed by climbing a rusted ladder bolted to the wall of the cabin beneath. Towards the back, there was space for a hold and a miniature gantry crane for winching goods between the jetty and the boat. Charlie never bet against the odds, but he would have laid money on the fact that most of those goods would fall in the category marked 'illicit'. Perfect!

He found the captain, bent over a hatch above the hold, shouting abuse at the sole deckhand below. A bully and an underling! Charlie was mentally ticking off his checklist—so far, so good.

"I need a ride across the lake!" he called, looking down from the jetty.

The captain raised his head and surveyed Charlie. He was old and fat, but the years hauling sails and battling the elements had made him hard, like gnarled teak.

"Take a ferry!" he snarled and he lowered his head back into the hold. Charlie heard him begin cursing again.

"I need a ride across the lake. I don't need a ferry," he called again and kept his voice sweet but firm.

The grizzled head reappeared. The suggestion had been made. The bait was in the water, and the fish was circling.

"This ain't no cruise ship, sonny."

"I need a ride, not a cruise. I need privacy, and you do have that."

"It'll cost."

"I can pay."

"Cash up front."

Charlie unstrapped his knapsack and fished around for the purse. The statue hadn't been the only thing he'd snatched from Varak's bedchamber in the moments before he'd fled. He held up a diamond the size of a quail's egg.

"This is enough to buy your boat a hundred times over, but all I want is the ride," said Charlie.

The captain was a suspicious man by nature and, given the business he was in, this was normally a healthy trait.

"How do I know that's real?" he asked, despite knowing the answer already.

"Fine," said Charlie, and he pocketed the gem and began to wander back along the jetty. "I'll find someone else." He was a master of negotiation and knew instantly when greed tipped the scales in his favour. He'd only gone a couple of steps when he heard the captain shout, and there was no mistaking the pleading whine in his tone. Charlie stopped and smiled.

"Wait! No, wait! It just so happens we're heading across the lake. I'll take you where you want to go."

Charlie sauntered to the edge of the jetty and tossed the diamond out in a perfect arc. It sailed through the air, and was snatched cleanly by the captain who concentrated on examining the stone closely as Charlie clambered down onto the vessel.

Charlie pushed open the door to the cabin. The room was small, but there was a bunk that ran the length of one side. He dropped his knapsack on a chair beside the bunk and swept a pile of clothing strewn across the foot of the bunk on to the floor. The bedding was damp and stank, but Charlie figured he could put up with it for as long as it took to cross the lake. He spread his coat over the top blanket and lay down on the bunk and closed his eyes.

He heard the sound of cables squealing across their pulleys as the captain and his mate spent the next two hours loading one of the holds with heavy cargo that thumped against the floor of the hold before being properly stowed. He heard voices outside the cabin: orders shouted, directions called, all interspersed with colourful language and pressed with urgency. He remained in the cabin until the last of the crates had been loaded and the hold cover slid shut and locked in place.

He heard the slap of footsteps passing forward and aft as the hawsers were cast off and stored and felt the first gentle rocking as the boat slipped its moorings and slid away from the quay. He kicked his feet over the side of the bunk and threw his coat back on over his shoulders. He tucked the knapsack beneath his arm and opened the cabin door.

The captain was out of sight above him in the wheelhouse, guiding the boat as it passed by lines of similar craft still tethered to the wharf. The mate gave him a quick glance. He was a freckled, rangy youth, whose thin arms were busy hauling the large triangular mainsail slowly up the mast. Charlie would be just another anonymous face as far as he was concerned.

Charlie leaned against the handrail that ran along the side of the boat from the bow down past the cabin and watched the water pass beneath the hull. This close in, it was still a bright opaque green sullied with the silt carried down by the river and effluent from the city drains.

The boat picked up speed as it neared the end of the pier and the last of the moored boats. Beyond lay the vast blue expanse of the great lake. He felt the wind stirring; cool and moist, so different from the hot oven airs that tortured the desert, and he inhaled the sweet freshness and let his eyes wander to the end of the pier as the boat drew level with it.

There was a woman leaning against one of the dock pylons that marked the end of the pier. The same breeze that Charlie was enjoying had plucked her long hair back from her face, and it fluttered softly behind her. Even at this distance, she was strikingly beautiful, tall and lean and athletic. She was looking at Charlie, and he remembered his past when he was constantly surrounded by such beautiful women, and he began to yearn for those occasions where women—*Wait a minute!* She was *looking* at him!

She had gripped the pylon and was leaning forward, peering intently in his direction. She brought one hand up to shade her eyes against the glare of the water, and he saw her whole body stiffen. *Who was she?* He racked his memory, but he was sure he would have remembered her. One thing was immediately certain—she had recognised him! She let go of the pylon and sprinted back along the pier, hurdling crates and ropes strewn in her path. He followed her until she disappeared from sight behind a ramshackle warehouse.

The boat caught the breeze as it cleared the last approaches to the wharf and the sail stiffened and billowed, causing the craft to rock as it ploughed through the waves kicked up by the wind. Charlie moved unsteadily to the stern of the boat and kept his eyes peeled on the diminishing wharf for any sign of a following boat but nothing captured his attention.

An hour out and the brown smudge that was the shoreline had dipped below the horizon. The bow was rising and dropping monotonously, and Charlie felt seasick. He held tightly to the handrail and staggered back to the cabin where he collapsed onto the bunk and tried to think of something other than his pitching stomach. *Who was she?*

Siobhan couldn't believe her luck. The city was teeming with people, and most of them gravitated towards the docks. The chance of finding The Magician amongst them was virtually zero. She needed to pause and think: what would she do in his circumstances? Anonymity was the key—he wouldn't want anyone to recognise him; therefore, he'd avoid crowds. He'd look instead to charter a boat from someone who wouldn't ask too many questions. This line of reasoning led her to the dilapidated rows of piers that lined the underbelly of the Goose Bay docklands. He would be somewhere here.

She began by asking questions, but that quickly led her nowhere. Anyone asking questions in this part of town was viewed with suspicion and treated with contempt, and besides, she had only a vague idea of what The Magician looked like. Trying to describe someone you've never seen to someone who thinks you're an undercover cop was never going to succeed.

She spent the next three hours combing the docks for anyone resembling The Magician: large, brutal, menacing, and protectively carrying a bag close to his body. She saw several large, brutal, menacing men, but none carried knapsacks. She left two of them unconscious beside a stack of ripped wool bales behind a warehouse: neither confessed to seeing the man she was searching for.

She'd made two sweeps up and down the piers to no avail. The Magician had disappeared off the radar. She began to have doubts about predicting his behaviour. Perhaps the best place to hide a tree was, after all, in the middle of a forest. She leaned against a pylon at the end of the last pier and thought about returning to the commercial sector of the port where the various ferries were berthed and waiting to fill with passengers. It was where Kareem would expect to find her.

She heard the sharp crack of canvas as a sail caught a flying fist of wind and glanced towards the sound. A wooden wide-hulled sailboat was passing out of the channel created by the adjacent piers and into the lake. She saw the deckhand lashing a wooden barrel to the deck and flicked across to a large man leaning against the handrail holding tight to a dirty khaki bag wedged beneath his arm. His coat flapped against his knees, and he looked like a bat about to launch into flight. She saw his face, looked into his eyes and everything she knew about The Magician, everything she'd ever heard about him, coalesced in the figure gazing back at her.

She felt faint as the shocking realisation that he was escaping the net hit her like a physical blow. He was escaping! She turned and bolted back down the pier. There was no time left to lose. She needed to charter, buy, steal or hijack a boat and try to follow him. She couldn't even afford to leave behind a message for Kareem to follow, but she had faith enough to know he'd manage to find her and catch up with her eventually. The Magician had seen her, and he would know he had been followed. They'd lost the element of surprise, and it was down to an all-out race. She knew if she lost the trail he'd be gone for good. She needed a boat! Now!

CHAPTER 10

*I*t still took them the better part of four days to complete the journey, despite Hawklight's considerable navigational skills. Kareem led the way. Kate suspected him of subtle sabotage. He started by veering off track ever so slightly which, given the distances involved, meant they would have missed Goose Bay by fifty miles or more. She doubted he was truly lost, despite the fact that the landscape was numbingly and relentlessly unchanging. They were assaulted by dune after dune; an ocean of sandy waves.

Hawklight's sense of direction was unerring, and he gently corrected the direction on each occasion. In no time, Kareem got the message that he was unlikely to lead them astray and he gave up trying. His sense of direction miraculously returned, and it then became a matter of pride to keep Hawklight from correcting him again.

Kareem also tried to leave clues along the trail in case a search party from Hornshurst was sent out, but Hawklight just as surreptitiously erased them. *Boys!* thought Kate, and she had to roll her eyes at their little macho games.

Despite this, they made good time through the desert, and by the morning of the fourth day they were overlooking the port from a similar hillock to the one from which Siobhan had first seen the city. Even from that distance, they could see the constant stream of travellers moving through the gates.

Kate and Hawklight sat together, a short distance from Kareem while they rested their mounts.

"How do we do this?" Kate whispered. They were both aware that Kareem was waiting for any opportunity to escape. Each night, Kate used a restraint charm to tether him by the ankle so that he couldn't sneak off into the night and the two of them could get some rest. Unrestrained, trapped in a milling throng of people, he'd give them the slip easily. In such crowds, it would be difficult to stay together under any circumstances.

Hawklight was silent. Kate suspected he was considering a number of options.

"Let's just zap him," she suggested. "Then we could roll him up in his blanket and pretend that he was ill." She twitched at the thought. Something about him needled her: his arrogance, his apparent ruthlessness, and his fearlessness. She was also unnerved by the way he looked at her. As a result, Rhyanon was never far from her grasp.

Hawklight ignored her. Instead, he beckoned for Kareem to join them.

The youth was truculent and restless, eager to reach the city. He squatted in the sand and glared at Hawklight who didn't seem to mind.

"Two possibilities spring to mind," Hawklight began while absently tracing patterns in the sand with a stick. "Either your friend is down there somewhere with The Magician, or he has escaped, and she has followed him. Wouldn't you agree?"

Kareem's face was stonily impassive. Kate just wanted to slap him.

"Either way, we need to find them, and we need to work together on this. We need you to promise you won't try to escape once we reach the city."

It was Kate's turn to glare at Hawklight. *What was he thinking?* The guy was as slippery as a greasy pole and Hawklight was going to try and hold him to a promise?

"Let me zap him, please!" she implored him again but Hawklight just smiled at the suggestion.

Kareem shifted his gaze to her. His face remained inscrutable, and she had to look away. She hated that he did that to her.

"Give me back my staff," he said, turning back to Hawklight.

"I can't do that yet. You'll get it back when we meet up with your companion."

Kareem considered his options. Time was ticking away, and if The Magician had indeed escaped, every second counted.

"I promise," he said at last.

Hawklight smiled and gave Kate a quick *That was easy!* look before they remounted their *Hon'chai* and pointed them in the direction of the beckoning gates of Goose Bay.

— *m* —

They collided with a carnival. They were swept along with a crowd the moment they passed beneath the imposing gates and were diverted away from the direction of the docks and towards the old centre of the city by the tide of partygoers.

Horns tooted and music blared, and the press of bodies grew tighter the closer they got. Eventually, they emptied out into the main plaza, which was awash with gyrating bodies gaudily dressed in every colour under the rainbow. Gangs of youths roamed with buckets of water and bags of dye; anyone was fair game and most of the onlookers were already plastered in dripping paint, ducking, screaming, and laughing. Towards the centre, the participants—masked and dressed in shimmering silver costumes—were holding aloft effigies on long poles, which they moved like marionettes in a puppet show.

Kate had never seen anything like it, and her gaze was drawn to the convulsive gestures of the towering puppets. Someone was running about beneath them. He was holding a cage of bamboo which sparked as if it had been interlaced with firecrackers, and he was like a crazy cow, ducking and weaving and chasing anyone who stepped into his path. She was too entranced by the atmosphere, so she missed the moment that Kareem slipped from his mount and disappeared below the sea of humanity that had isolated him from the others.

It was already too late when she screamed across the short gap at Hawklight.

"He's getting away!"

Hawklight tried to dismount, but there were just too many people. He searched the plaza from his mounted vantage point.

"There!" he cried, pointing towards the opposite corner of the square. Kate was able to make out the familiar black curls tied back in a tail down his neck. She cursed him and cursed Hawklight in the same breath.

Kareem reached the exit and pushed past the latecomers struggling to find a way into the plaza to join in the fun. He turned briefly and glanced back across the square. He could see Hawklight pointing at him, and he glanced across at the girl. He flashed her a grin and flicked a mock salute at her before dropping out of sight once again. His final vision of Kate was of her finely balanced astride the *Hon'chai* levelling her staff at him, trying to get a bead on his head.

There had only been one opportunity, and Kareem had snatched it. What was a promise to those people who told him that they trusted him with their mouths but whose actions said otherwise? Well they were right not to trust him. Varak, with all his corrupted power, had still sought the collective wisdom and knowledge gathered over millennia inside the *Toki-Moai*. That was power! Why else would two soldiers from Hogarth be following except to claim the same prize for the legendary golden girl who had defeated Varak? The talisman belonged to Hornshurst. He had been entrusted to return with it. He would not be a pawn in another power struggle.

The man was as good a tracker as Kareem had ever seen; better, even, than his old mentor back in Hornshurst who could track the path of an animal by the changes created by the mere passing of its shadow across the ground. Despite the urgency, he spent two hours laying subtle but false trails across the city, dead-ending them within the labyrinth of twisted alleyways and back yards. He was meticulous in concealing evidence of his exits, using rooftops and leaping between buildings, hitching rides on lumbering wagons, treading in the footsteps of others directly in front of him. He could afford to leave nothing to chance, but after two hours, even he was satisfied with the result.

He'd kept an eye out for any sign of Siobhan throughout, but there had been none. She had to be down at the docks, and he needed to be especially careful there. The other two would head in that direction as soon as they lost his spoor, but he had the advantage. The big man would be hard to miss in a crowd, and Kareem's eyes were sharper than most.

He backtracked almost to the plaza and allowed himself to be carried along in the midst of the revellers before sneaking away down another side street. He paused in a darkened doorway and waited, watching, but nobody followed. He was safe.

He passed a livery stable and froze. He recognised the *Hon'chai* inside one of the stalls. It was the animal Siobhan had been riding. An old man was mucking out the adjacent stall and never heard Kareem approach.

"The woman who left that mount," whispered Kareem and the old man leaped back, startled. "Did she leave a message? Did she say where she was headed?"

"What do you mean, creeping up on an old man like that?" the little man retorted, clearly angry.

I don't have time for this! thought Kareem, and he picked up the man by the lapels of his leather jerkin and suspended him from a coat hook drilled into one of the beams that held the loft.

"Hey! Hey! Put me down!" the old guy shouted, kicking his legs that were now eighteen inches off the floor. Kareem stepped back and pushed the barn door closed, and the man's agitation was suddenly laced with fear.

"Who are you? What do you want?" he asked.

"Tell me about the woman," said Kareem, keeping his voice level and calm.

"What do I know? She paid me to look after the animal. Said if she didn't return, I could sell it. What's it to you?"

"Where did she go?"

"She didn't say. She headed towards the docks. She was in a hurry."

"There was a big man. Did she follow him?"

"What? I didn't see any big man. She looked to be on her own. Just dropped off the animal and left, I'm telling you."

Kareem squinted at the man, trying to find some telltale sign he may have been lying. He took one step forward, and the man's eyes widened in fear, and he raised his hands in front of his face.

"Don't hurt me! Don't hurt me, please! I don't know what this is about!"

He was telling the truth. Siobhan had promised to leave a message behind, and she would have left it with this man, knowing Kareem would recognise the *Hon'chai*. Something had happened! Something that wouldn't wait! The answer lay somewhere on the docks.

Kareem pushed open the barn door again.

"Hey! Hey, where're you going? Hey! Come back! You can't leave me here!"

But, of course, he did.

There was no sign of the two Hogarth soldiers. Kareem kept to the shadows and scoured the docks for any sign of Siobhan. Night had fallen and had swallowed her up. Almost!

He discovered the faint outline of her boot in the dust outside an abandoned wool shed at the entrance to one of the last decrepit piers at the far end of the docks. She'd been running—sprinting—back along it. She had to have been standing at the edge of the pier and seen something, someone! She'd caught sight of The Magician!

He stared out into the dark as if he still hoped to catch a glimpse of her out there on the water somewhere. She would be following behind in another boat, making sure the trail did not grow cold. He needed to catch up with her before that happened.

He followed the signs along the wharf—a faint tread mark, freshly splintered timber, a scuffed barrel she'd collided with—to where they led out to another pier. He remained in the shadows, moving slowly along, occasionally peering over the side. Halfway along, he spied a vacant berth, a gap between two moored boats, and knew she'd found a craft. It was his turn.

He heard the sound of approaching voices and ducked behind a crate draped with a mould-speckled tarpaulin that had dried in the wind and stiffened like cardboard. Two men materialised out of the gloom; one carried a lantern and both were armed with long truncheons that swung from their belts.

". . . right out from under his nose. One minute it was there, and the next bleedin' time he checked it was gone, can you believe it?"

"Yeah, well, this part of the docks ain't no angel's quarters," said the other. "Mind you, I ain't complainin'. More work, more pay, and with all of us scurryin' about like rats up a drainpipe, ain't no one gonna try that again in a hurry."

Kareem's teeth flashed in the shadows. *Don't bet on that!* he thought. He waited in the deep shadow until the two security guards disappeared back into the darkness and the sounds of their footsteps thumping on the wooden planks receded. The world was silent, save for the slosh of waves against the pylons beneath his feet and the occasional grind of hull against pier.

He raised his head cautiously and checked the pier for any sign of movement. He was alone for now, but there was no telling how soon the night watchmen would reappear on their rounds. He needed to work quickly but stealthily.

He crab-walked across to the edge and paid closer attention to the various craft tied up to the wharf. Most were too large for one man to handle alone; he needed something smaller, something sleek and swift. A light came on two boats down, and he ducked back out of sight. He heard footsteps clamber down a ladder and across a deck, followed by the slamming of a cabin door. It was a warning to be careful. The world was full of prying eyes.

He spotted the boat he wanted, but it was moored against one of the adjacent piers. It was a smack, a small fishing boat with a single mast, about twenty-four feet long. Kareem knew how to sail—he had crewed on dhows during his short spell on Earth. This vessel was ideal.

He picked his way among the shadows back along the pier and gradually worked his way around to the opposite side of the narrow channel that had separated the two. He easily avoided the night watchmen who were resting on a couple of crates with their feet up, out of the wind. Once again, he sat in the shadows and watched the pier for any sign of movement, anything out of the ordinary. Only when he was sure he was alone did he venture further along the pier to where the boat floated alongside a narrow jetty reached by a set of creaking wooden steps.

The wharf was alive with the creaks and groans as rotten timbers protested the slow weathering and gradual decay. This close to the lake's surface, the water was trapped and stagnant and lapped at the planks that formed the tiny jetty.

Two guy ropes, forward and aft, held the boat steady in place. Kareem slipped the first one clear of the iron hoop and tossed it into the boat. He reached for the other just as a flash of light briefly punctured the darkness above and a long blue-glowing plasma cord wrapped around his neck and pulled tight. Kareem twisted in surprise and toppled into the boat, struggling to wedge his fingers between the cord and his neck while the cord reacted to his struggles by contracting even tighter. He couldn't resist and gave up. He lay on his back and stared up at the stars that were visible between the clouds.

Two shadows slowly descended the stairs. The smaller shadow held a staff from which the blue plasma binding emanated, and Kareem's heart sank as he recognised them.

"You might want to think about loosening that off a bit," he heard Hawklight say and immediately felt the tension around his neck ease. One of the moons low in the sky poked out from behind a cloud, and Kareem stared up into the icy blue eyes that caught the moonlight. Her head was still hidden behind the cowl of a cloak, and when she tossed her head and flicked it back, he could see the patchy honey coloured aura of her skin.

He rose on to his elbows carefully. The glare of the blue eyes was merciless; she didn't need any encouragement to choke him.

"How did you find me?" he asked, puzzled. He had taken every precaution to keep hidden.

"You certainly didn't make it easy for us," admitted Hawklight, and he glanced towards the girl, "but then again, I've had my fair share of practice." Kareem caught the slight smile that curled the edges of her mouth.

She stepped into the boat, and Hawklight followed, a little unsteadily, tossing their meagre belongings ahead of him. Kareem derived little satisfaction knowing that his own staff was amongst them.

"Congratulations," he said, and hoped that the sarcasm was evident in his tone. Neither of the two reacted. "What now?"

Hawklight sat heavily in the boat beside Kate, and the small craft rocked gently with the movement. Hawklight did not look comfortable.

"Since you've gone to the trouble of stealing the boat, my guess is that you know The Magician has escaped and that your friend is tracking him, and you have a fair idea where they are going. I suggest we follow them."

"What if I refuse to cooperate with you any further?"

"Then there would be nothing to prevent us from handing you over to the little man you left hanging in his barn. He wasn't very happy about that, you know."

A sudden pulse of energy passed along the rope and caught Kareem like a jolt from a stun gun, leaving him flopping like a fish on the deck for a few seconds.

"He made us promise to do that to remember him by," said Kate. "You'll notice that when *we* make a promise, we keep to it." She gave him the same look she'd given him when he'd last looked at her from across the crowded plaza. This time there was nobody between them. Kareem edged backwards uncomfortably, and the plasma hummed about his neck.

"On the other hand," Hawklight continued as if nothing had happened, "our offer still stands. The sooner we leave, the less likely The Magician will give us the slip. You are an exceptional tracker. You now know how good I am. We would work better as a team, don't you think?"

"Again, I ask: why should I trust you? You didn't trust me."

"And how right were we?" Kate interrupted. "You dumped us first chance you could."

"Because you want the talisman for yourselves," Kareem snapped back at her. "You'll deliver it to your precious golden legend. Is that what you want? Another Varak?"

Kareem hadn't recognised her! He'd only heard about the legend of the golden girl who had conquered Varak. He hadn't learned about the personal cost that had caused her aura to fade to a mottled honey brown. He didn't know who she was. Hawklight was on the brink of saying something, but she silenced him with a quick knowing look.

"You're wrong," she whispered.

"Am I?" he asked. The anger had gone from his voice, replaced by sadness that suggested he wished he was wrong but wasn't.

He heard Kate whisper but couldn't make out the words. The plasma cord about his neck suddenly disappeared. Rhyanon's tip glowed blue and faded, and Kate placed her staff at her feet.

Kareem was confused. What was going on here? He rubbed his throat where the cord had nearly strangled him.

"We don't have much time," said Hawklight. Kareem heard voices in the distance. The night watchmen had resumed their patrol and were headed along the pier beside them. He nodded reluctantly, then leaned out of the boat and released the single rope that kept them tied to the jetty.

He pointed to the tiller and said to Kate, "Swap places and sit back here and steer this thing while I get us under way."

The boat wavered as they edged past each other, and Kareem noticed that Hawklight held a firm grip on the side of the boat. He unfurled the sail and hauled on the rope, and the triangular canvas slid up the mast. The breeze stiffened the sail and the small boat edged silently out into the channel. Enough moonlight reflected off the surface of the water for Kate to see to steer, and as they sailed past the end of the jutting pier, they could just make out the frustrated cries of the two security men who'd now lost another boat.

The prevailing breeze carried across the lake, and Kareem reasoned it would not only be easier but also faster to sail with the wind. The Magician would have gone that way; Siobhan would have followed in his wake.

Two hours in, the wind picked up. Kareem had been watching the stars, and he noted the glint of satisfaction in Hawklight's eyes as he maintained a steady course. Two hours in, the cloud suddenly rolled in and blotted out the night sky, and the waves grew in size. Kareem had resumed his seat at the tiller, steering with one hand and controlling the boom of the sail with the other, feeling the vagaries of the wind and judging the growing tension against the guide rope. The signs were not good.

Water sloshed over the bow as the vessel dipped into the troughs of the waves. Kareem shouted above the wind to the others.

"Grab some buckets and get bailing!" They needed no further encouragement as more water covered the bottom of the boat. Kate could see lightning illuminate the sky in the middle of the lake and the peal of thunder rumbled across the surface of the water. A storm was bearing down on them.

"Can we turn back?" she yelled as the first raindrops splattered about her.

Kareem shook his head. "Either way it will catch us. We can't outrun it!" He called her over and handed her the tiller.

"Keep the bow pointed into the big waves!" he instructed and scurried forward to furl the sail and strap it securely against the boom.

The wind had gusted close to gale force and the edge of the storm hit hard. Waves ploughed into the boat, and it began to take on more water. Hawklight bailed with one hand; he refused to let go of the side of the boat with the other. Kate squinted into the stinging rain that blinded her as she attempted to keep the bow pointed into the oncoming waves. She saw Kareem pulling open a compartment hatch at the bow, and he hauled out an armful of canvas, which trailed a series of ropes from its edge. It looked to Kate like a crumpled parachute. He stumbled back towards the stern.

"It's a sea anchor!" she heard him yell above the din of the wind. He quickly knotted the trailing rope to a cleat in the stern and heaved the canvas out into the boiling lake like a fisherman casting a net. The canvas sank below the surface but began to fill with water as it trailed behind the boat. As the rope stretched taut, Kate felt the tension in the rudder ease as the anchor acted to pull the boat in line with the driving waves.

"We have to ride it out!" Kareem screamed through cupped hands. "Let's get busy bailing!"

The three of them fell to furiously bucketing the water from inside the boat. As quickly as they tossed it out, more spilled back over the bow and sloshed about their ankles. The night was pitch black, and Kate could barely make out the light of her aura surrounding her skin. She had ditched the heavy cloak and her head, arms and lower legs were bare and dripping wet. Her hair was plastered across her forehead, and she was soaked and shivering with the cold, despite the constant activity of bailing, for there were no muscles to help generate heat. How ridiculous to have come this far only to drown in some nameless lake!

The wind continued to shriek, but Kate heard something else; a deeper sound, like a long, low groan and she stopped bailing to lift her head and listen. Kareem heard it too, and she saw him staring into the blackness beyond the heaving bow. Hawklight had glanced at them before he quit bailing also, and the three of them waited, staring into the rain-lashed void, motionless, as the groan intensified.

At first, it was just a horizontal white line as if someone had run past a black wall and swiped it with a white paintbrush, but the line grew in size and loomed higher as it bore down on them.

Kareem threw down his bailing bucket and screamed: "Hold on tight!"

Kate immediately dropped and wrapped both arms around the base of the mast as the rogue wave rose above them and the tiny boat began the impossible task of scaling the steep leading wall. It nearly made it, but the rope from the trailing anchor pulled up short of the crest, and the craft strained like a dog at the end of its leash before it tilted to the left and was bowled by the force of the wave.

The three of them were flicked into the lake and driven deep below its surface as the boat rolled through three hundred and sixty degrees above their heads and the giant wave passed by. Kate followed the line of bubbles upwards as she clawed her way back to the surface. She broke through with a gasp that sounded like a languishing sob and was on the brink of being drawn back beneath the waves when a strong arm grabbed her from behind and held her head above water.

Kareem cradled her close to him, tucking her between his arm and his body, trying to keep her head above the thrashing, pounding waves, but she fought against him and slipped from his grasp. Moments later, she resurfaced beside him, and as he reached for her once more, she gripped his head between her two hands and screamed into his face.

"*Hawklight! Find Hawklight!* He can't swim! Leave me! I can make it back to the boat!"

He opened his mouth to argue, but she yelled him down.

"Don't you understand? *Find Hawklight!*"

A flash of lightning lit her face. Her eyes were wide, fearful, and pleading. He nodded, hesitantly at first, but she fixed him with such a terrible, intensive stare that he agreed. She let him go then, and drove through the water to where the boat drifted at the end of its anchor.

The lake dragged at her clothing and filled her boots, but she refused to kick them off. By the time she reached the side of the boat, Kate was almost to the point of exhaustion. She made three attempts to latch on to the gunwale before her hand clawed a hold, and for a moment she was stretched between the safety of the boat and the sucking dead weight of her waterlogged clothing. She could feel the strength in her arms ebb away; it was now or never.

She caught hold with her other hand and hauled upwards, screaming with all the passion and intensity she could muster. She forced one elbow over the edge of the boat, and then the other so that she was hanging from her armpits. Her leg slithered and scraped the wooden hull as she twisted her body to the right and she kicked out and hooked her knee over the gunwale. And then, with one final determined effort, she pulled herself back into the boat and floated about in the water trapped in the bottom.

She wanted to lie still, to close her eyes and sleep away the aching tiredness, but that was impossible. She rolled to her knees, thigh deep in sloshing water, grabbed a bucket that floated by and began a slow steady rhythm of bailing once more. The water level inside the boat did not go down, but it wasn't going up either. And all the while, she whipped her head about searching for any signs of Hawklight or Kareem.

The raindrops peppered her face and her hair was pasted across her eyes. Shafts of lightning exposed the lake like the blue-white snap of a camera flash. All about her, the whitecaps pitched and boiled and drove past the boat in surging waves.

"Hawklight!" she screamed at the night. *"Hawklight!"*

There was still no sign of either man. Kate was alone, adrift in a twenty-foot tub that was not designed to weather storms. Even if she survived the night, she couldn't sail and was out of sight of land. She couldn't even begin to worry about that now; her first priority was to keep the boat afloat.

Another wave washed over the bow creating a smaller wave that ran past her feet the length of the boat. She struggled to suppress the sob that lodged in her throat at the futility of emptying the boat; that one wave had erased all her efforts of the previous ten minutes.

She slumped against the hull defeated and exhausted, and searched the lake surface fruitlessly. Her face was streaming water, and this time the rain had mixed with her tears that she was powerless to prevent. It had been more than half an hour by her reckoning, perhaps as much as forty-five minutes since she'd left Kareem in the water. *What had she been thinking?* She should have stayed behind, to have floundered and dived into the cold, black depths, flailing about hoping to bump into Hawklight. Instead, she had lit out for the boat and surrendered Hawklight's fate to someone who had tried to kill the both of them.

A hand hit the gunwale at her shoulder and was accompanied by a soulful agonised cry of despair. Kate whirled about and latched on to the wrist before it slipped back out of sight. She rose to her knees and looked out and over the boat.

Kareem's pale face stared up at her. His lips were turning blue, and he couldn't manage to spit the water from his open, gasping mouth. One arm gripped the gunwale, and his other was locked under Hawklight's upturned chin. Hawklight's eyes and mouth were closed, and water continued to splash across his face.

"Help me!" moaned Kareem, cut short by another mouthful of water. He tried again. "Help me get him into the boat!"

He pulled his other arm tighter and Hawklight's head washed into the side of the boat. Kate let go of Kareem's wrist and bent down and caught hold of Hawklight's shirt. She manoeuvred both her hands beneath his armpits and hauled back with all her strength. He was bulky and heavy and waterlogged, and she only managed to haul him partway out of the lake before he slipped back in.

"He's too heavy! I can't lift him!" she cried.

Kareem had clutched the gunwale with both hands, resting his head against his outstretched arms. He turned to Kate and said: "Then let him go."

"No!" she screamed at him. "Push him from below!"

Kareem was wholly spent, yet he let go of the boat and drifted back to where he was able to wrap his arms around Hawklight's waist.

"Again!" she cried. "Now!"

She hauled as hard as she was able. She pressed her legs into the side of the boat and used the strength of her thighs for extra leverage. One of Kareem's hands gripped the edge of the boat once more, and she felt him shoulder Hawklight's weight to boost him upwards. Hawklight's shoulders rose above the gunwale, then his chest, and then, with one final concentrated haul she yanked him into the boat. His head splashed into the water rolling about the bottom and she quickly stooped and lifted it clear and propped him half-lying, half-sitting against one of the wooden planks that served as a seat.

She turned and expected to see Kareem scrabble aboard, but there was no sign of him. She rushed to the side just as his body began to float away from the boat. She leaned out and stretched her arm towards him and nearly toppled back into the lake again. Her fingers brushed his sodden jacket, and she locked her fingers into the leather and pulled him back to the boat.

After Hawklight, his light frame was almost a breeze to haul aboard, and she dragged him and laid him alongside Hawklight. She sat back and gazed for a quiet moment at the two unconscious forms slumped together in the boat, and she smiled. Suddenly she had purpose once again. She reached for the bucket and resumed the steady rhythm of bailing.

The clouds were layered thick and heavy grey and the rays of the breaking sun burned their bellies with the angry red that advertised the foul weather was far from over, but at least the storm had abated. The rain was gone, and the high swells had shrunk to a confused wind-blown chop.

Most of the water that had threatened to swamp the boat had been bailed overboard during the night. Kate had continued emptying bucketful after bucketful until she passed out through exhaustion, leaving the boat to bob about at the mercy of the elements until the dawn.

A faint breeze brushed lightly against her cheek, and the tickling of her hair across her face teased her awake. She felt as if she were moving. Her eyelids fluttered as she took a moment to reorient herself. The first thing she saw was Kareem, bedraggled and soaked like a drowned rat, pale and barely awake himself, holding the tiller and steering to maintain maximum trim before the wind.

She was leaning against Hawklight who appeared to be sleeping. Sometime during the night, Kareem must have shifted her. She never felt a thing. She watched him through hooded lids for a long time as he sat alone at the stern, his face a pale impassive mask.

Eventually, she stirred and slowly sat up. She felt stiff, cold and sore, and she stretched as if to ease the aches. Kareem watched her. She was aware of the distance between them, far greater than the few feet of boat that separated them.

"Last night, I—" she began and then hesitated, lost for words. Finally, she just looked into his eyes and said: "Thank you for everything."

His face softened, but his eyes remained glazed and cold. She glanced away; at Hawklight, to one side, and at their belongings, securely lashed, to the other. She eased forward and loosened the rope that secured them, and then carefully unrolled the thin blanket that had protected their staffs.

She withdrew Kareem's, and fondled the beautifully inlaid filigree that was the mark of extraordinary craftsmanship. It was heavier in her hand than Rhyanon, but just as finely balanced: a perfect weapon.

"Here," she said and she handed it across to him. He looked at it briefly as if considering the nature of the gesture, and then reached out and took it from her. He laid it carefully at his feet, and then his eyes rested on her face once more. She scrutinized him closely, searching for some sort of acknowledgement. She thought maybe his eyes had softened slightly as well, but she couldn't be sure.

He broke her gaze to check the luff of the sail. She leaned back against Hawklight's shoulder and stared out moodily across the endless tossing whitecaps.

CHAPTER 11

harlie spent most of the first day flat on his back in his cabin. He had all the symptoms of seasickness, apart from the most obvious one of heaving violently over the side of the boat. Nevertheless, he certainly felt as if he had a full stomach that was threatening to rebel from the endless rocking motion. He managed to stagger off the bunk to wedge a chair against the handle of his cabin door. He knew to expect a visit at some stage; he just didn't want it to happen when he was incapacitated.

He tasted the change in the air later in the afternoon as it wafted in through the porthole that had rusted and jammed in a partly open position. He had finally drifted off to sleep, and when he awoke he felt far more settled. He slipped his bag across his shoulder and tucked it safely beneath his arm, then gathered his staff, tipped the chair aside and stepped unsteadily out into the late afternoon sun and leaned on the handrail that ran either side of the bow.

The deckhand was somewhere below deck, and the captain's weathered pigskin of a face could be seen through the cracked windscreen of the wheelhouse. The wind had balled the sails and the boat was skimming along the lake tossing up spray in its wake.

Charlie could see a vast, towering mass of black thundercloud away to his right. That explained the change in the air: cooler and fresher and ionised with ozone. The captain followed his gaze and rolled down the window.

"Nothing to worry about, squire," he called. We're well west of her and running with the wind. She'd be a big'un though. Smart money would be to head for shelter if you looked to be caught up in her."

Charlie nodded absently and kept his eyes on the horizon, which seemed to be the only stable line in an otherwise rocking universe. He could make out a faint olive-green line with another smudged line of thin grey cloud above it.

"Is that the other side of the lake over there?" he called out to the captain.

"Aye," replied the captain. "There's a bay, slightly northwest of us. We have to anchor there briefly to unload the cargo. It might be an idea to stay inside your cabin then, squire. Lips can't lie about what the eyes don't see, eh? Might take a couple, three hours. Then, after that, we're all yours."

Charlie nodded again and briefly considered that fact that he'd been constantly immersed in criminal activity over two lifetimes. He wondered if there was such a thing as fate after all. He headed back to the cabin as the vessel altered course and tilted slightly with the wind.

He replaced the chair against the door and left his staff propped upright against the bunk head. He leaned his back against the lumpy pillow, fished into his bag and pulled out the preciously wrapped package. He peeled the velvet layers away to expose the strange, silver-coloured statue.

The emerald eyes, the lapis necklace, and the ruby heart: any of these alone would be worth a minor fortune. If all else failed, Charlie would take to it with a knife and prise out the precious gems. They would pay for a small army; maybe it would be third time lucky for Charlie.

However, Varak had resisted the temptation to plunder. He'd spoken of the power within—the power to control destiny and the infinite knowledge that came with it. If that were true, then the value of the gems paled into insignificance in comparison.

There were three locks, and Varak had somehow managed to open two of them. As he twisted one of the metal arms and felt the soft click as tumblers aligned inside the lock, Charlie's mind cast back and made the sudden connection he'd never before suspected.

He remembered the two old men—druids, according to his network of Hornshurst informants—whom Varak had dedicated the better part of a decade to locating. They had been captured just before the time Charlie had been appointed Head of Security, at a time when he was out of the loop but far enough inside the trusted circle around Varak.

Charlie had witnessed some of the sessions between Varak and the two old men, which had forced even him to turn against the sweating block walls of the dungeon in disgust. The levels of pain were exquisite because Varak had been meticulously patient, waiting on the confessions he knew would escape their lips. Still, Charlie had to wonder what secrets were of such value that they forced the men to keep their silence for so long. He would have broken one hundred percent.

The druids broke too—it was always just a matter of time. Twice, Varak bent his ear to their ravaged whispers, and twice he rushed from the room. There was no third time.

The inner circle had been infiltrated, but it only took one man. He ended the suffering with two rapid high-energy pulses before turning the staff on himself, which left Varak in a homicidal rage for days and resulted in the summary executions of many of Hornshurst's leading citizens. Anyone else who knew the combinations had been swept into hiding, and when the two druids were assassinated, access to the *Toki-Moai* went with them.

Until now! Charlie was determined to change all that. Two down and one to go: those were pretty good odds where the prize was Master of Destiny.

The muffled voices outside brought him back to reality with a thump. The truth was he was alone and on the run with a statue that didn't do much, and stranded on a rust bucket connected with a criminal organisation beyond his control. He suspected things would get worse before they got better.

He heard the splash of an anchor and the loud clanking as the anchor chain ran out over the side. A moment later, he felt the sudden jolt of another craft banging against the hull as it drew alongside. There were voices, conversations in a language he didn't recognise or understand. The boat rocked as the crates and bales that had been hidden in the hold were winched up and transferred across to the other vessel. He sat with his back to the wall, facing the door with his staff across his knee and waited.

The image of the woman at the end of the pier crept back into his mind, and he tried again to recall if he had seen her before; perhaps met her somewhere. He doubted it though—he knew he would have remembered her. So she was a stranger, and she had recognised him. He had been looking directly at her and had seen her face change, had seen the momentary flash of panic pass across it, and watched as she turned and ran.

He didn't believe she could have followed him from Cherath. She must have lived in Goose Bay—that was it! But his little inner voice piped up, intruding on his line of thought and interrupting the moment. *She is connected to the talisman!* it was telling him. *Somehow she knew you had it!*

Well, tough cheese, he replied. She's too late; she *missed the boat,* and he smiled inwardly at his private joke. I've got a whole coastline to get lost along. But despite his show of confidence, he felt a residual tickle down his back as if he were being watched, and he made a mental note to be more careful in future.

The promised three hours had stretched to four before Charlie heard the last of the heavy footsteps descend the gangplank, and the sound of the deck hand straining against the windlass as he slowly winched the anchor back to the surface. He heard the lapping of the water against the hull outside the cabin as the boat picked up speed. He hopped off the bunk and peered through the grimy glass of the porthole and watched the bay recede as the vessel made for deeper water and started the run parallel to the shore.

One advantage of having a criminal mind is that often you can guess what the other guy will do before he thinks of it by himself. The duck-egg diamond had virtually guaranteed the reaction.

Charlie knew the captain wouldn't move against him while there were others around. It would have been the safest move, but it would also have meant sharing the booty. He would wait until he'd offloaded his cargo, wait until he was well out in the lake and alone. There were bound to be more diamonds ripe for the picking if Charlie had chosen that one just to purchase a ride across the lake.

He was a burly man, so he knew they would make their move in the early hours of the morning when he would be expected to be well asleep. He still had a few hours up his sleeve until then, provided they were true to form.

He carefully rewrapped the *Toki-Moai* and tucked it in place at the bottom of his bag. He then removed the thin mattress from the top bunk and rolled it tightly and secured it with strips of material torn from one of the sheets. He peeled back the rough blanket that covered the bunk, and laid the roll on the bed, then tucked the blanket back into place, and stood back to review his handiwork.

In the dark, the roll would look like a sleeping body. He hoped the dummy would provide the distraction and give him the time he needed. Satisfied, Charlie picked up his bag and tucked it over his shoulder out of the way. He gripped his staff in two hands and leant against the door, listening for any sounds of movement.

Everything was quiet. He lifted the chair away and opened the cabin door a crack. The evening was fading fast; only a dull grey glow lit up a section of the horizon and many stars had already made an appearance.

The deck was empty. The deck hand was most likely in the wheelhouse with the captain. Charlie could see across to the hatch covering the access to the hold. It was partly open. Perfect!

He ducked and darted for the hatch. The wheelhouse was facing forward near the bow. No one would have seen a thing. Charlie tested the hatch; it was heavily greased and slid back in its rails silently. He stepped on to the metal ladder and lowered himself just far enough so that he could see through the slit when he pulled the hatch back into place.

They were early because they were greedy. Charlie felt the speed of the boat slacken, heard the flapping of canvas as the sails deflated, and saw two shapes pass beneath the lantern that hung outside the door to the wheelhouse. *Coming, ready or not!* thought Charlie and he gripped his staff in one hand and the ladder with the other.

He noticed that the captain let the deck hand lead while he hung back. They stopped outside the cabin door, and the deck hand reached out and slowly turned the handle. The door opened a fraction.

Then all hell broke loose. The deck hand burst through the cabin door, leading with his staff. The captain immediately followed, and there was a muffled, shouted command and a brief flash of flame. At the same time, Charlie slid the hatch back and vaulted on to the deck covering the distance between the hatch and the cabin in the same time it took the older captain to figure it was safe to enter.

Charlie loomed in the doorway and watched as the old man coshed the rolled mattress with a short length of lead pipe. As he peeled the blanket back, Charlie spoke.

"It's lumpy to lie on, but it still doesn't deserve that sort of treatment."

Both men whirled at the sound, but the cabin was cramped and the deck hand couldn't raise his staff in time. Charlie clipped him with a speciality he'd developed over the years in Varak's service that added a little spicy extra to the body slam punch it delivered. It usually left the recipient unconscious with his eyes wide open because it was quicker acting than the blink reflex.

The captain stood, stunned by this sudden turn of events. Charlie almost could hear his mind whirring as he scrambled for a plausible explanation for being in the cabin with malicious intent. He shook his head.

"Don't bother," he said. "I can't think of one either."

He had the captain drag the deck hand to the stern of the boat, then settled in and sat facing them until dawn broke. The boat had floundered in the water and was drifting slowly in some unseen current but was still perhaps a good half-mile from shore. Charlie looked up at the limp, flapping sail and thought: *How hard can it be?*

Off to the east, the sky still looked ominous, and the occasional bolt of lightning lit the clouds from within. To the west the sky was a deepening blue. Time to keep moving, he decided.

Aloud he said: "Alas, gentlemen, we have come to the parting of the ways. Unfortunately for you, I still need this tub to get me to the shore." He gestured to the lake with one hand and pointed his staff with the other. "If you'd be so kind—"

"Please, squire, I beg you—" the captain began, but Charlie silenced him with a finger to his lips.

"I can't swim," he whimpered and ogled the lake fearfully.

"Then you need to hang tight to the boy," replied Charlie as a pulse that quivered through the air like a spreading umbrella flew from the tip of his staff and blew them both backwards over the gunwale and out into the lake.

They spluttered to the surface, and Charlie watched on, amused, as the captain clung to the deck hand and loosed a string of obscenities. He strolled to the edge of the stern in order to wave back at them when something bumped the boat. It rocked as something large and dark and sleek passed beneath the hull headed for the two men splashing about on the lake surface. Charlie watched transfixed as it dawned on them that they were not the only ones in the lake that morning, and the deck hand screamed and struggled and swam away from the sinking captain. The older man managed to remain afloat momentarily before he was suddenly seized from below and jerked beneath the lake so swiftly he didn't even leave a ripple to mark his passing.

The deck hand tried to swim towards the boat as the large shadow further out made a slow lazy turn back towards him. He had gotten to within twenty yards of the boat before he was gripped by the legs, and his body was thrashed from side to side before it exploded in a cascade of sparks.

And then it was Charlie's turn. The shadow had circled the boat twice before Charlie sensed the danger he was in and ran to the wheelhouse. He'd only just passed through the door when the boat was rammed from beneath and rocked through an eighty-degree arc. Charlie was flung against the opposite wall of the wheelhouse. He clung to the wheel as the boat swung back again, and this prevented him from being catapulted out the door and into the water.

He watched the shadow pass out from beneath the other side of the boat and curve round to begin another large circle. Whatever it was, it was slightly longer than the boat, and Charlie felt acutely exposed out on the water. He swung the wheel, which moved easily, and as he wound it, he felt the boat respond and the bow swung towards the shoreline. A gust of wind caught the sail broadside, causing it to billow wildly, and the whole vessel rolled to the left. He let go, and the wheel spun back, causing the boat to yaw but at least it righted itself once more.

Too close! thought Charlie. He gripped the wheel once more and turned the boat steadily so that it was running with the wind again, parallel with the shore. This time, the boat was hit from behind, and he heard the splintering of timber deep down in the hull. He had to be taking on water.

He swung the wheel once again, and the vessel veered towards the shore. The dark shadow circled in front of him, to come around at him from behind again.

The shoreline was closer now, but still too far to swim to; he wouldn't make fifty yards anyway before he was taken. He concentrated on keeping the boat steady as the wind filled the sail and the boat picked up speed. He noticed that the water was changing colour, becoming lighter and shallower, but the thing rammed into the stern and this time he knew the damage was serious enough to cause the boat to sink.

Water poured in below deck, and he felt the speed slacken as the aft end became ponderous and heavy in the water. He wound the wheel furiously and pointed the bow in a steeper angle to the shore. The water was green from the sandy bottom, and Charlie could make out the blacker shadows of rocky outcrops below the surface.

He scanned the surface for any sign of the circling monster, and saw it turn towards him from way out left where the water was deep and blue. He watched as it closed in on a collision course, staggered that something so large could move so quickly.

He felt the hull rise slowly as it crossed over a blunt reef he hadn't seen and blew a sigh of relief as the shadow suddenly veered off course and disappeared back into the depths of the lake.

By now the bow was riding considerably higher in the water. The boat was sinking, and the wheelhouse was tilted towards the sky. Charlie couldn't see where he was going, which was why the wind drove him crashing onto a second reef jutting out of the water.

He hit the front of the wheelhouse and almost knocked himself out on the windscreen with the impact. He clambered to his feet groggily and pushed open the wheelhouse door. He was greeted by a shrieking tearing sound as the timbers of the hull splintered under the relentless pressure, and the whole boat was pushed on to its side.

He was still a hundred yards from the shore. The boat was wedged solidly between two rocks poking from the lake like large teeth. He scrambled down the ladder and leaned against the side of the wheelhouse while he secured his staff to his bag and pulled the straps tightly across his shoulders. He would like to have retrieved the diamond, but it was probably lying at the bottom of the lake.

Satisfied that everything was safe and watertight, he clambered down on to one of the rocks and slipped into the water. The moment the water surged over his head, he panicked and fought the desperate urge to thrash about wildly. With a supreme effort, he turned on to his front and began a slow, casual breaststroke towards the shore. All the way there, his little voice railed at him because the monster fish surely was rushing up behind him, but he closed his ears and concentrated on the shoreline, stroked quietly and steadily and the fish never materialised, never knew he was there.

His feet scraped the pebbled bottom, and he stood, dripping water, and shuffled heavily on to the dry land. He eased the bag from his shoulders and checked that the contents were still there, and then he found a rock to sit on and watched the boat break apart while the wind dried his clothes.

Siobhan woke with a start. She had fallen asleep with her arm across the tiller, but the loose flapping of the sail had snapped like the flick from a wet towel and she'd jumped. She was exhausted. She hadn't rested since she'd led the army from Hornshurst.

She was alone in the stolen boat barely larger than a dinghy. With no one to relieve her, the steady breeze and the regular slap of water against wood had conspired against her and had lulled her to sleep.

When she awoke, she had no idea how long she had been asleep, or even what day it was anymore. She checked the position of the sun in the sky enough to know it was mid-afternoon. Off to the east, a massive storm had materialised, brooding and full of menace like a fighter entering a ring. The air ahead of it was ruffling as if it knew something was amiss, and it was time to pick up and leave.

She knelt and leaned over the side and splashed handfuls of brisk, clear water over her face. The cold was invigorating against her skin, and she felt the cloying fug of sleep withdraw its tendrils for the time being.

She eased the tiller right, and the tiny craft began to move with the wind. She knew The Magician would have had to come this way; the alternative was to sail directly into the eye of the approaching storm. *But where would he go?* She needed to review what she already knew.

He had avoided the commercial ferry lines and had chartered a small trader to avoid being recognised. From what Siobhan had seen of the boat as it sailed past, it had been poorly maintained and was probably a trafficker in illegal cargo; anything from drugs to slaves. This would mean the boat would avoid the larger ports, seeking refuge in smaller settlements where few questions were asked. She tried to recall the geography of the lake shore, but there were too many possibilities: Tahola, Mosomane, Hackettstown, Copainalá . . . the list went on and he could have been headed for any one of them, or none of them.

Siobhan felt despondent. She'd come so close at Goose Bay; two or three extra hours could have made all the difference. Instead, she was surrounded by water that stretched to the horizon wherever she looked while he slipped further away with every minute that passed. She screamed in frustration at the sky.

Where was Kareem? She cursed herself for being too cautious. She should have known The Magician would have kept the talisman. Instead, she had sent Kareem off on a wild goose chase when they ought to have stayed together to track their main quarry. What had she been thinking? She needed his skills now more than ever, and she fumed at her own sense of helplessness.

She had to put it behind her. There was no use worrying about what might have been. It was a waste of her time and energy, and she had to make do with what she had. But what *did* she have?

She had seen The Magician and now knew what he looked like. She knew she could pick him out in a crowd. She had seen the boat he had chartered. That would be the next step. She would keep the wind at her back and sail toward the distant shore. Once she had covered the distance, she would turn and sail parallel to the shoreline, calling in at each settlement she encountered to search for any sign of the boat. That would mark the beginning of the new trail. *She would find him:* she made that promise to herself.

Siobhan needed another day and a half to reach the northern banks of the lake and by this time she was too exhausted to continue. She detested the thought, but she found a sheltered, sandy beach and anchored in the shallows. She furled the sail and waded ashore.

The beach was entirely deserted. She clambered up the nearest hill and surveyed the area. It stretched away in bush and low scrubland, but she saw no paths and no indication that the area was inhabited. When she was satisfied, she clambered back down and made herself a bed in the soft sand. She needed a clear mind for the next step and tiredness was a minefield of poor decisions and honest mistakes.

The storm was miles away and blowing south. Above her, the sky was clear blue, and the sun radiated its warmth against her upturned face. She was fast asleep within seconds of her head hitting the sand.

She woke once. She was surrounded in pitch black. Overhead, the night sky was ablaze with the light of billions of stars from millions of galaxies. Space was so infinitely large and yet the sky would look the same no matter where in the universe you were. Stars twinkling in the sky were the one constant connection above. Siobhan rarely thought of Earth, but whenever she took the time to gaze at the heavens, she remembered, sometimes with immense sadness and regret.

The next time she awoke it was morning. She undressed and bathed in the shallows where the sand was clear of the beds of underwater reedy grasses, and swam to ease the stiffness from having lain cramped in the bottom of the boat. Siobhan was a strong swimmer, and her strokes were relaxed in the manner where everything was honed by perfect technique. There had never been enough time to enjoy it on Bexus; there had only been the need to fight to survive.

She stood and shook the water from her hair and gazed down at her body. Her skin was the walnut colour of a worn leather book. Her aura was now patchy and much dimmer after all the fighting—all the killing—since she'd arrived on Bexus. She felt the loss: a vague kind of emptiness, and coolness as if a sea breeze had found a way to her skin beneath her clothing. Her aura had been unblemished lemon-white, but if she'd had the choice to do it all again, she wouldn't have changed a thing. Some things are just worth fighting for.

Siobhan dressed and tied her hair back and clambered back aboard the boat. She hoisted the sail and, once clear of the bay, she turned west and followed the line of the lakeshore.

She discovered the boat just before noon. The shoreline was harsh and jagged, and the land had dropped off steeply in eroded cliff faces to lay hidden just beneath the surface as broken shoals. Siobhan had steered back into deeper water to avoid colliding with them, and as she rounded a bleak-looking promontory she saw the wreckage wedged against the rock.

The mast had broken and lay half submerged in the water, tangled in the sail. The stern was under water, and the boat was bent across the rocks where its keel had snapped in two. There was no sign of life.

Siobhan dropped the sail and checked that her staff was within easy reach. She lifted a set of oars that had been stowed in the bottom of the boat, set them in place in the oarlocks bolted to the gunwale, and rowed towards the wreckage.

The boat had to have been driven up on to the rocks deliberately; the question was why? She brought the dinghy alongside the wreck and tied it to one of the cleats before climbing out. The deck beneath her feet was steady. The boat was held fast, and only a heavy storm would be able to dislodge it.

She edged along the deck to the wheelhouse. The door swung back and forth on creaking hinges in the breeze. Siobhan poked her head inside, but the wheelhouse was empty. The glass in the windscreen had cracked around a dome-shaped hollow—whoever had collided with it would have a sore head for a few days.

She backed out and climbed down the rusted bridge ladder to the main deck. Water sloshed around her feet near the cabin door. She turned the handle and pushed. Something had fallen behind it—an upturned chair—and she had to bump her shoulder hard against the door to open it.

The cabin was a mess. She saw the tangled and torn blanket; saw the rolled up mattress tucked beneath it, and noticed the burn marks on the bedding. A short lead pipe had been dropped in the middle of the floor. Siobhan began to understand what might have happened here. There had been a fight; she knew that much, although it looked as if it had ended as soon as it had started. Once again, The Magician had outwitted his opponents.

She checked the cabin thoroughly for any sign of the *Toki-Moai*, but it had disappeared along with The Magician. Siobhan stood in the doorway and gazed towards the shore. The beach was littered with boulders. The bedrock poked through in places. There was no sand, and no footprints that she could see, but The Magician had to have come ashore on that beach. Somehow, she was determined to pick up his trail once more.

She dropped back down into the dinghy and cast off from the floundering wreck. She had been extremely lucky to catch this break. She might never get another chance like it, but she was determined she would never need another one.

She took her time. She beached the dingy and carried the anchor up the shore and wedged it between two large boulders. She gathered her scant belongings in a pile before beginning a careful search of the beach, which she traversed in a grid. Her keen eyes picked out the places where rocks had been dislodged, and she followed the line to the base of the short cliff, about twenty feet high.

The Magician had passed this way. He had been clumsy: dislodging loose stones, breaking brittle branches, leaving a boot print in the dust of the clay bank. Something else caught her eye—a tiny patch of material, fluttering on the end of a short, sharp branch that had torn the clothing that had brushed by and been caught.

Siobhan slung her roll over her shoulders and picked up her staff. She climbed the faint path, following in the footsteps left behind by The Magician. She paused at the top of the hill for one last look at the vast expanse of the lake before heading inland, leaving behind a clear trail for Kareem to follow.

CHAPTER 12

lthough they had called a truce, the tension in the air was still palpable. Kareem had laid his staff at his feet, but the casual way in which the handle was raised fooled no one: he could arm himself in an instant. He had insisted that his bandolier of knives be returned, and Kate had handed it across to him without a word.

So when Hawklight finally woke, the first thing he saw was a fully armed and dangerous young man eyeing him apprehensively. It had been Hawklight's decision to keep him unarmed, but Kate had apparently ignored it. He decided she must have had a good reason for doing so and the fact that he had almost drowned once again was probably a large part of it.

He had a vague recollection of hitting the water and being dragged under by the weight of his clothing. He had struggled to the surface, and the few lessons in dog paddle he'd had kept him on or near the surface. He remembered the third time he had submerged: he couldn't stay on the surface and he sank, still clawing frantically at the water and watching the silver bubbles rise past his face and then . . . Blackness!

He had no idea how he came to be resting in the bottom of the boat. He felt Kate stir briefly beside him, and when he moved slightly, her head flopped forward. She had been sleeping against his shoulder.

She woke and turned sleepily to check on him.

"Welcome back to the land of the living," she smiled and yawned. "You gave me a fright back there. You really must learn how to swim, you know," she admonished.

Kareem watched them silently, slumped against the stern.

"How are you feeling?" she asked.

"Like last time," Hawklight replied, and they both chuckled. "Thank you," he said.

"Thank the Captain," Kate said. "He found you and brought you back." She didn't add at what cost, and that she had feared she had lost them both to the lake.

Hawklight nodded and smiled and closed his eyes as if he'd just pieced the puzzle together and was trying to think how best to apologise, but he never got that far. His head lolled sideways, and he began to snore softly.

Kate glanced at Kareem who looked to be in a half-crazed stupor in an effort to stay awake at the helm. She eased away from Hawklight and crawled towards the stern. Kareem watched, glazed and full of suspicion as she drew level with him.

"You need to rest, Captain," she said. "Just show me what to do."

"I'm fine!" he retorted and his hand gripped the tiller tighter. He checked the sail again because he couldn't meet her gaze.

"You're dead on your feet and you'll be no good to anyone, especially yourself, once we make landfall."

He couldn't think straight. His head buzzed, and he desperately wanted to collapse. He didn't trust the girl and he didn't understand why—when she'd implored him to find the drowning soldier—he hadn't hesitated, to the point where it had nearly cost him his own life.

"Please. Just show me what I need to do," and she grasped his arm in her hand to turn him back to her. Her touch shocked him, repulsed him at the same time that he wanted to fall against her and surrender in the arms of sleep. He shook her hand away angrily, confused.

"I said, I'm fine!" he snapped, and saw her flinch.

He waited on the outburst, but she'd changed. Her voice was tinged with regret.

"I get it. You still don't trust me."

Once again he couldn't meet her eyes. He stared ahead blankly.

He was too tired, and she moved too quickly. Her staff appeared in her hands as if it had been conjured from thin air. His hand was locked about the tiller like a cramped claw, too far from his faithful shuriken blades strapped across his chest.

"*Colligacionis faciamus!*" she murmured, and a blue light flashed from her staff. The plasma rope uncoiled and fastened tightly about her neck, and she felt the choking pain as she instinctively reacted against it. She forced herself to remain calm, and then she handed Rhyanon to him.

"You need . . . to sleep," she rasped, and her tongue felt thick in her throat from the effort.

Kareem stared at her. She confounded and confused him. Her eyes were the colour of the lake water. He recoiled from her.

"That's not necessary!' he said and thrust her staff back at her.

She sat and looked at him for a long moment before she hacked the command and the plasma binding dissolved.

She massaged her throat where the binding had been. "It's not very comfortable, is it?" She smiled awkwardly at him.

He was too tired to argue anymore. He gestured for her to take the tiller and then he stood unsteadily.

"Just keep the sail stiff," he said. "Don't let it flap with the wind. Wake me if we hit the other shore."

He stumbled to the middle of the boat and collapsed alongside Hawklight. Together, they set up a chorus of snores and Kate couldn't stop grinning.

They slept for more than fourteen hours, and the shore was just visible above the horizon when Kareem woke. His head was clear, and he felt refreshed as if he had come out from the other side of a nightmare that he could dismiss finally at the onset of the new day. He sat up and rubbed his eyes that felt as if someone had flung sand at them.

He checked his bandolier. Not one of the blades was missing. He turned his head and saw they were within sight of the shore, so he stood and edged his way past Hawklight to where Kate still sat at the tiller. Hawklight nodded as he passed.

Kate shuffled to one side and offered him the tiller.

"Thank you," he said and sat beside her. "You did good. How long was I out?"

"Long enough," she replied. "You look better."

He smiled. "Call me Kareem," he said.

"I'm Kate," she replied, and she shook his hand. "And you already know Hawklight."

"It was you, shouting his name, that guided me back to the boat," he said.

"These things have a way of working out," she replied.

The flotsam in the water was their first clue that the lake had claimed another victim. Soon after, Kareem spotted the wreckage as they sailed past the weathered headland. There was a much smaller boat grounded in the bay and anchored well up the shore, but there was no activity, no sign of life.

Kareem guided the small craft between the gaps in the reef shoals lurking just beneath the lake surface, and he smiled as he saw Hawklight's knuckles whiten where he gripped the gunwale as they slid by with only a foot or two of clear water to either side. He filed the weakness away. The alliance had been forged for now, but there was no telling how the cards would fall when they eventually retrieved the talisman. He couldn't deny his growing respect for the two soldiers of Hogarth beside him and he hoped the alliance wouldn't end the way it had begun—violently.

The boat coasted into the shallows, and Kate and Hawklight leapt out and waded ashore, dragging the prow behind them until the keel struck the pebbled bed of the lakeshore and ground to a halt. Kareem furled the sail and lashed it to the spar, then threw their belongings onto the beach. He hopped out of the boat and helped pull it far enough up the shore and out of the reach of the vagaries of the weather that could cause the lake to lick higher up the beach.

Both Hawklight and Kareem scoured the bay and the land leading down to it, and almost immediately both found the evidence they had been seeking. Kate searched for any signs of human disturbance, but the stony beach gave up no clues to her, and she was mystified by the ease with which the other two read the spoor, and just a little miffed this was something she couldn't do.

"The Magician, certainly," said Kareem, pointing to a spot where the rocks were encrusted with a pinkish lichen. "He moves easily across the stones for such a big man."

"And yet, here—" Hawklight continued, "—he appears to favour his right leg."

"Yes, I see, although it can be no more than a knock, as though he banged his leg, perhaps when the boat smashed on the rock."

"Will you two just cut it out?" Kate was exasperated. Hawklight smiled at Kareem, and the young man grinned back at him. Kate stomped off and sat on a rock.

The two men grew serious again as they discovered the second set of telltale prints that had scuffed the rock.

"These are the tracks my companion made," said Kareem. He knew the narrow boot tread, the length of her stride, and pointed out the signs she'd left to mark the trail. Hawklight privately marvelled in the faith of the woman, and her confidence in her captain to locate her trail on this one isolated beach among so many others along the expansive northern lakeshore. He saw that her tread was light and evenly spaced as it disappeared amongst the rocks as if she were already beginning a steady slow run to grind down the distance that separated her from her quarry.

He beckoned to Kate. Kareem had already started up the slope away from the lake, and they needed to follow along behind to avoid disrupting the spoor. He thought they were four, maybe five days behind the woman, judging by the signs of her passing. She was pitted against The Magician; Hawklight hoped she was up to the challenge. They desperately needed to make up the lost time to even the odds stacked against her.

Kate fell in behind him, and they began to jog after Kareem who had already climbed the short cliff face and dropped from view behind it.

CHAPTER 13

harlie sheltered in the lee of a scree ridge, crouched over a small fire that crackled sparks occasionally as it cooked the dried, encrusted salt sticking to the wood. The air was crystal clear and chillingly cold, and the collar of his dusty greatcoat was turned up against his ears.

He'd marvelled at the passing countryside and cursed it simultaneously. The land was desolate, buffeted by wind and stinging wind-blown sand and covered in a patchy mix of tussock and thorny scrub, all of it baked a dull yellow-brown under the relentless hammer of the sun. Things slithered and skittered away as he approached, sounding like rats across a bed of dry leaves. He caught snatches of occasional movement: brown blurs beneath the stunted branches, nothing more, but he kept his staff in a tight two-fisted grip nonetheless.

There were no settlements, nobody huddling inside smoky adobe shacks. There were no roads, not even the thin worn path of a passing *Cacia* herd, animals that vaguely resembled goats. The rolling plateau stretched beyond the horizon. He paused often, trying to maintain a northerly heading, piling on the miles between him and Cherath. The bad news was there were no towns ahead of him; the good news was there was no one trailing behind him, and he gave up the notion that he needed to cover his tracks continually. The shifting sands would do that for him.

He reached across and threw another log from the pile on to the burning embers. Sparks leapt into the air and were carried aloft by the swirling wind; there was a soft *whuumph!* and the log burst into flame. He leaned back against the scree wall and felt the bulge of the statue press against his side through the bag. Charlie grinned to himself. He couldn't resist the familiar urge to unravel it from the velvet blanket and caress its metallic hide.

It was cool to his touch and basked in the red reflection from the firelight. It looked a little more worn, less polished, stained black in places. He supposed the skin had oxidised in the moist air above the lake.

He unfolded the two bent arms. One was loose at the shoulder as if something inside had been forced or broken. He examined it closely looking for any sign of the third and final lock, but if there was any other moving part or concealed slot, he couldn't spot it. Not for the first time did he begin to doubt its authenticity and claims that it held the collective wisdom and source of power of untold generations of Hornshurst's noblest citizens. And yet, he reflected, Varak had kept the city subdued from the moment he had stolen it.

The night was still, and Charlie was altogether lost in thought, so the sudden noise startled him. It sounded like the squeal of a rusted hinge and was immediately followed by another, a scream like a rabbit—its leg broken inside a trap. It came from the statue cradled between his hands.

Charlie dropped the talisman, and it rolled in the sand at his feet. The screaming ceased, and the only sound that remained was the *tick-tick* rocking of the loose arm. *Where had that come from?* Charlie glanced about him nervously, instinctively, in case the screams had alerted someone or something close by. He rolled away from the firelight and pressed his back against the rocky bank, his staff poised nervously, and he waited.

Nothing slunk into view from the blackness beyond. The fire sparked and danced in the breath of the soft, swirling wind. Still, he waited and watched.

After five tense minutes, he relaxed and crawled back into the light. He reached forward and picked the statue out of the sand and brushed the particles of sand away that had lodged between the ridges of its carved surface. He pressed the open arms back into position and felt the gentle click as each locked back in place.

As he rotated the little figure in his hands, it resumed a soft cooing noise like a baby cradled safely back in its mother's arms. *What was inside this thing?* he wondered. He tugged against one of the arms again, and it swung loose. Immediately the screaming resumed, louder than before and he hastily pressed it back into place. The screaming dropped to a whimper.

Charlie had had enough for one evening. The darkness pressed in on him, and he didn't like what he couldn't see. He quickly bundled the talisman back into the velvet cloth and stuffed the package into his haversack. The moaning noise was muffled and indistinct and no longer a distraction.

He sat for some time in the dwindling light of the fire, occasionally feeding it logs, which were being steadily devoured. The question was: why? Why now, after all this time? He supposed the good news was that there was more to the statue than he'd first assumed, which reinforced his belief that the tales of unimagined power and knowledge stored inside were likely to be true.

Beneath this, however, was a sense of unease. The more he thought about it, the more he was convinced of only one possible explanation. The statue was calling out for help! And, if this were true, there was only one other possibility—he was being followed, and the chase was drawing closer. He closed his eyes, tried to relax and clear his mind and waited.

An image swum into focus of the woman standing erect on the pier at Goose Bay, staring at him as he'd sailed past. It had to be her! He concentrated on that memory and remembered her face, her long auburn hair. She'd been alone at the end of the pier, he was certain. Charlie smiled. This was going to be easy, maybe even fun. He wasn't stupid enough to underestimate her; after all, she'd managed to follow him this far, and he hadn't seen a sign of anybody on his trail. He'd have to be careful, but the game was tilted in his favour.

He missed the muffled footfall, so engrossed was he in the prospect of setting a carefully laid trap. He caught the briefest sour scent in his nostrils, but the wind came in behind and cleared the air and silenced the alarm. But a single pebble rolled free from the top of the scree wall and the noise as it clattered down cutting through the silence was almost as startling as a sudden gunshot.

Charlie instinctively rolled to his right away from the sound but away from where his staff leaned against the wall to his left. He scrambled to his knees and crawled frantically on all fours towards his staff, and that was when something landed on him from above. He collapsed under the force but twisted at the same time and hit the ground with his back, and whatever was clinging to him grunted with the impact and loosened its grip.

He tore himself clear of the weakened grasp and managed to get one hand to his staff. He turned on his buttocks just as a dark shape sprung through the air at him. Charlie swung the blunt handle in a tight arc and caught the creature a glancing blow on its torso, just below the neck. There wasn't enough power behind the swing to cripple it, but the creature was knocked aside and it cannoned into the rocky wall. Charlie heard a sharp yelp of pain as the creature continued to tumble head over heels and he rose to one knee, brandishing his staff like a club, waiting for the next onslaught.

The dull firelight picked out a pair of gleaming eyes across from him, and he heard a low animal growl. At first, he'd thought the woman had attacked him, but whatever else it was on the other side of the fire, it wasn't feminine.

"What are you waiting for?" he screamed. "Come and get it!"

The eyes blinked once, and the shape behind them began to assume a form as his assailant moved cautiously forward. Charlie rose to his feet and backed against the wall and reversed the hold on his staff so that it was pointed, business end out, towards the fire.

His attacker moved into the light, and Charlie got his first clear glimpse. It walked upright on two legs but there the resemblance to anything vaguely human ended.

It was squat and stocky and might have come up to Charlie's shoulder on a good day. It was reptilian in appearance: its head was covered in a mottled maroon-coloured leather-like skin, and its face was slightly elongated with two vertical ridges mirroring each of the bony eye arches running lengthwise and tapering into two nasal slits in the middle of its face. Its lips were puffy and swollen tight as if they had been pumped full of collagen in a beauty treatment where the surgeon had blundered horribly. It growled once more and the plump lips stretched into a kind of grimace, revealing twin rows of small, pointed, and probably extremely sharp, teeth.

"God, but you're ugly!" Charlie hissed through clenched jaws.

"Got, boot yer ooglie!" the creature hissed back at him, and Charlie was startled to realise that it was easily capable of mimicking speech. Did it also understand?

It continued to advance towards him and stepped over the ashes of the fire. Charlie now saw that it was clothed in a suit of animal skin. The suit reminded him of the skins of crocodiles; armour-plated ridges protected the chest and torso while the arms of the uniform were pliant and minutely knobbed like the skin on a gecko. Protruding from the sleeves of the garment were hands sculpted in long, tapering fingers. Charlie doubted if they would be able to master the use of chopsticks; the hands could grip, but they looked awkward and clumsy.

Its legs were sheathed in tight pants cut from the same material. The calloused plates ran in vertical rows down the legs, protecting the thighs and ended where the pants tucked into calf-length boots of supple fish leather.

The creature turned sideways, transfixing Charlie with one eye, and tilted its head skywards. The thick lips barely parted, but it gave a shrieking high-pitched whistle. Charlie grew alarmed when he heard an immediate reply that didn't appear to come from too far away and answered Charlie's question: *Were there more?*

The situation was turning sticky, and Charlie was an ardent believer in the pre-emptive strike. On Earth, that took the form of a head butt or a savage knee to the groin, but Charlie didn't want to get too up close and personal. He pointed his staff at the circling lizard-boy and was about to issue an offensive blast, but he never got the chance.

The thing was more than six feet away from him, so the tongue caught him by surprise. It was a long, ropy, purple blur, longer than the body that encased it. Before Charlie had even registered what had happened, it had flicked from between the turgid lips, its tip catching the staff just above Charlie's leading hand, and it tore the staff from his grasp. The tongue released its grip mid-flight and the creature neatly caught the staff, then tossed it aside while Charlie was still left wondering where the tongue went after it disappeared back inside the mouth.

Charlie charged, and it was Lizard Boy's turn to react too late. Charlie hit him in a perfect rugby tackle—surging upwards and lifting him off his feet, driving him backwards, through the hot coals and on to a slab of flat rock poking above the sand. Charlie was reaching for his throat when the tongue made an unexpected curtain call and wrapped around Charlie's head and across his eyes. Charlie caught a whiff of vomit just as the gelatinous saliva that coated the tongue began to burn his head and eyes, and he let go of the creature and tried to rip the tongue away. He couldn't get a tight enough grip and the mass slipped through his fingers as it unwound.

Charlie blinked and tried to wipe the goo away using his sleeve, but like so many of the chemicals on Bexus, the lizard spit had the ability to create the sensation of pain by interfering with the energy fields that defined Charlie's soul. Charlie lashed out with his fists and boots, but by then, the creature had wriggled free and stood panting a safe distance away. It whistled once more, and Charlie heard the nearby rustle of shrubbery and the noise of many boots scuffling through the sand.

They surged through to the clearing and hit him all together like a tag wrestling team. He was buried beneath a mound of bodies, and he tried to curl into a foetal position in order to protect himself from the pummelling. Something—a rock, perhaps—grazed his skull, and he saw stars briefly. He shook his head and tried to rise to his knees, but a tongue curled around his right wrist, and his arm was jerked out from under him. Another found his left wrist, which was pulled in the opposite direction, and he was hung out to dry.

His head was still buzzing and he was on his knees, suspended like a crucified man between two of the baleful creatures. His wrists were stinging from the saliva, and his eyes were still streaming. He blinked the tears away and saw about a dozen blurred shapes standing in a semicircle in front of him. His shoulder and left thigh began to throb, and he wasn't surprised to notice he'd been bitten twice. Tiny sparks fizzed from the wounds as his body attempted to repair the leaks. One by one, they spluttered and were snuffed out as the punctures closed over, but the incessant throbbing remained.

"Wit ere yo doong hair?"

The voice was harsh as though the creature's larynx had been brushed with sandpaper. One of the creatures knelt before him and grabbed a fistful of hair and yanked his head back. Charlie found himself staring into a pair of slanted blue eyes that were as cold and merciless as they were blue. He realised the creature spoke and understood his language though the accent needed more attention to detail.

What are you doing here?

The creature dropped its eyes as if it were sizing up his stretched neck for a chance to chew out his jugular. The reason that there were no signs of human habitation suddenly became clear to Charlie. He was mesmerised by the creature's fleshy-tipped tongue as it licked its lips.

"I . . . uh, I . . . uh . . ." He stammered nervously. Something caught his eye at the edge of the firelight. One of the creatures had rifled his bag and was holding the velvet blanket, which it was now slowly unravelling. Charlie forgot his predicament momentarily and cried out.

"Wait! *No! Don't touch that!* Be careful!"

Lesson One in cultural awareness—don't disrespect the hosts. Boss Lizard yanked harder on his hair and leaned forward, opening his mouth and peeling his lips back for a decent bite. Charlie smelled the fetid breath of trapped and rotting tissue and closed his eyes. At least it would be quick.

Its jaws clamped over half his throat, and he felt the needle sharp teeth begin to prick his skin. At the same instant, he heard a cry of alarm, followed by the shrill shrieking of the talisman that had fallen from the velvet to the sand once again.

The pressure around his throat disappeared as Boss Lizard looked up from his work. Charlie had been staring at his face and witnessed the change from bloodlust to amazement that passed across it. All movement froze, like a snapshot at a birthday party. The long fingers loosened their grip on his hair and the tongues that held him pinioned slipped from his wrists. He pitched forward into the sand and lay panting like a dog on a stoop in summer.

The cries from the talisman continued to cut through the night, intruding into Charlie's consciousness and drawing him back from the edge of the black abyss on which he'd just been standing awaiting the final bite. He opened his eyes and slowly sat up, feeling sore and disoriented. He glanced up at the half-circle of creatures whose gazes were focused on the dull metal object. He noticed one arm had swung loose when the talisman had bounced on to the sand.

Wearily, he crawled towards the statue. None of the creatures made any move to stop him. He flopped on to his buttocks and picked it out of the dirt, gently blew away the sand still lodged in the carved crevices and folded the arm back into place. It locked with a soft *click!* and the shrieking ceased. He sat with the statue cradled between his hands and calmly met the stares of the lizard-wannabees.

They erupted in animated conversations of clicks, whistles and strangulated cries, and Charlie noticed that they were slowly backing away as they argued amongst themselves. He almost could smell the scent of alarm, and he suddenly realised that they had recognised the talisman from somewhere.

What did they know?

Charlie had been handed a lifeline that might just prevent him being served up as the main course. He decided to chance his luck.

He stood and slowly drew himself up to his full height so that he towered above his captors. He cupped the talisman in one of his meaty hands and extended his arm towards them. They backed away, and some of them even cowered before him, but Boss Lizard stood his ground—a little hesitantly, Charlie noted.

He felt for the loose arm with his thumb and flicked it out of its slot. Immediately the shrieking recommenced—louder, if anything—and Charlie saw a flicker of fear in the blue eyes. He took a step, keeping his arm outstretched, and was unable to repress a smile as Boss Lizard dropped his gaze and knelt in the sand. It was the signal Charlie so desperately needed. One by one, the others submitted; only Charlie remained on his feet.

He had no idea what he was holding; only that it wielded the power to have saved his life. He had no idea what the lizards already knew, or how they came to know it. They certainly didn't know it had been stolen, and he didn't want to be around if or when they found that out.

He picked the velvet cloth out of the dirt and shook out the sand that clung to it. The whining was driving him crazy, so he folded the arm back into place. His ears continued to ring in the ensuing silence, so he used the time to re-wrap the statue and place it carefully back inside his pack.

He had regained the upper hand and needed to illustrate this point quickly. He searched for Lizard Boy, but they all looked the same. He chose one who looked haggard and most covered in dust and swung a boot into his side. The creature squealed and rolled away. None of the others made a move.

Satisfied, Charlie squatted in front of Boss Lizard.

"You can understand me?" he asked, although it was more a statement of fact than a question.

Boss didn't reply, so Charlie reached forward and tucked his finger under the creature's chin, gently tilting his head so that Boss was staring into his eyes. Charlie held the gaze, and in the end, Boss broke away and nodded slightly.

"Good! Then understand this! I am the Keeper. What I am doing here is none of your business, but you have made me greatly displeased. Do you hear me?"

Boss nodded again, and this time kept his eyes averted. He was distracted and made nervous by the constant cooing, muffled by the velvet, from Charlie's bag. Charlie wished the bloody thing would shut up, but he didn't know how to keep it quiet, and he needed to appear all knowing.

"However, there is something you can do to regain my favour."

He paused and waited. Boss was taking his time processing this. Something shifted inside the reptile's brain, and he met Charlie's gaze once more.

"There is someone—possibly a woman—following me. I'm certain she is somewhere close by. It would make me very happy if she no longer continued to do this thing." Charlie finished the sentence by dangling his bag in front of the creature.

He smiled. Boss returned the smile when the implication dawned on him. Charlie patted his cheek and stood.

There was light on the horizon to the east. Dawn was breaking. The bleak darkness of the night was replaced by muted greys and shadowed forms. Time to move on. Charlie would have liked to ask for a guide, but he was treading on thin ice as it was. Truth was that the talisman was beginning to make *him* nervous; he didn't want a travelling companion to pick up on the fraud he was perpetuating.

He rubbed his wrists absently; the pain was abating and they were beginning to itch. He cast one final glance towards his erstwhile attackers who were huddled and subdued as they listened to Boss. Whoever she was, he didn't want to be in her boots; these guys meant business.

He turned and headed off, using his staff like a walking stick, keeping the sun to his right and his bag tucked firmly beneath his arm. He was whistling softly.

CHAPTER 14

*S*iobhan awoke with a start. She was curled in a tight ball, wedged beneath a weeping bushy shrub that looked to be weighed down with thin copper-coloured leaves. The night air was chilled and its breath had wormed beneath the short cloak she'd brought with her. She was dog-tired, for the pursuit had been relentless, and she still hadn't caught sight of her quarry moving across the high plateau of wasted scrubland.

She yawned once and rolled onto her back, keeping her knees bent. She had scattered a family of tiny furry creatures the size of rabbits when she'd first crawled under the bush, and she heard scuffling that suggested a couple of them had returned and were hunkered down on the far side. Keeping out of sight in this environment was a sensible option. Travellers tended to avoid these central plateaus as they did the fecund forests—there were too many 'unknowns' and the routes through them were dangerous. But, she thought, desperate times called for desperate measures. She was relying on the fact that The Magician would be taking as much care to keep himself safe as she was. If he lost the talisman now, it might disappear forever.

She turned onto her side and pulled the cape down, drawing her knees up inside and wedging the bottom of the cape around her body to preserve some of the warmth. And that was when she first heard the screaming.

It sounded like an animal in considerable pain some distance ahead. Her first thought was that The Magician's luck had finally run out, but something about the depth of despair in the cries seemed strangely familiar, and the urge to run blindly out into the night to seek it out was overwhelming.

She gripped one of the branches tightly and held on. Her entire body was trembling from the effort, and the temptation to break free and run was almost hypnotic. A small, insistent voice of reason inside her head was telling her this was a very bad idea, but the internal debate was soon settled when the screaming subsided.

Siobhan was shaken and suddenly felt terribly vulnerable, alone in the wilderness. The furry animals had bolted once more, and the night air was still and oppressively silent. She took long, slow breaths to calm herself though her mind continued to race.

She was confused and unable to explain the weird seductive effects of the plaintive cries. They brought memories flooding back of her death on Earth; she'd been drawn across the barrier to Bexus unwillingly, leaving too much behind to be able to let go in peace. That anger and resentment had stayed with her; had helped her become the fearless warrior general she was as if nothing that anyone could throw at her could match the hurt and sense of loss she had already experienced.

She knew instinctively that the cries had been directed at her. That ruled out The Magician, which left only one other possibility—the *Toki-Moai*. Somehow, it knew she was close by and was leading her on.

By now, further sleep was impossible, but so was pursuit. The night was blazoned with stars, but there wasn't enough light to see clearly, and the land remained cloaked in dark shadows. She would need to wait for the dawn. She couldn't risk generating light from the end of her staff, tricky enough to do at the best of times, because she'd lose the element of surprise and probably draw every night predator from miles around. She had to be patient.

Another scream cut through the night, and she was on her feet immediately, staring in the direction of the sound as if the night would peel its veil back and she could see clearly. A sob escaped her lips, and she noticed she was crying. The force drawing her forward was almost too much to bear, but the noise was cut short before she'd gathered up her staff.

She began to pace back and forth in front of the bush, torn between the desire to take off into the night or to pick up the trail at first light. She peered towards the east; the horizon was inky black and only silhouetted by the backdrop curtain of stars, but dawn was not far off. She would wait.

She slumped beside the bush and fidgeted. Twice more during the night she heard the talisman calling her and each time she had to resist the impulse to run off into the darkness to try and find it. The second time she pressed her hands over her ears to block out the sound, and she nurtured the steely resolution to rescue the talisman. Whatever happened to The Magician in the process was not her concern.

Eventually, the black sky to the east morphed into grey and the few, layered clouds that hovered above the land became stitched with the pink edges that marked the approaching dawn. Siobhan had long since bundled her belongings together, and she set off as soon as there was enough light to see.

She followed in the direction from which she thought the cries came, and kept one eye peeled for any sign of movement above the stunted brush. Initially, that was an impossible task, but as the redness burned from the sky and the first rays of the sun lit the landscape, contours and forms were thrown into sharp focus. It occurred to Siobhan that if she could see The Magician moving across the scrubland, he could just as easily spot her, and the element of surprise would be lost. So, despite the urgency, she forced herself to move cautiously and with care, which was why she spotted the footprints in the sand.

She paused to try and read the signs, but the space was muddled and confused with imprints stamped upon others. A group, maybe seven or eight, even upwards of a dozen or so had cut across the clearing. Recent too: the wind had not yet begun to blur the edges or wipe them clean. The situation had just gotten trickier.

Siobhan suddenly felt exposed, and gingerly lowered herself to the level of the surrounding scrub. The sun was to the east, rising over her right shoulder, throwing long shadows across the plain and making any movement easy to spot. She knelt immobile, squinting and scanning the land, waiting for something to show. Her eyes flicked past a wispy thread of smoke as if a smouldering campfire still burned, but when she looked again it had disappeared. Perhaps it had never been; her imagination was already shunting in overtime. She blinked once and checked again: again, there was nothing to note out of the ordinary.

Yet something was not quite right. Reason dictated that she needed to keep moving fast to cut into the distance that separated her from her quarry, but some sixth sense had triggered a silent alarm, and Siobhan knew better than to ignore the signal. So she waited and watched.

An hour drifted past, and the sun climbed steadily higher in the sky. The air grew hazy as the land heated up and the wind began to tease at the scrub, rocking it gently. Siobhan had seen nothing to alarm her, and yet the sense of unease continued. She had to make a decision.

She stood, slowly, warily, and her eyes fell to the stomped clearing once again. Whoever they were, they were headed in the same direction, towards the sounds of the talisman screaming. Either The Magician had managed to evade them, or they were now in possession of the statue. Siobhan had no choice, really: she had to continue on to find out for herself which one was true. If ever she'd needed Kareem by her side, now was the time.

That thought reminded her to leave behind a clear path for him to follow. She had no doubts that he was behind her somewhere, already looking to catch up. Once more, she rued the decision to split up as she broke some branches from the surrounding bush and laid them in the middle of the track beside a clear imprint of her own boots. The scrub would buffer the effects of the wind and keep the print fresh for longer.

She moved on, intrigued by the footprints. *Whom did they belong to?* She'd not seen a living soul since leaving Goose Bay. They could have come from some ragtag remnant of Varak's army; his reach, in his heyday, had been extensive and these had been a part of the conquered lands. However, she had never seen the style of boot tread before and the feet that wore the boots were curiously splayed outwards.

She moved like a wraith, ghosting across the rolling terrain—a wisp, a moving shadow, briefly sighted, then lost from view, pausing occasionally to mark her passing. By now the sun was overhead, and the light was harsh and bright, the air hot and dry. The sense of dread had remained trickling like sweat down her exposed back, and she would stop randomly to check that nothing was approaching from behind.

She halted suddenly. The tracks dispersed in different directions, like spokes on a wheel; like a prearranged action. She crouched and waited, gripping her staff in readiness. She rechecked the spoor. The boot prints were still all of the same tread. Whoever it was, they hadn't encountered The Magician—yet.

She decided to keep heading in a northerly direction, trying to keep a line that would take her close to where she thought the shrieking sounds had been. Apparently someone else had the same idea, judging by one particular set of tracks. She peeked above the bush first, and then stealthily moved on, stooping and staying low.

Her senses were on heightened alert, and though she saw nothing, she smelled something: something sour, faint but out of place. She hesitated, then dropped abruptly and rolled to her left, bring up her staff in one fluid motion.

"*Exstinguere!*" she cried as a dark, mottled shape burst between two adjacent thorn-bushes. A bright blue pulse of energy the size of a glowing tennis ball erupted from her staff, passed through the shape and exploded out the other side in a deafening static blast. Something slammed into the ground beside her head, just before she took the full impact of the falling body that almost rendered her unconscious. She fought the blackness that threatened to envelop her, and skittered to one side in the sand.

As her vision cleared, she found herself staring at a quivering maroon-coloured mass lying at her feet. It looked like a person in a pink lizard mask, but the resemblance quickly ended there. A long tongue protruded from the creature's mouth and lay caked in sand; this was the object that had nearly crushed her skull. The blast from her staff had caught the creature across the side of its face. Half the lower jaw was gone, and the back of its head had been blown away. Deep red blood seeped into the sand and the animal began jerking spasmodically in a final death throe. It gave a long shrill whistle that ended in a wet, throaty gurgle before its eyes glazed over and it lay still.

Siobhan heard the whistled responses, each from a different direction. They were all around her, closing in on her. She needed to be anywhere but here, and the quicker the better. Her hand closed around a fistful of smooth pebbles, and she tossed them stiff-armed over her head as far as she could throw. They clattered against some exposed rock out to her left.

She thrust the staff into its sheath that ran diagonally down her back and kept low, crab walking through the brush. A piercing whistle immediately ahead caused her to freeze and slip for cover beneath a drooping thorn bush that was choked with windblown leaves. She lay still, her staff out of reach for now, and waited.

Moments later, she watched as a pair of scaly black boots ran past her bolthole without pausing. The creatures were running upright now; the ambush had been blown and they were actively seeking her, heading in the direction she'd tossed the stones. They'd soon discover the deception, and probably find the body of their comrade not long after that. *Time to move!*

They knew she was headed north, and they'd suspect she'd run for safety back south, the way she'd come. She ducked and headed west, into the sun. No sense in making it too easy to spot her. She'd crab walked another hundred yards when she heard the collective wails and whistles, so they now knew they were one member down.

Siobhan reached behind and withdrew the staff again. If this was where it would end, then she was determined to take a few of the creatures with her. She thought of the *Toki-Moai* and she knew she couldn't afford to fail. She'd have to try to cut around in a wide circle and come upon The Magician's trail again later. She hated the fact that he was once more gaining some distance between them, but to get to him, she needed to survive this round.

Hopefully, the creatures would have to split up in order to try to find her. With luck, only one or two might follow. The trick would be to take them out before they could alert the others. That way, she still stood a chance.

She did her best to hide her tracks in the sand, skittering between slabs of rock or brushing the sand behind her as she crept along. She forced herself to have enough patience and courage to tread warily and resist the temptation to stand and flee. The creatures kept up a constant stream of communication as they searched, although Siobhan noted with some satisfaction that some of the high-pitched trills sounded further off.

She crossed a couple of ancient, dried-out riverbeds that once must have kept the land irrigated, and probably still did during the seasonal rains, and she noticed that the ground was beginning to fall away. She had traversed a shallow rolling hill and would be hidden from view as it sloped away.

She stopped behind a grey-coloured fleshy-leaf shrub and gradually raised her head until she could barely see above it. She scanned the skyline for any sign of her pursuers. The coast was clear. Time to put some miles between them. She turned and ran.

The terrain began to break up into a series of shallow, narrow gorges with steep sloping sides. The brush petered out, and she was pounding across flat bedrock that had been thrust upwards over many millennia. She'd half-clamber, half-slip down one bank, cut across the eroded channel and scramble up the opposite bank, only to have to repeat the process every couple of hundred yards.

Siobhan was midway across one of the exposed tops when she heard a long drawn-out whistle carried on the wind. She looked back over her shoulder and saw the silhouetted outlines of two of the creatures breasting the distant rise down which she'd crawled.

She had a gap of a couple of miles—maybe slightly more—and she didn't know what advantage that held. She wasn't sure she could outrun them, so she needed to continue to evade them.

She dropped into the next shallow gut but instead of climbing the other bank, she turned and ran up the old riverbed. It twisted through a series of shallow bends and the banks grew steadily narrow and steep. The rock faces were smoothly granular, like sandstone, and fissures had appeared where the rock had slipped and worn away.

She came to a fork in the old riverbed where three tributaries once met. Great! The pursuers would have to search each arm and this would split their numbers once again. She chose the right-hand fork since that appeared to lead back the way she'd come and they wouldn't be expecting that. If she could draw them out far enough, she might be able to double back completely and pick up The Magician's trail, which was growing colder with each passing hour.

She could hear faint whistling behind her as the hunters regrouped, and she hurried on. She scrambled over larger boulders and wondered at the sheer force of water that would have rushed and tumbled its way through this ravine, tossing these boulders aside as it surged along.

Another whistle echoed off the rock face, and this time it came from somewhere up ahead. At least one of the creatures was in front of her, perhaps having circled around when he heard the calls of discovery. She eyed the walls, but they were worn smooth, and there were no handholds that would enable her to climb out of danger. For the moment, she was trapped!

Siobhan was no shape-shifter; she'd always preferred to stand and fight than run and hide. However, she had no choice. She needed to remain free to search for the talisman. She looked for options.

A few of the boulders were big enough to hide behind, but she knew the searchers would be vigilant. She hurried closer to the biggest one, and that was when she spotted the fissure—a narrow crack in the rock not much wider than her shoulders. She peered down.

It was like a narrow chimney, about twenty-five feet deep, with smooth walls ending in a bed of sand. It would have been eroded by rushing water, and so it had to go somewhere.

She lowered her legs into the crack and looked down. Once in, she'd have to work out how to get back out again, but this would buy her time. She dropped her staff into the gap, and it fell with a whispered thud in the sand piled at the foot of the fissure. She braced her legs against each side of the vertical walls, bent her elbows and stiffened her arms against the rock to support her weight. Her head disappeared as she inched her way down, using her legs as brakes while she alternated the pressure left to right through the strength in her arms.

She'd gone about a third of the distance when she heard another whistle. Something was extremely close and getting closer! She had suddenly exhausted all her options. She took a deep breath and held it, pressed outward with her arms, and brought her legs together away from the wall. Then, in one fluid movement, she pulled her arms across her body and dropped like an arrow down the shaft.

As she hit the bottom, she bent her legs and rolled with the impact. The sand was soft and piled deep, and it broke her fall. She was immediately on her feet, retrieving her staff and adjusting the roll that was strapped to her back, which contained the few possessions she carried with her.

Down here, the fissure was more like a cleft in the rock as if some of it had simply split away from the wall. Ahead of her, it disappeared like a narrow, dark cave beneath the overhanging cliff that formed one side of the river gorge. Most important, it was hidden from prying eyes from above.

She whispered a command and a soft red light sprung from the tip of her staff, just enough to see by in the darkened crevice. She moved into the darkness, hoping it would lead somewhere, never looking back. She never saw the shadow block the sunlight fleetingly, leave, and then return for a closer examination of the freshly disturbed sand along the bottom.

Siobhan had been negotiating the twisting narrow path for the past three hours, and she was totally disoriented by the time she rounded another bend and saw a faint glow in the distance. The cave had forked numerous times and twice she ended in a blind chamber and had to retrace her steps. She had listened intently for any noise that signalled pursuit, but the cave was quiet, apart from the flap of tiny wings high above her head.

She approached the cave opening with caution. Outside, the light of late afternoon was subdued, but after three hours in pitch-blackness with only a weak red light to see by, it was bright enough to cause her to squint. She paused just inside the exit to allow her eyes to adjust to the light, while searching for any signs of movement. She saw nothing to alarm her, and tentatively stepped into the opening.

The exit was a hole in a sloping scree edge that helped form the side of a wide basin. The walls were composed of loose rock and sliding shale: impossible to cross without setting off cascades of loose stones with each footstep. The bottom of the basin was lumpy, filled with outcrops of rock, windblown hillocks of shifting sand and islands of dun brush that had managed to colonise the higher ground. Opposite, the walls had been swept away and the materials had been scattered across the outer flatlands in a fan-shaped stony pan.

Siobhan searched for any familiar landmarks. She noticed a line of purplish hills in the distance out to her left, pushing like a bony spine above the flat horizon, and recalled them as being on her right as she had made the tedious uphill climb across the plateau. The sun was now throwing shadows right to left, so she was facing south once more, back the way she'd come. The cave system must have led her in a wide arc below ground. In the wet season, water would gush from the gash and flow out and down, back towards the lake.

The problem was, she'd also lost the spoor she'd been following. The only thing she could hope to do was to traverse back and forth across the plateau until she found it again. Meanwhile, there were pink lizards on the loose.

She checked the angle of the sun in the sky. It was a hand-span above the western horizon and sinking steadily. She had between one and two hours of daylight left. She pulled the leather strap over her head and let the bag drop into the sand, then knelt and started to untie it. She decided to camp overnight just inside the cave, which was almost invisible: a slit in the rock that wouldn't be noticed from the plateau below. Besides, she was elevated and could see well out into the badlands. If the lizards were there, she felt sure she'd see them coming first.

Siobhan dozed fitfully at first until the stresses of the day took their toll and she slumped, exhausted, into a dreamless sleep. She awoke after the sun had arisen the following day, with a constant headache and equally as weary as she had been the night before. She could have slept for a week; she ought not to have slept at all.

She gathered her belongings together and repacked them in the roll and slung it across her back. Then she crept to the opening in the rock and sat motionless for thirty minutes, watching the shadows shrink, waiting for signs of movement on the plains below. She hadn't expected the lizard gang to give up quite so easily, but maybe she was being paranoid; maybe she had chanced a lucky break.

She held her staff tightly as she slipped down the slope, then moved warily over the boulder-strewn pan that emptied on to the sloping plateau. She moved in a crouching zigzag run, pausing frequently to listen for any unnatural sounds. In this way, she made one traverse, looking for any signs she'd left the first time through. Nothing seemed familiar, so she turned, keeping the line of jagged hills to her right and slightly behind, and set off again, scrutinizing the ground in front of her, heading north and west once more.

The land rolled slightly like an ocean swell frozen in time. She topped one gentle crest and was flitting among the bush cover on the other side like a bee pollinating a flowerbed when she heard the familiar whistle, out to one side. She immediately dropped on all fours and waited—poised for action. It sounded again.

Siobhan inched upwards and peered through the bush cover. At first, she saw nothing, and then a squat uniformed body rose out of the sea of scrub, and stood gazing back at her. She could see the thick maroon lips peel back in a kind of sneering smile before the creature tilted its head and whistled a third time.

This time, another answered the call, in back of and to the other side of her. She swivelled and saw the second hunter stand. Then: a third hunter, directly behind her. All three began to converge on her position.

She bolted. Ahead and to her left was an outlier, a kind of *kopje*, which afforded some high ground and a defensible position, and she ran towards it, but two more lizards popped out of the shrubbery ahead of her and forced her to turn away.

As she ran, she tumbled to the fact that they'd anticipated her moves, just as another lizard popped up and steered her left once again. She glanced back. Her pursuers were catching up, but they were in no hurry to run her to ground. They were shepherding her forward, flushing her out like beaters at a pheasant hunt, directing her into the bottleneck where the ambush would take place.

She swerved right and ran directly at the last lizard to surface.

"*Recëde!*" she cried, aiming her staff. A yellow translucent sphere shot from the staff and exploded into the unfortunate creature, blowing him off his feet and sending him twenty feet backwards in a sailing arc. He crashed out of sight below the brush and didn't reappear.

They didn't expect that! she thought maliciously as she tore through the gap in the attack.

Two others moved to cut off her escape route, closing in quickly. Siobhan felt their presence and pointed her staff back over her right shoulder as she ran.

"*Exstinguere!*" she commanded. The energy pulse blew a crater in the ground in front of them. The shrapnel of broken rock levelled one of the pair, but the other had anticipated the blast and sidestepped it. He ran wide, out of lethal range, and forced Siobhan to turn aside as she ran. They worked her, the way sheepdogs muster a flock, darting in and snapping at her heels and retreating before she could retaliate.

She took out another who leapt out at her from his hidey-hole a fraction too soon, cutting him in two, and she heard the howls of anguish and anger from the others who followed and saw their comrade fall.

She weaved back and forth and tried to force another path as another hunter materialised nearby and joined in the chase. She'd neutralized three, but seven were closing in, and she was tiring; she wasn't going to outrun them.

She'd have to stand and face them, but she needed to choose her place and time. She crested another ridge and the land fell away in front of her as if it had slumped in the centre. It was like charging down the slope of a gigantic boot print where the sharply defined edge continued to rise in a sheer wall the further along she ran.

She glanced behind her and saw that all seven remaining hunters had bunched together in a single line and were eating into the gap she'd tried to maintain. Fine! Let them come!

When she'd covered about four hundred yards, she swerved and raced towards the rock wall. There was a tear in the wall where some of it had collapsed, and under normal circumstances she would have been able to find handholds and easily climb out. But this was anything but normal, and they'd be all over her before she'd gotten beyond the first five feet.

At least her back would be protected. She made it to the base of the wall and ran up on to a small mound of compacted stone that had formed after the last slip. She turned astride it, gripping her staff in both hands and faced her attackers who halted and separated out, cutting off any possible escape route. She was cornered; she knew it, and so did they.

"Come on! What are you waiting for?" she yelled but she was breathless and the words caught in her throat.

No one made a move towards her. They were forty yards out; waist high in scrub burned every shade of brown. One by one, they sank out of sight and disappeared.

Siobhan waited and watched, panting and trying to regain her strength after the chase. Nothing moved.

She looked to where she'd last seen one of the creatures sink to its knees.

"Displode!" she cried and sent a bolt of energy coursing from the tip of her staff. It ploughed into the patch of ground and sent a pile of rocks and rubble ten feet into the air. The surrounding bush caught alight and began to burn, but the creature had gone.

A rock smashed into the wall barely missing her head, and she felt the prickle of cuts from stone shards as it disintegrated. She caught a brief blur of movement out of the corner of her eye, swirled and aimed another fire-bolt at the spot. A soft *whuumph!* of sand billowed up like a giant brown mushroom and the bush caught alight again, but she'd missed her target.

Another missile struck her left shoulder, and she lost her grip on her staff momentarily. One more careened into her leg just above her knee and the blast she'd just commanded was deflected down, shattering the rock about ten yards out and creating another patch of flaming scrub.

Some of the neighbouring bush had begun to catch alight also, and smoke drifted in towards her. It was pale and yellow and hung above the vegetation, distorting and masking the ground beneath it. Siobhan squinted from the acidic bite of the smoke and tried to spot movement beneath it, but it was impossible.

Missiles began to rain in on her from all sides. Many of them were no larger than small stones, but they were distracting, and every now and then a larger chunk would hit home. Many rocks also missed and bounced harmlessly into the wall, dislodging others that clattered noisily at her feet.

Suddenly the barrage stopped, and the lizard creatures rose to their feet one by one. She counted seven of them, so none of her defensive blasts had been effective. They were closer, no more than twenty yards from her and the semi-circle had constricted.

They all took one step closer, and Siobhan levelled her staff so that she could sweep it in an arc in front of her.

Another handful of stones clattered down behind her, and she realized too late that no rock had caused them to dislodge. *There was an eighth!*

Something long, wet and pink snaked around her staff, and it was wrenched from her grasp from somewhere above. She heard the shrill whistle, the signal to attack. Seven maroon bodies launched themselves at her, and their sleek tongues had pinioned her flailing arms before she had a chance to land a single blow.

She was buried in a tangle of bodies and bitten savagely on the arms, legs and neck. Sparks flew from the puncture wounds, and she cried out in pain.

The brawl was disrupted by a shrieking wail, and the bodies on top of her began to peel away one at a time until she was left, spread-eagled over the rock, unable to move. She could see the eighth hunter as he climbed down the rock face above where she had made her final stand. He carried her staff in his hand.

He leapt the final eight feet and landed heavily on the gravel beside her head. He handed her staff to another nearby, then knelt beside her and grabbed a handful of her hair, and pulled her head towards him. He gazed at her curiously and tilted his head to one side as if he'd been given a kitset toy with no instructions on how to assemble it. The tip of his tongue protruded between his lips as though he were testing the air and tasting it for any sign of fear.

Siobhan glared at him defiantly. She'd already died once; could this be any worse?

He seemed disappointed: slightly miffed that she wasn't trembling or begging for mercy. He shrugged and let go of her hair, and her head bounced back painfully onto the rock. He stood and looked about him, and she could tell he was counting how many of his men had survived. Siobhan took small pleasure in knowing he'd come up short, but the pleasure was short-lived.

He bent and picked up a boulder. It was flat, chiselled at the edges, and larger than her head. He towered above her, and his smile was grim as he raised the rock with both hands above his head, about to bring it crashing down and crush her skull like an eggshell.

CHAPTER 15

ifteen hours after they'd left the beach, Kareem called a halt. The night was pitch black and ablaze with stars. Kareem had been following an unseen trail with the aid of a feeble red light that glowed from the tip of his staff. Kate could barely see her hand in front of her face, and she had to marvel once more at the young man's skill—he must have had eyes like a cat—but they'd come across a flat pan of hard rock and the trail apparently disappeared.

Kareem consulted with Hawklight, and the two of them began a slow, methodical examination of the ground while Kate rested against a rock. She heard Kareem curse quietly to himself and knew they'd finished for the time being.

They'd gone fifteen hours without a break, moving at a steady jog—Kareem, then Hawklight, with Kate trailing at the rear in a single file. That would never have happened back on Earth, Kate reflected; she'd have whined and moaned about the ache in her legs and the size of her blisters, argued, and cried. She'd come a long way since then. She'd grown up.

So she'd followed along silently, determined not to be the one to slow the pace. She knew that Kareem would be watching her closely, testing her resolve with the cruel and relentless drive forward. She'd responded by biting her lip and lowering her head. She'd focused on the footprints of the others in the sand, and just concentrated on putting one foot after the other.

She'd caught Hawklight's eye too, and he had that stupid smirk plastered over his face. He'd noticed the game that was being played, and he was awaiting the outcome with interest. And when Kareem had looked backwards and seen Kate trailing doggedly, keeping up, the smirk had grown to a grin.

Hawklight was on her side. He knew her strength of will and the belligerence she showed in the face of adversity. She was stubborn beyond belief; he'd had first-hand experience of that, and he knew it would take more than a few hours of steady running to grind her down. Kareem had met his match with this one.

The cloak of night had declared a stalemate. Neither Kareem nor Hawklight was able to find any further sign of the path in the darkness. They couldn't risk pressing onward and losing their way. They had to wait till the first light of the new day.

They returned to where Kate sat and dropped to the sand beside her. Kate had removed her leather boots and was busy chewing a couple of leaves of Mother's Glove, a bush whose leaves held medicinal, healing properties. She'd chewed them to a slick paste and was carefully spreading the goo across her heels, plugging the trickle of sparks where her boots had rubbed her skin raw.

Her long slender calves were bare beneath her tight breeches, and the skin along both legs had remained unblemished and glowed with a muted golden radiance. She caught Kareem staring at them.

"What's the matter?" she asked. "Haven't you seen a pair of girl's legs before?"

He clamped his jaw shut, and Kate imagined she saw his skin darken. *Was he blushing?* she wondered. He'd heard of the golden girl of legend; perhaps he was putting two and two together at last.

He looked at her heels. "You should have said something," he muttered.

"This?" She shrugged in response. "Nothing, really. They'll be fine by morning."

A long silence followed, which Hawklight broke by announcing, "We need to post watch. Two-hour shifts apiece ought to just about cover it till dawn. I'll take first watch, then Kareem, then you, Kate. Okay?"

They nodded and the moment of awkwardness passed. Kareem slithered to his right, and made a shallow hollow in the sand, then drew his cloak over his shoulders and nestled in, turning his back on Kate. She finished dressing her blisters and followed Kareem's lead, tucking her bare feet into the hem of her own cloak. Kareem started to snore, so she dug him in the ribs with the butt end of her staff. She smiled with satisfaction and shut her eyes.

Hawklight, who had continued to watch the pair of them, shook his head and sat silently, peering into the darkness.

Kareem sat huddled against the chill night wind, trying to remain focused and alert, but his mind kept wandering back to the girl. On the one hand, she seemed strangely familiar, but he couldn't quite place her; on the other hand, he'd never met any other girl quite like her. And then, to top it off, he recalled the smooth gold skin of her legs and the aura that surrounded it.

It had initially made no sense why Hogarth would send these two as emissaries in the quest to retrieve the sacred statue. Hawklight—well, yes, he was a skilled and battle-hardened warrior, someone Kareem would be loath to meet across a battlefield. But the girl—?

If she were the one who had faced Varak and beaten him, then he had grossly underestimated her. He had tried to wear her down during the trek inland, and maybe even knock her sideways off the arrogant perch she seemed to straddle, but she had stayed with him and matched him stride for stride. Now, in the privacy of his own thoughts, he could admit to being relieved at losing the path that Siobhan had used so he could call a halt and rest.

Her stark, blue-eyed stare also unsettled him. The older girls of Hornshurst would hide their eyes and giggle and whisper as he passed. He didn't know how to react to that and would hurry on by. Kate was different, and he was curiously drawn to her, and this made him feel uncomfortable. He had been so surprised by the glow of her skin that he almost reached out to touch it, and it was only a distant voice in the back of his head warning him that she would deck him if he tried that stayed his hand.

He shook his head vigorously to clear that image from his mind, and peered intently into the blackness trying to refocus, but she crept back in like an insidious foul smell. He'd all but drowned back on the lake, looking for Hawklight, when the smart thing would have been to do nothing and reduce the number of those rallied against him. She'd controlled him with her gaze. The same gaze that held him in her sights across the crowded square in Goose Bay and he smiled at the pang of regret he'd experienced when he thought he'd never see her again.

He'd looked for reasons to hate her, feeding off her constant threats to zap him until she pulled the stunt in the boat where she harnessed herself in a painful noose and handed him the staff to hold. She was vengeful, but she was strangely vulnerable too, and it confused him and consumed him as he sat guard over their camp.

He'd been on duty three hours. He felt guilty about force-marching her and had decided to let her sleep and to cover her shift. He turned to look at her once more that night and caught the glint of starlight in her eyes. She was awake and watching him.

The pasty dressing across her heels had dried to the consistency of papier-mâché, and he watched as she peeled it back like the skin of a ripe orange. She sat and pulled on her woollen socks and boots, then sidled across to where he sat, skirting Hawklight's sleeping form.

"Why didn't you wake me?" she whispered to him. It sounded like an accusation. He bristled momentarily.

"I—," and then he bit his tongue. "I wasn't sleepy. I was enjoying the peace and quiet."

He felt her looking across at him, and he kept his face neutral and casually scanned the dark horizon where the belt of dazzling stars abruptly ended. He knew she was waiting for an accusation of weakness that she lacked the strength to keep up, and he didn't want to feed her anything that would suggest it. He waited.

"Thanks," she whispered. "I should have woken. I guess I was tired."

She was tired! But he smiled inwardly.

"How long till dawn?" she asked him.

He glanced at the sky, and saw the constellation he was seeking hanging low in the heavens.

"An hour. Not much longer. How are your feet?"

"They're fine. I still can't get over how quickly things heal here," she replied. "I wish we'd had Mother's Glove back on Earth."

They settled back into a comfortable silence, staring out into the immense void that was the universe. She sat beside him, and their arms brushed. He resisted the urge to pull away from her, and he noticed that she didn't pull away either. He could feel the warmth of her body through his cloak.

Sometime later, Hawklight awoke and he saw them silhouetted together against the backdrop of a red dawn. They were both staring towards the light. He grinned and rolled on to his back and stretched, and from the corner of his eye he saw their shadows part. His hip ached slightly where he'd lain on a hard slab of rock. He thought: *I'm getting too old for this.*

The sky to the east was turning a pale blue, and the sun hadn't yet risen above the horizon when Kareem picked up the trail once more. He pointed out to Kate the broken branch and the copper leaves of the shrub that had been wiped of dust as something had passed by. When he'd shown her, she was amazed that it seemed to stand out so clearly from the surrounding bush features, and even more amazed he'd spotted it in the first place. It was like one of those "Where's Wally?" cartoons—hard to see, then impossible to miss.

Kareem quickly fell into the same loping, effortless stride from the previous day. Kate noticed that Hawklight hung back, and she was now running sandwiched between the two of them. She also noticed that Kareem glanced back more often, checking her stride for any signs of limping. She didn't want to give him the satisfaction of slowing down "for the girl", so she ignored the residual soreness that the poultice of leaves hadn't quite managed to remove.

For whatever reason, he'd changed somehow this morning. Kate had to admit that the pre-dawn silence the two of them shared had been blissfully peaceful. He'd known enough to keep quiet, and for the first time, the accidental contact wasn't repulsive. Kate had her own problems dealing with that. Only one other person had broken past the wall she'd erected around herself in the past year, and he was dead and gone. She had not gotten over the loss of Jaime; she was still raw with guilt and grief, and the mottled patchiness of her once golden skin was a constant reminder of the fact she'd been implicit in his murder. She had kept everyone at arm's length since that time. Kareem was a complication she didn't want to acknowledge.

Up ahead, Kareem slowed to a walk, a signal that he'd lost the spoor temporarily. She stopped and waited, but he turned and waved her forward. She approached cautiously, taking care to follow in his footprints in order to avoid contaminating the area with her own tread marks.

"What's the matter?" she inquired.

His eyes never left the ground, which was a junkyard of rock and sand.

"Tell me what you see," he replied. Their eyes met briefly before Kareem resumed scanning the area.

Kate looked over the area. There were no conveniently broken branches; no outlines of footprints embedded in a sand dune, nothing to suggest anyone had passed this way.

Yet Kareem had already spotted something, and it was as if he were testing her. Hawklight stopped further back and was patiently squatting on his haunches, watching with interest.

She scoured the harsh wasteland for clues. The ground was a tumble of rock, bleached grey with the sun, streaked and banded with a kind of resilient, encrusting form of lichen that tended to colonise the shaded southern faces of the protruding boulders. But the surface was solid, and there was nowhere for a footprint to—

"There!" She pointed to a small flat rock where the pattern of blackened lichen had shifted as if the stone itself had been rotated somehow, and the banding was more eastward facing. She was aware of the ghost of a smile flicker past Kareem's lips as she continued to search beyond the stone. About twenty yards further on, she saw where another rock had been dislodged—part of it was devoid of any encrusting settlement, which meant that part had to have been buried in the soil and sand.

"I think she went that way," she said.

"Yes. Well done! What else do you see?"

Kate was searching for any other displaced rocks when something caught her attention. There was a flash of—something, a reflection—that didn't fit with the surroundings.

She pointed. "That?" she asked.

Kareem nodded in reply and beckoned Hawklight forward. The three of them walked to the spot that Kate had indicated.

She saw a smear of something that had brushed the rock, then been baked in the heat, like the gossamer film of snail slime.

Kareem bent and rubbed some of it with his finger and then examined his fingertip. Light, white flakes clung to it. He looked at Hawklight.

Hawklight shook his head. "I don't know. I've never seen it before." He nodded towards a similar stain ahead of them. "Whatever it is, it's moving and headed in the same direction. Maybe more than one."

Kareem stood. "We'll need to pick up the pace," he said, and he looked at Kate as he said it.

"I'll be fine."

He nodded once, picked up the trail and started jogging. Hawklight indicated the way and said, "Ladies first."

Kate laughed. "Try to keep up, old man. You're too heavy to carry."

The land sloped gently uphill, and the brush was waist-high in some parts. It had seeded more thickly, and the spoor was easy to follow where Siobhan had pushed on through. They ran throughout the day and half the night, pausing only to rest for a few short hours. Kate collapsed in the sand and was almost instantly asleep. Kareem and Hawklight sat talking.

"What are you thinking?" Kareem asked.

"Your friend passed this way, and so did The Magician." Kareem waited. "The tracks are more recent; we must be getting close."

"I agree."

"They're being tailed—ten, maybe upwards of a dozen tracks. Not animals: whoever it is, is wearing boots, but the feet are splayed out. I don't think they're human."

"Any thoughts?"

Hawklight shook his head. "You?"

"Could be a band of *Uaneacs*. They're natives; walk like men, look like lizards. They're hunters, and they're cunning—they roam in packs like this."

"How do you know so much about them?" Hawklight asked.

"The people of Hornshurst formed a loose alliance with them, but this was a long time ago now. I've seen statues of them around the city. We even established settlements out this way and back then we were welcomed. Then, a couple of centuries ago, Varak conquered this land and, the story goes, he tried to wipe them out. After that, they didn't trust us, any of us; didn't see any distinction between good and evil men. They hate us with a passion, and now they'll kill us if they get half a chance."

Hawklight glanced at Kate, sleeping soundly. "All the more reason to want to stay awake."

"I'll take first watch," Kareem volunteered, but Hawklight waved him off.

"I'm not tired, and I don't sleep well. Besides, we need to make haste if these *Uaneacs* are on the prowl. You'll need to be alert tomorrow—that's just the way of it."

He was right. Kareem thanked him and looked for a spot on the ground. There was a patch of sand near to where Kate was lying, and he crossed to it self-consciously, knowing Hawklight's eyes were on him. He ruffled his cloak about his shoulders, and then twisted onto his side, facing Kate. He watched her through heavy lids until sleep took him and he tossed with troubled dreams and conflicted emotions.

He awoke with a start at first light and realised that Kate was lying on her side, facing him. Her long hair was tousled, falling half across her face, but her liquid blue eyes were open and they were staring at him. She didn't try to look away as some people do; nor did she flash him a smile. He felt like an object under a microscope being scrutinized dispassionately. Her gaze was steady and cool, and he had the ridiculous notion that her eyes were pools of water into which he longed to leap.

He blinked to break the spell and sat up. Hawklight hadn't moved but looked relaxed and alert.

"We should get going," Kareem suggested.

"Do you have enough light to see by?" Hawklight asked, and Kareem nodded.

Kate was already on her knees, rolling her cape away and securing it to a strap. She slung the roll over her shoulders and picked up her staff, Rhyanon.

"What are we waiting for?" she asked and Hawklight smiled at the return of her sense of playfulness.

Around nine in the morning, they stood at the top of a scree slope that fell away to a bed of sand at the base. Even from there, they could see the disturbed sand and the tracks of many boots. Kareem had lost Siobhan's spoor, but they assumed she was being followed by the band of *Uaneacs* and had pursued their trail instead. They'd sped up considerably but now, staring down, they feared the worst.

Kareem wasted no time and ran nimbly down the steep slope, quickly followed by the others. They skipped to one side and waited while Kareem examined the prints in the sand, trying to decipher what had happened.

"She has not been here!" he exclaimed. He probed the sand with two fingers and traced the outline of a boot print. "But The Magician has! He was attacked here—and here—" he pointed to one side, "—but his footprints lead off in that direction. He was spared. The others appear to have regrouped, and they lead off back this way."

He was perplexed and re-examined the evidence. Kate thought it all looked like the aftermath of a beach volleyball contest, but she knew better than to intrude while Kareem was checking the ground.

He stopped mid-step and paled slightly, then bent to inspect a small round dent in the sand. He sat against the sloping wall, and his face was a mask of despair.

"The talisman was here. It spoke to them. They let him go."

"'Spoke to them'? What do you mean, 'Spoke to them'?"

Kareem looked at them.

"The *Toki-Moai*, it's not just a sacred statue. It is a vessel full of sacred souls. They carry the wisdom, the knowledge, the power inside—they're alive. Our high priests can speak with them; understand them. This collective wisdom of these elders has guided our city for centuries. Some of them would remember the *Uaneacs*—they would have intervened."

"To save The Magician?" Kate was incredulous.

"To save the bearer of the talisman."

"You're guessing!"

"No." Kate had not seen Kareem so intense before. His eyes were almost wild. "It left behind a trace. It knows me, knows I am from Hornshurst; knows I am following!" He paused. "It has called to another."

His eyes flicked to the dirt, searching out a sign. "*Not here!* But she must have been close by." His gaze followed the path made by the *Uaneacs*. "That's where they've—"

His voice trailed off.

"Do we continue to follow the talisman?" Hawklight's voice snapped him back to the present.

Kareem leapt to his feet. "No! We can't just leave her! Please!" he implored them.

"Then we have no time to lose," replied Hawklight and he took the lead, setting off along the path trodden flat by the hunting party.

They traversed rolling country and saw where some of the group had splintered away in a flanking manoeuvre, but they continued to follow the main bunch. The land became more broken, badly eroded and gouged by numerous rivers, now just dry and dusty gulches. Kareem spotted the faint outline of a familiar boot tread.

"She passed by this way!" he exclaimed, and Kate heard a measure of hope return to his voice.

They came to a fork in the riverbed and Hawklight pointed out the signs that showed the entire band had re-grouped after having hit each branch further along and created a pincer movement. But there was no sign of the woman—somehow, she had escaped, which meant she had known she was being pursued.

"They've headed out into the open plateau," Kareem noted. "They wouldn't just give up the chase, so that must mean they anticipated her movements and were trying to skirt around ahead of her."

"Would she think of that?" Kate asked.

"I think so. But this is *Uaneac* country, and she won't see them coming."

"Then let's go!" replied Kate.

They climbed out of the gorge and followed the natural curve of the land. They crested a rise and Kate spotted a thin sharp outline of a mountain ridge poking above the horizon. They raced down a shallow trough and crossed to the other side, climbing steadily once more.

Hawklight skidded to a halt at the front as the other two caught up. He was standing on the edge of a short cliff face. Below them, the ground fell away sharply, and they stood overlooking a vast brush-covered tableland. The cliff stretched either side of them like the lip of a large shallow bowl. Hawklight began searching for a safe way down.

"Wait!"

He turned. Kareem had one hand across his forehead, shading his eyes from the glare of the sun. He pointed at a spot somewhere in the middle of the bowl.

"There! Do you see?"

Both Kate and Hawklight peered in the same direction he was pointing. At first, Kate saw nothing, then—yes—tiny dots of movement. One was well out in front, and Kate realized she was witnessing a chase: a well-organised chase that seemed to be guiding the prey in towards the wall where there was no hope of escape.

Hawklight had already assessed the situation and searched for the spot where the chase would end against the wall. They had the height advantage and needed to keep it to keep track of the chase.

He sprinted left, dropped lower out of sight and ran parallel to the edge of the wall. Kate and Kareem tore after him. Twice they ran back to the cliff face to collect their bearings, and Kate could tell they were closing the gap. The second time they saw the unmistakable blue smoke of a brush fire and they knew the woman had turned to face her attackers in a last-ditch stand.

They were running downhill, and Kate could see a cleft in the edge of the ridge directly above the billowing smoke. Almost immediately, they spotted something moving across the gap of the cleft. One of the attackers had managed to scale the wall! Her first thought was that they'd been spotted, but his attention was directed at the battle below, and the wind was blowing in their direction, masking the sounds of their approach. Quite suddenly, he dropped from view over the side.

They had about four hundred yards left to cover when a jangling shriek pierced the air. Kate could hear the painful cries of a woman as the sound died away, and they redoubled their efforts to reach the cleft before it was too late.

Hawklight reached the gap in the rock first. He saw that the cliff was no higher than twenty feet at this point. Below him, a woman lay pinned to the ground, surrounded by what looked to be a group of men wearing large, pink-headed lizard masks. He saw the look of defiance on the woman's face; she was down but not out!

Kareem arrived at his side at the same moment one of the *Uaneacs* bent and picked up a large boulder in his hands. The creature stood over the woman and raised the rock above his head.

Kareem leaped from the top of the cliff and crashed into the *Uaneac,* and the impact sent both of them sprawling. The rock thumped into the ground a foot from Siobhan's head. Meanwhile, Kareem had rolled with the impact and risen into a defensive crouch. There was a blurred movement, followed by a painful scream as a flying *shuriken* left his hand and sliced through one of the rope-like tongues binding Siobhan's wrist. Another followed, burying itself in the neck of the *Uaneac* gripping her other wrist. He made a wet, choking sound and the tongue dropped into the sand and twitched like a writhing snake.

Siobhan struggled into a sitting position, but before she could utter a warning, one of the nearby lizard men had wrapped his tongue around Kareem's neck and choked him. He dropped to his knees and wrestled with the muscular tongue, trying to prise it loose, but he began to lose consciousness and one hand fell slackly at his side.

There was a loud explosion, and the *Uaneac* was blown off his feet. Kareem was jerked backwards as well, and Siobhan could see a bloodied mess where the lizard man's arm had been severed from his shoulder. The tongue slackened and Kareem lay gasping on his back on the rock.

Two other shapes landed in the middle of the battle, and they stood, back-to-back, firing bolts of energy, sending two more assailants scattering for cover in the underbrush. That left the two remaining *Uaneacs* whose tongues were curled around her ankles, crouched with their mouths agape, shocked into submission by the sudden, vicious surprise attack.

Siobhan picked up a rock that fitted neatly into the palm of her hand, and fired it at the nearest *Uaneac*, catching him fully between the eyes, snapping his head backwards. The other retaliated immediately. His tongue let go of her ankle and disappeared back down his throat. He launched himself forward and slammed into her as she tried to stand. They rolled together in a tight bundle but came to a stop at the base of the cliff, and Siobhan was pinned beneath him, unable to free her arms. He raised his head and screamed, and his lips peeled away exposing the razor-edged teeth as he lunged at Siobhan's face, intent on peeling it clean with one tearing, savage bite.

He never got the chance. He was punched from her by some unseen force and catapulted into the rock wall where he lay crumpled, unconscious and bleeding. Siobhan rolled on to her side and sat up groggily, waiting for her vision to clear.

Images floated into focus. She saw the maimed bodies of six of her captors. Three lay motionless, the others twitched spasmodically. She saw Kareem with his head between his legs, massaging his neck. She saw a tall, black-haired warrior sheathing his staff and moving from one of the lizard men to another, checking if any still remained a threat. She saw a young girl moving slowly towards her, pointing a staff in her direction, and realized this was where the knockout blow had come from.

The girl stepped closer and lowered the tip of her staff. Her eyes widened, and her mouth parted involuntarily, and she paled. She tottered unsteadily then sank to her knees, and tears began streaming from her eyes. Siobhan thought she had been grievously wounded and was about to yell for help when the girl spoke.

"Mum!"

The girl pushed her hair back; it had fallen across her face, and Siobhan stared into the two ice blue eyes she'd come to love and had to leave behind.

"Kate—?"

171

CHAPTER 16

"**K**ate!"

It was the same voice from her memory, the one that sang her to sleep: the same voice she thought she'd never hear again called out to her from across the universe of time and infinite distance. The voice that uttered that single word had been the pillar of Kate's being for the first nine years of her life. Her final image of her mother had been of a woman dying of pneumonia, lying pale and still between two crisp sheets. Kate had held her hand and begged her not to leave, and it had been Gran who finally prised her hand away and carried her out of the hospital ward.

Kate was vaguely aware she had dropped Rhyanon into the sand. She'd lost the strength to stand, and her whole body began to tremble so intensely she could not control it. She wept as if the floodgates that held back all the lost love over the years had finally burst open.

She felt strong arms envelop her, and she was pulled and held in a tight embrace. She nestled her head against the nape of her mother's neck, and that once familiar soothing smell overpowered her completely. She felt herself being rocked gently and heard soothing words whispered in her ear as she clung tightly, too afraid ever to let go.

Kate cried until she was drained of all reserve; until she was lulled to a point where she felt safe enough to pull back slightly without the fear that everything would end in a terrible dream. Her mother's face, too, was streaked with tears, but lit with a smile so radiant, it drew Kate in and she began to giggle as she wiped the tears and her nose with her sleeve.

Siobhan held her daughter at arm's length to appraise her. She'd grown into a beautiful young girl, but with a quality of strength and hardness she would never have suspected.

"Katie, darling!" she laughed. "But you're so young still. Whatever happened to you? How did you get—?"

She stopped mid sentence. She had glimpsed the golden skin that ran beneath the patches of brown mottling like a rich river, and Kate's aura was unmistakeable. Rumours of the golden girl who had vanquished Varak had swept the planet like a wildfire. She'd overheard the tales of the saviour of Hogarth—of Bexus—back in Goose Bay. The insignia on the shoulder of Kate's uniform was that of a soldier of Hogarth.

Siobhan put her hand to her mouth as the awful truth dawned on her, and she shook her head from side to side.

"Oh, no!" she sighed. Somehow, she knew Kate had been taken; had been brought to Bexus. But Kate had survived, and the spectre of Varak was gone. The only thing that mattered now was that mother and daughter were reunited.

Hawklight sat, speechless. He watched the two women embrace, chatter excitedly, and embrace again. He could not fathom the circumstance he had just witnessed, and knew only that Kate Gallagher had to be far more remarkable than any of them had dreamt. He felt distinctly uneasy that her future appeared to be so preordained as if she were a pawn in a much larger game and no one knew who was moving the pieces. Hawklight did not believe in coincidences, and he wondered what lay in store for all of them.

He heard his name called, which brought him out of his reverie. Kate was grinning and waving him across. He stood and brushed the dust from his leather pants and ran his hand through his hair.

"Mum. I want you to meet Captain Nathaniel Hawklight. He's brilliant and so courageous, and I've lost count of the number of times he's saved my life here." She held her hand out to him, and he took it. "Hawklight, this is my mum."

"Hello Kate's mum," he smiled and shook her hand.

"Please, call me Siobhan," she smiled. Her hand was firm and dry and warm, and Hawklight could sense the strength within. She had pale green eyes that hinted of the blue gene hidden beneath, and Hawklight saw the family likeness shine through, framed by long, dark lashes.

So, too, did Kareem. He knew now why Kate had seemed so familiar to him. *Mother and daughter!* It occurred to him that he would have died for one of them and killed the other, and was thankful he'd had to do neither.

"Apparently Kareem needs no introduction," Siobhan said, and she broke away from the other two and wrapped her arms around him in greeting. "Your timing was impeccable," she said. "Thanks."

There was so much to say, so much lost time to make up for, but it was a luxury they couldn't afford. They had to find the talisman and that meant finding The Magician.

"I was so close," Siobhan said. "I could hear the elders calling to me."

"Then that's going to be a problem," Hawklight replied. "The talisman will alert him that someone is close at hand. We are not going to be able to surprise him. It might prove costly."

Siobhan eyed him coolly. "This is not your fight, Captain Hawklight; neither yours nor my daughter's. In fact, I would be eternally grateful to you if you would see to it that Kate is kept out of harm's way."

"That's not his decision to make!"

Siobhan had forgotten about Kate, and she turned towards the voice. She caught the flash of defiance in the blue eyes, and realized that her daughter had grown into a stranger in the intervening years.

"Mum, we left behind two armies on the brink of war, with only the soldiers of Hogarth separating them. We promised to do whatever we could to bring the talisman safely back to its rightful owners. We only have a sliver of time left before they give us up for dead, and then all the fighting will begin again."

Siobhan heard the desperation behind her daughter's plea. She smiled. The four of them would make a formidable alliance.

"Then try to keep up," she replied.

"What is it with Hornshurst that everybody has to turn everything into a foot race?" Kate grumbled to herself, and glared at Kareem when he burst out laughing. She noticed Hawklight seemed distracted, staring out above the swathes of bush, some of which were still smouldering.

"What are you—?" she began, but he cut her short with a warning look before his eyes sought Kareem's. A silent message passed between them before both unobtrusively slipped from the clearing and disappeared into the undergrowth.

"Come and sit with me," she heard her mother say.

"What's going on?"

Siobhan kept her voice low and even. "There are two more *Uaneacs* out there somewhere. With luck, they're probably still watching us, but they'll go for help soon. We can't afford to be—distracted."

She smiled and reached for Kate's hand, and they sat silently as the sun plodded across the afternoon sky. Kate saw or heard nothing beyond the occasional cries of flying creatures—*Bienguls*—

wheeling above, so she was taken by surprise when the two men suddenly reappeared.

"We can go now," was all that Hawklight said, but it was enough to signal that the problem had been resolved.

They knew the general direction in which The Magician was headed, but it wasn't until early the following morning that they rediscovered his unmistakeable spoor. The area was also criss-crossed with the tracks of wandering *Uaneacs*, but none seemed to have picked up on his passing, slight as it was. But not so slight that Kareem missed it.

Kareem studied the ground for clues.

"We are in luck," he said, pointing to a rambling thorn bush that seemed to settle heavily over the sand like a nesting bird. "He is wary and cautious. He hid there out of sight of the *Uaneacs* that passed by here. He doesn't want to risk another encounter, and that is slowing him down. He was here a day, maybe two, before moving on. See here—" he pointed, "—where the tracks are fresh and sharp-edged."

Kate could make out the occasional scuff mark in the sand, but she couldn't see any difference. She thought that he was showing off, but Hawklight was nodding agreement and her mother listened and looked on intently.

"How long?" she asked.

"Three days ago, maybe four."

"Three," said Hawklight, and Kareem shrugged.

Siobhan pointed to the spot where the sand had been carelessly kicked aside. "We need to be just as careful," she added.

"But we can smell them," said Hawklight.

Both Siobhan and Kate turned to him. Kate wasn't sure whether or not to laugh out loud.

"It's true," added Kareem. "They have a distinct odour. We're headed into the wind, so as long as they don't hit us from behind, we will be able to detect them."

Kate couldn't help herself. She wrinkled her nostrils slightly to test the air and saw Kareem grinning at her. It was as if she'd been caught picking her nose, and she bristled inwardly because for some stupid reason it mattered to her what he thought of her; she couldn't dismiss him out of hand any longer.

At the same time, Kareem realized he had embarrassed her unnecessarily, and he hastened to cover his mistake with the girl.

"It's not that easy," he hastened to explain. "Right?" He looked to Hawklight for some support, and Hawklight nodded in agreement, though he hid the twinkle of amusement behind his eyes.

Kareem quickly bent and snapped a leafy branch beside his leg. The dust had been smeared, and its surface looked faintly greasy.

"Here." He offered the twig to Kate.

She narrowed her eyes but took the twig and lifted it to her nose and sniffed. There was a faint musky scent, like sour body odour, like nothing she'd ever smelled before."

"Yes?"

"Yes." Kate flicked the twig away into the bushes. She saw her mother's gaze flick between the two of them as if she'd just missed something crucial, and then she glanced at Hawklight for confirmation. There had been tension between the two young adults that wasn't born of animosity. Her daughter was growing up.

"Which way?" she asked and intruded on the moment.

"This way," Hawklight responded, and they turned and followed him in a loose single file.

Siobhan wrapped her cloak about her shoulders and lightly stepped away from the two sleeping forms lying nearby. She clutched her staff in one hand and crossed the sheltered patch of sand at the bottom of the natural crater they'd encountered as night fell.

She climbed the slight rocky slope towards the inert shape of Hawklight who maintained watch at the lip of the depression, and settled beside him. He didn't turn to face her, although he'd undoubtedly heard her approach.

For a while, they sat together in comfortable silence as they scanned the edge of the bush for any signs of movement.

"I think she likes him," she whispered.

Hawklight didn't reply. Her presence signalled the end of his watch, but as he turned to leave his station, she caught the reflection of a thousand stars in his eyes and saw their merry twinkle and the upturned corners of a smile on his face as he left her to ponder the situation that, for her, had suddenly grown more complicated.

Kate closed her eyes and pretended to be asleep as Hawklight quietly scraped some sand into a mound for a pillow before settling to sleep. She waited until she could hear his regular, rhythmic breathing before she opened them again.

She peered across at Kareem who was lying on his side with his back to her, lost in sleep. She could make out the long tangle of loose black curls and the broad outline of one of his shoulders. He lay just beyond her reach, neither too close nor too far away.

He confused her. A look, a stray sentence, that stupid grin—he made her bristle with impatience, and she would not allow herself to look weak or foolish in his eyes. And yet, at the same time, she found herself making feeble excuses to be close to him: to walk behind him on the trail, or to share the secrets of sifting information from the faint outline of a footprint.

They would kneel together on the ground, and Kareem would point and show her the subtle signs and explain the passage of the tracks, but then their shoulders would brush together, she'd feel his warmth through the sleeve of her shirt, his words would melt away, and she would be left kneeling in the sand trying to remember what he'd just said.

She had also felt Hawklight's scrutiny, and whenever she'd turn suddenly and catch him watching the two of them with his mouth turned up in a lopsided smirk, she could feel her ears burn and had to look away and fume silently with embarrassment.

She rolled on to her back and stared up at the stars, trying to clear her mind but her thoughts were insistent and leaked back like water into a sponge. She sighed loudly and shut her eyes, but sleep was proving impossible. The thought of Kareem's ease in sniffing out the signs of the lizard men and the look in his eyes as he spoke made her angry once again and she silently cursed him for not leaving her in peace.

She twisted again in the dirt, but it was no good. Finally, she sat up and glanced to her left. Both men were fast asleep, though neither one snored for both were light sleepers. They would be awake and fully alert at the slightest intrusive sound. She stood quietly and picked up her sleeping cape, and crossed the dip to where her mother sat keeping guard.

Siobhan watched her daughter approach. She had grown into a lithe and beautiful young woman, so different to what she had been as a child on Earth. Siobhan had missed six vital years since the time her frail body had wasted away and had privately mourned the loss ever since. Her fear had been that Kate would not endure the loss of both her parents and would somehow crumble under pressure, but at least she had a chance at life—until the accident.

But now she was here, and the story of her survival had transformed her in the process. She was both strong and fearless beyond her years and Siobhan flushed with the glow of immense pride in her daughter. At the same time, there was something else—a hint of fragility hidden beneath, and Siobhan saw it in Kate's eyes as she sat beside her mother.

Siobhan reached out an arm and pulled Kate close. Kate's arm snaked about her mother's waist and she was once more that young child burying herself in the security of her mother's embrace.

Kate's head rested against her mother's shoulder, and Siobhan gently stroked her hair until she finally felt the head beneath it grow heavy and begin to slump forward. She eased out of the close embrace and lowered her daughter so that Kate's head rested in her lap. She continued to stroke her hair and smiled as she watched the troubled frown that creased Kate's forehead relax and disappear.

"Sleep well, my love," she whispered.

Charlie watched the last of the *Uaneacs* trudge past from his position tucked well beneath an overhanging copper-coloured bush. They seemed to be everywhere, like an infestation of vermin. He couldn't wait to be beyond this arid land, but he'd needed to curb his desire for haste to increase his chances for survival. He had managed to survive one encounter with the lizard men, but he wasn't willing to gamble that he'd survive another. He moved with caution, and when he rested, he took the precaution of masking his presence as best as he could manage.

Like now. He had brushed the sand around the opening beneath the bush, then piled a few rocks in place and dusted them with sand and dirt. He'd dug a shallow pit long enough to conceal his body and then scraped the sand back in place so that only his head and shoulders were exposed above ground.

He buried his bag, as well. The talisman would utter the occasional squeak or moan, but these were kept muffled by the layer of dirt on top. His luck had continued to hold, but he didn't want to press it. He was fairly certain the lizards had taken care of whoever had been following him—most likely the woman. He took pleasure in imagining her final, terrifying moments, surrounded by these beasts as they started in to dismember her while she was still alive. The talisman had stopped the wail of squawking once the *Uaneacs* had released him and the silence, punctuated only occasionally by pitiful chirrups, seemed to confirm he was on his own once more.

He could hear the whistles coming from the bush. This wasn't a hunting party, obviously, but it would be unwise to make a move too soon. The bed of sand was warm and reasonably comfortable, so Charlie figured he might as well haul up for the day and snatch some sleep; give the critters time to put some miles between them.

The heat of the afternoon sun was oppressive and very little breeze penetrated his shelter. Charlie slept fitfully until the shadows grew longer and the sky turned a shade of light ash blue and the air began to lose some of its heat. He had scraped the sand away that had covered his body, and he was nestled on his side in the shallow trench.

Something faintly disturbing intruded into his dreams, like long, probing fingers stroking the strands of sleep aside. His eyelids were heavy and reluctant to part, and he never quite surfaced before he dozed off again, but the odd disturbance was insistent and eventually he opened his eyes.

The air was pleasantly cool to his skin, and he could feel the breeze tickle across the leg of his breeches—except, there was no breeze across his face. Charlie froze. *Something was moving down there!*

He remained still and slowly twisted his head. Crawling up his leg were two dark, deep red bulbous shapes the size of a teacup. They had thick, jointed legs and a shrunken undersized head that seemed stunted compared to the bloated abdomen that was dragged along behind. Another one surfaced through the sand between his feet and Charlie could make out the slight rise where it had burrowed towards him.

ALAN CUMMING

One of the creatures on his leg had stopped moving. Tiny palps either side of a short black tube at the end of its head began waving, stroking the material of his pants. Charlie was mesmerized with terror; it reminded him of the way a terrier seeks out a rat hole, sniffing and testing, searching for the entrance. Without warning, it thrust downwards violently and the creature's head disappeared through the material, punching a hole through his skin like a grotesque gigantic tick.

Charlie felt a momentary stab of pain, which was quickly replaced by a sensation of mild euphoria. He wanted to lie back and give in to the pleasant sensation that flooded outwards from the puncture wound. He could hear a faint suckling sound above a buzzing in his ears and began to giggle as if on a giddy high. He was vaguely aware the other creature had also penetrated his leg and saw tiny sparks leaking out around the buried heads.

He was drunk with rapture, but some part of his brain registered his revulsion as the two creatures began gorging themselves. Somehow he found the strength of will to reach for his staff. He touched its narrow end against the bulbous red-black body of the larger of the two creatures.

"Incendere!"

It was little more than a ragged whisper, but it was enough. The bloated shell burst apart, spewing a greenish custard-like fluid in all directions. Some landed on the neighbouring creature which squirmed and wriggled as if it were trying to extricate its head that was firmly wedged in his leg.

All pleasant sensations disappeared; in their place was a blinding stab of pain from the wound made by the first creature.

"Incendere!"

The second animal met the same fate and Charlie's leg felt as if it had been stabbed through with a length of red-hot wire. The anaesthetic they had injected had bled from his leg in a shower of sparks and Charlie was left writhing in pain, scrambling from the trench while dragging his deadened leg behind him. The third

182

tick-like creature had burrowed back into the sand, but Charlie was taking no further chances.

He pushed the mound of rocks he'd placed at the edge of the opening aside and tumbled out from beneath the bush. He gripped his leg either side of the wounds and fought the urge to cry out. Instead, he clenched his teeth and uttered an outburst of profanity beneath his breath while he waited for the pain to subside.

The wounds continued to throb savagely, crippling him. He ripped a hole through his pants and examined the wounds. Sparks of his energy fizzled from the punctures, but Charlie could see that the two heads were still buried just below his skin.

He tried to stand, but the pain was excruciating and he fell backwards on to his behind. Glancing about, he spied a thorn bush off to his right that bristled with long, lethal looking spikes. He crawled across the rocky ground to the nearest low-lying branch and cautiously broke off one of the spikes, almost the length of his finger and needle sharp.

"This is going to hurt me more than it hurts you, me old China," he muttered, addressing one of the heads, and he drove the point of the thorn into his skin beside the head and began to lever it up and out. He cried out once with the pain, and the head slipped from the thorn, still firmly embedded in his leg. It took another ten minutes of prodding, digging and squeezing before the head, which was the size of his fingernail, popped from his skin like a pip from a ripe orange.

He couldn't face further surgery, but it had to be done. He could have done with a few of these beasties when he worked for Varak. His eyes swam with tears, and the tip of the thorn broke off in his skin, so it was almost twenty minutes later before he was able to tear strips of clothing to bind the punctures and flop back exhausted with his back against a rock.

Finally, the pain abated enough for Charlie to take stock of his situation. He had half an hour, tops, before the last of the daylight disappeared. He needed to find a safer spot than this to hole up for the night, but first he had to retrieve his bag and the talisman.

He forced himself to crawl back beneath the bush. He used the thick end of his staff to prod at the sand, but nothing moved. His palms were sticky from the goo that had splattered over the sand and rough particles of sand stuck to his hands as he dug for the buried bag. He pulled it free using the shoulder strap and dragged it behind him back into the open.

He unbuckled the flap to check on the *Toki-Moai*, and dislodged another of the creatures that had burrowed its way inside. It rolled on the ground and came to rest on its back, waving its clawed legs in the air as it tried to right itself. Charlie dropped a rock on it.

Satisfied that the talisman was safe and secured, he slung the bag across his shoulder and used his staff like a walking stick, leaning heavily on it to ease the pain in his leg as he walked. He'd spied an outcrop of rock in the distance and imagined he could see a chink in the wall like a shallow crevice where he could find shelter for the night. It wasn't far, but it took the better part of three hours to cover the distance. He wondered if his luck was changing.

Thirty-six hours later, Kareem was kneeling in the sand. He had already crawled beneath the bush and had found the abandoned shallow trench. He had rubbed some of the sand between his fingers where it had stuck together in thin narrow ropes, and noted that it was still moist and sticky.

When he emerged, he saw that Hawklight was examining something in his outstretched palm.

"What is it?" he asked.

Hawklight showed him. There was a broken thorn and the head from a *Chathor*, a large blood-sucking parasite. Kareem knew of men who had bled to death from the bites, usually after the creatures had gorged themselves and crawled back into the soil, leaving the men unconscious, heavily sedated from the narcotic in their saliva. He also knew of men who had hacked off their limbs to ease the pain, once the narcotic had worn off.

Hawklight smiled. "He's been bitten—twice."

They discovered a pasty red mess slathered beneath a flat rock and clear tracks in the sand, which appeared to head towards a group of rocks jutting above the rolling bush. Kate could see the deep indentation made by The Magician's staff as he'd hobbled away. For the first time, he hadn't taken any precautions to try and disguise his footprints. He was getting careless.

Kate walked the point with Kareem, and he revealed the telltale signs where The Magician had tired and had begun to drag his wounded leg in the sand as he walked.

"He's slowing," he said to her. "We have a good chance of catching him soon if the *Uaneacs* don't find him first. See here, he is leaning more heavily on his staff."

Kate noticed that the holes in the sand were deeper, and the edges around the holes were ragged and broken where the staff had been yanked roughly.

"Do you think he'll stop to rest up?" Kate asked.

"I would do, if I were him," Kareem replied. "Though he probably won't want to lie in the sand again after what he's been through. It depends on how badly he was bitten. He dug two heads out of his skin, so I don't think they could have been in for too long for him to do that. He'll be in pain for a couple of days, and after that the effects of the bites will begin to wear off. He's a day away already, so we don't have much time to close the gap between us."

Within the hour, they arrived at the pancake-layered rocks, and it was soon clear that The Magician had sought refuge in a crack in the walls. It was wide enough for a man and sheltered from the sun. Kareem and Hawklight were like dogs straining on a leash. The Magician had rested here; the prints in the sand were remarkably fresh and the steady breeze that blew across the plateau had not yet deposited sand to cover them.

Kate stood to one side, and she saw a single set of footprints that led around the side of the rock. She bent to examine them and was dismayed by what she found. There was no evidence that he was using his staff as a crutch any longer. He might be limping, but he was well enough to walk.

She called to the others. They hurried across and quickly reached the same conclusion as Kate. Their window of opportunity had ended.

All four of them heard the faint, piercing scream. It sounded to Kate as if a mother were cradling the broken body of her dead child in her arms and wailing to the world.

Siobhan heard it, and she recognized it—she was once again within earshot of the *Toki-Moai,* and it was calling to her! She whirled and scrambled to the top of the rock spur and the others quickly followed behind.

She searched the land ahead of her for the source of the sound. They had reached the edge of the bush, and the shrubby vegetation thinned, giving way to a prairie of dry grass. It was brown and stunted from drought and resistant like tussock. It was unable to conceal a tiny figure isolated in the middle, with no place to run and no place to hide.

Charlie had left the bush and the constant threat of the lizard men behind. He'd waited until mid morning, testing his leg cautiously. He'd slept sitting up with his back against the wall of the snug crevice, and during the night the pain had eased back to a dull ache.

He had examined the puncture wounds, unwrapping the cloth that bound them. His skin had formed a tough tissue that sealed the holes, which still appeared to be inflamed around the edges.

The good news was he was no longer leaking bursts of energy. He wondered if his body could replenish it like blood, though he didn't think so; he figured part of him was gone for good. It didn't pay to get too injured on this planet.

Time to go! He saddled his bag across his shoulder, feeling the familiar weight of the talisman bumping against his hip. He rounded the base of the rock and saw to his delight that the bush petered out into a field of grass. He could make up the lost time, and maybe even come across some signs of humanity. Someone had to be living out this way!

He was humming quietly to himself when the talisman screamed, so loudly that he instinctively flinched with fright. He was momentarily stunned, and he didn't grasp its significance at first. Then he glanced back over his shoulder.

He saw no one until he picked out the rock formation he'd just left. Four tiny silhouettes climbed into view, straddling its top, looking back at him. *How could this be?* The talisman cried out once more, this time in a chorus of voices, and Charlie had no idea how to shut them up. Anyway, it no longer mattered. He watched as the distant figures disappeared from view, and then he turned and ran.

The four of them spread out in a loose line once they reached the boundary where the bush gave way to grass. Siobhan held the middle, following the line of The Magician while Hawklight drifted out to her right and Kate and Kareem angled out, flanking her on the left. It had come down to this—a footrace—one that Siobhan was determined not to lose.

The land continued in a series of long looping rolls. At times, Siobhan lost sight of her quarry as he disappeared down one side into a trough, only to catch another glimpse as he wove his way upwards again. They were gaining on him, and the screams grew louder and more plaintive with each wail.

She lost sight of him once more as he dipped below another rolling ridge and she sped up, concentrating on the ground in front of her, careful not to trip and fall. She reached the crest of the hill where she'd last spotted him and stopped short.

The land spilled away below her, but there was no sign of The Magician. She heard the constant wail of the *Toki-Moai* somewhere close by, and she swivelled her head slowly to get a bearing on the sound. It came from somewhere in front and to her right and she started forwards slowly, scanning the area for any giveaway movement. She was aware that Kareem and Kate were circling back in her direction, but they were still a couple of hundred yards distant. There was no sign of Hawklight.

The noise was shrill and immediately close by. She paused—tense and alert—and waited. Something caught her eye, something glinting through the grass, catching the morning sun. She took a step sideways and saw the talisman lying on a patch of bare ground leaning against a clump of grass.

The Magician had dropped it, or thrown it, and was hiding somewhere. No matter. They'd come for the *Toki-Moai*. She ran to the spot. It had rolled from the purple velvet cloth lying nearby and was lying on its side, covered in dust. Siobhan laid her staff aside and gently reached out and picked it up. She felt the vibrations of the agitated energy trapped inside and immediately the wailing ceased.

That was Charlie's signal. He rose from his hiding place in the grass behind her and out of her line of sight. Her head was bowed, and she was transfixed by the statue. *Not for long,* he thought. He aimed his staff at her back.

Siobhan heard the soft *pffizzz!* of an energy bolt and instinctively rolled to her left. Clods of dirt and grass rained down on her as the bolt exploded where she'd crouched moments before. She dropped the statue and continued to roll sideways into a defensive stance like a cornered cat. As the smoke and dust settled, she saw the prostrate, smoking form of The Magician draped across the grass. And then Hawklight materialised out of the dust cloud, his staff still pointed towards the unconscious Charlie.

CHAPTER 17

harlie saw stars. It took a moment or two for him to realize they were real and that he was lying on his back staring up at the night sky. He was stiff and sore, and his head pounded in a relentless headache. He tried to sit up, and that's when he discovered he couldn't move.

His head and feet were bound together and linked to a loop around his neck, which tightened whenever he struggled. He gave up and tried to remember what had happened.

There had been no place to run. His only hope had been to hide, but the bloody statue wouldn't shut up! He'd ripped it from his bag and tossed it to one side, then dropped out of sight in the tall grass and waited.

He'd seen his pursuers spread out behind him and cursed; he'd have to try and take them out one at a time. He'd spotted the woman early on, the one he remembered seeing on the jetty in Goose Bay. She had been alone then, and he had been certain the lizard men would have taken care of her. Apparently, she'd had help.

The two out to his left had circled widely in an attempt to cut him off from fleeing in that direction, but they'd gone out a bit too far. He'd glanced to his right but hadn't seen anything. He'd racked his brains to check whether he'd seen three or four figures on the top of the rock; it must have been three.

He'd needed to act quickly before the other two came within range, and so he had waited, not daring to move. When the screaming had stopped, he'd poked his head above the tips of the waving grass and saw he had the perfect shot. He'd lined her up. Then he'd been blown backwards by the blast that came out of nowhere.

He slowly twisted his neck to survey his surroundings, careful not to trigger the noose around his neck, and discovered he was back beside the crevice in the rock where he'd sheltered and rested for a day. They must have carried him back here, and he figured he must have lain unconscious for many hours. A moan escaped his lips.

"Well, well, The Magician is awake at last."

He heard the woman's voice as her face swam into view. She was standing, looking down on him. Three others joined her: a girl, a young man, and a tall, brooding soldier he'd overlooked. That had been a mistake.

"Who are you?" he muttered, his voice thick and groggy still.

"You stole something from us," she replied. "We wanted it back."

"You followed me?" He was incredulous.

"From Cherath." She smiled. "You didn't make it easy, but you did make it possible."

Charlie returned the smile. "Well, it was worth a try at least." He fell silent for a moment or two and then he asked, "So, what now? You have your statue back, no harm done. You could let me go, and I'll be on my way, and you won't have to worry about seeing me again."

The soldier shook his head.

"I'm afraid we can't do that. You have a large fan club waiting for you back at Cherath, and they're planning a surprise party for you. It would be such a shame to miss it."

A chill finger of fear swept down Charlie's back. He would be facing too many victims with too many long and painful memories. He turned his head away so they wouldn't see his face.

Kate cupped the statue between her palms. She thought it looked ugly and primitive and yet there was something strangely compelling about its form. Kareem and Siobhan sat either side of her. She lifted one of the arms and heard a *click* as it swung outwards. She pulled the other out as well, although it swung loosely as if the hinge inside the shoulder had been broken.

"These are the first two locks," her mother explained. "Thankfully the key to the third has remained hidden." She knew of the abductions of both elder priests and was overcome with a feeling of melancholy as she considered the cost of surrendering the information to Varak over the years. But he had not succeeded in breaking the code and the *Toki-Moai* was back with its rightful owners once more. She knew that the secrets contained inside were powerful enough to restore the city of Hornshurst to its former glory as a key city-state on Bexus.

"How does it work?" Kate asked.

"Only the elder priests knew for sure," Siobhan replied, "and only one still survives.

The trappings of power—the great castles, the armies, the wealth, and the land—these are all transitory. You saw that with Varak. His empire crumbled the moment he was defeated. The city of Cherath is nothing more than a shadow of its former glory, and all in the blink of an eye. But the secret to power—the accumulated knowledge and wisdom of a civilisation, and the ability to apply these things—these things last! Our priests discovered a way to contain the energy of our revered leaders, our wise men and women inside a vessel—this statue—so they are, in one sense, immortal. The priests could communicate with them, seeking advice and guidance that kept our city strong. Varak took us all by surprise, and when he threatened to destroy the statue he tamed the city and kept us under his thumb.

If the vessel had been destroyed, the energy that it contained would have been lost forever. Think of the civilisations back on Earth—the Egyptians, the Aztecs and Incas, the empires of Persia, Greece and Rome—they all lost the essence that made them strong and their empires crumbled. Without the talisman, the same thing happened to Hornshurst."

Kate was silent as she continued to rotate the statue gently in her hands. She thought about the crystal she had wrested from Varak, how others had lusted after the power it bestowed.

"What's to stop another Varak from Hornshurst taking control?" she asked.

"That would be abuse of power, not use of power," Siobhan answered. "Those inside the talisman would not permit it."

Kate saw the irony and smiled. "So The Magician would never have been able to use the talisman for himself?"

Siobhan laughed. "No. But if he had succeeded in opening the talisman, the days of Hornshurst as a great city would have been numbered. We weren't worried about him *using* it; we were worried about him *losing* it."

They started back at first light. Siobhan released the bindings around Charlie's hands and feet, but the plasma noose about his neck remained tight in place, leading out from the tip of her staff.

"You very nearly made it, you know," Hawklight said to him as the others were assembling their gear.

"What do you mean?" asked Charlie.

Hawklight answered him by pointing back towards the grassland. They were standing on a high spot just below the summit of the rock spur.

"You can just see it from here," he said.

Charlie squinted out over the ash blue haze that hung like a mist above the grass. From this height, at this early hour, he could just make out the sooty smudge against the horizon from the smoke of a hundred houses. It would have taken him less than two hours to reach them. He closed his eyes and whispered a profanity. Luck was deserting him in droves.

The prospect of re-crossing the bushy plateau, home to hordes of *Uaneacs*, was not a pleasant one, and the group adopted a defensive array in the shape of an arrowhead, with Hawklight at the tip, and Kareem and Kate either side of Siobhan, who carried the talisman and was tethered to the prisoner via her staff.

This time, too, the wind was at their backs so any raiding party would be downwind of them, reversing the advantage they'd held previously. No one spoke; all eyes were peeled on the landscape, and they walked bent over to reduce their upright profiles. Even Charlie was cooperating; he had no desire to have his spark extinguished at the end of a pair of gaping jaws and ripping teeth.

Kate was getting a crick in her neck from the constant swivelling. She had to maintain a hundred and eighty degree line of sight in case the marauders came at them from behind. After several hours, she began to hallucinate from the constant strain, and every branch that wavered in the wind marked the passage of a lizard man moving behind it.

When Hawklight called a halt to their progress, they bunched together in a defensive circle and took turns to rest up and revive. Kate massaged her stiff neck and lay down and stretched out in the sand with her head on her mother's lap and her legs brushing lightly against Kareem's. It occurred to her that, despite the apparent danger lurking behind every bush, she was extremely contented.

By the end of the first day, they started to encounter the bold limestone formations that were characteristic of much of the plateau. Wind and water had eroded holes and guts into the rock over time, and there were plenty of places to take shelter for the night.

Hawklight found a small cave opening at the base of a hill that sloped downwards in a long tunnel that was only waist high. The floor of the tunnel was carpeted in a thick layer of grey sand. Kareem volunteered to check it out, so he disappeared down it, half-sliding in the sand on his hands and knees.

He'd been gone no more than a couple of minutes when he reappeared at the entrance.

"It's perfect," he grinned. "The tunnel only goes about forty feet, and then it opens out into a wide underground chamber which looks as if it could have been carved out by a river at some time in the past, but it's dry now."

He led the way back down. At the bottom of the short tunnel, Kate was able to stand. The underground chamber was wide and as high as fifteen feet in some places. A spot of diffuse light shone on the floor from the outside; otherwise, the chamber was gloomy and dark at either end.

They tethered Charlie hand and foot again while Hawklight and Kareem crawled back up the tunnel to collect dry brush for a small fire. The nights had been brisk and they had not lit any fires through fear of drawing unwanted visitors from out of the night, but down here, they were safe from prying eyes.

The fire crackled and threw flickering shadows against the wall of the old watercourse. Its light and heat brought comfort to the weary travellers, and for once, they were able to relax completely. Hawklight took up position at the foot where the tunnel rose upwards as a precaution and Siobhan sat beside him so they could exchange information and work out the quickest route back to where they'd left the boats tethered on the shore of the lake.

Kareem reached forward and threw another log onto the fire, then settled back with his face hidden in the shadows.

"What are you going to do when you get back?" Kate asked him.

He shrugged. "Stay in the army, I guess," he replied. "It's all I've known since I was a boy. I'd like to stay with the general—your mum—at least till everything settles down a bit. Who knows? Maybe there'll come a time when we don't need armies. Perhaps then, I'd like to travel." He looked across at her. "Maybe I could come and visit Hogarth one day."

He was met with silence. He wondered what she was thinking, and not for the first time, he wondered if he'd blundered into a situation he didn't quite understand. He searched her face in the glowing firelight for some clue.

She gave him a coy smile and whispered, "I'd like that."

"What about you?"

"I'm not sure. Hogarth is home to me, I have a few real close friends there, and I don't feel I belong in any other place. But I never dreamed I'd meet up with Mum again, and I don't want to lose her a second time around. So, maybe, I could come and visit Hornshurst one day."

Kareem couldn't help himself. He broke into a broad, elated grin.

"I'd like that."

The following two days passed uneventfully. Hawklight's sixth sense for danger proved unerring: they had to take evasive action three times, and hid amongst the rocks while roving bands of *Uaneacs* filed past. The creatures were unsuspecting and less vigilant than if they'd been part of a hunting pack. Kate had no idea what they did or where they went to when they weren't out hunting, and she had no desire to find out either. The Magician had been cooperative throughout, but there were many times when Kate felt his eyes drilling into her back as she walked. *He's planning something*, she thought to herself.

They passed landmarks that looked familiar—a broken spine of mountains out to their left, a wide, shallow basin, a swathe of burned scrub—as they ran in a half crouched manner and made as little noise as possible. No one spoke throughout the day; communication was through a variety of hand gestures: stop, eyes peeled, quiet, look left, check behind.

Around midday of the third day, they heard the first whistle, behind and to the left. It was faint and distant, but others answered it closer by. Hawklight called the group in tighter.

"We've been spotted," he said matter-of-factly. "We're too exposed out here, and we need to try and lose them." He surveyed the area quickly. "Keep below the brush line and head in that direction—" he said, indicating with a nod, "—and stay together. We should hit the dried up riverbeds, and we'll have a better chance with our backs against a wall if we need to make a stand. With luck, we'll outsmart them yet. Stay alert! If they're going to hit us, they'll do it before nightfall."

He glanced across at Siobhan. Her staff tethered Charlie with the plasma noose. They couldn't count on it if they were ambushed. He briefly considered the idea of setting Charlie loose; with luck, he would divert the hunting *Uaneacs*, and they would escape with the talisman intact, but Siobhan's face was set and he knew without asking that she would reject the idea. The Magician needed to settle his accounts with the people of Cherath and Hornshurst. Justice should prevail. He said nothing more; just turned and slithered on his hands and feet beneath the brush.

They followed his example, keeping close together. Kareem brought up the rear, brushing their trail clean and guarding against a surprise attack from that direction. Kate hung back with him and assisted with disguising their tracks.

The whistling appeared to come from every direction, but it was sporadic and Kate thought she could detect frustration in the keenness of the shrill calls. Eventually they ceased altogether, and she hoped they had done enough to escape detection.

They regrouped at the first of the steep riverbanks and slid down the loose slope to the dry, rocky bed. They were dusty and scratched from the thorns where they'd pushed through the underbrush, but still in one piece.

They wasted no time. Hawklight set off downstream. They were careful not to bunch together and kept to the rock as much as possible to avoid leaving tracks. They followed the course of the riverbed until it began to veer north again, so they scaled the opposite bank and scooted across the flat, broken plateau until they found another that flowed in the direction they wanted to go.

This one was steeper, narrower, and The Magician nearly hung himself when he slipped and fell while negotiating the sheer side. He almost pulled Siobhan with him, but he reached out and grabbed a rock and clung on, choking on the plasma that seemed to cut into his neck.

Siobhan released the tension and he lay panting and dry retching, gripping the rock with one hand and massaging his neck with the other. He stared up at Siobhan through watery eyes.

"Can't we work something out?" he asked, but he was met with a stony, impassive stare. He felt the noose settle and shook his head, then picked himself up and continued to clamber down the slope, taking more care to search for secure footing.

The ancient river had sliced through the porous rock, carving a gorge where the water would have tumbled through a series of waterfalls. Now the dry cascades were vertical rock faces littered at their bases with piles of massive boulders worn smooth over time.

They stood at the edge of the first drop and stared down. There were cracks and knobs and crannies enough for handholds, but it was apparent they could not keep The Magician harnessed during the climb down. Two would negotiate the falls first, and then Siobhan would send Charlie down.

Hawklight led the descent, closely followed by Kate. She remembered being afraid of heights, although her time on Bexus had cured her of that. She watched where Hawklight placed his hands and feet and before long they were standing together on a large, flat boulder at the bottom, watching The Magician negotiate the rock face.

"He's going to try something for sure," Kate said as she watched him stretching for a handhold.

"I agree, but not just yet," replied Hawklight. "He's going to want to stay with us until we're clear of the *Uaneacs*. I think he'll wait until after we cross the lake."

Charlie jumped the final few feet, and then turned and smiled as if to say, *That was easy!* before seating himself on a nearby rock to wait for the others. Siobhan and Kareem made the descent look deceptively easy.

Charlie was left untethered although the remaining stony cataracts were shorter and less formidable, and within the hour, they were standing on the boulder-strewn bottom where the riverbed flattened out once again. The torrents must have been powerful indeed for the water had cut a narrow chasm in the rock only slightly wider than Hawklight could have reached with arms outstretched.

A faint fizz signalled that Siobhan had looped the noose about Charlie's neck, and they adopted the same single file formation as Hawklight led the group into the narrow cleft.

A tired breath of wind wafted through the gut and Kareem's nostrils flared as he caught the sour scent.

"Ambu—!" he cried but the word was cut short when a falling body hit him from above. He crashed on to the rocks and tried to roll with the impact, but he was flattened by the weight on top of him. He feinted, twisting his body one way then quickly reversed when he felt the body above move to counter him, and was able to use the momentum to flip his attacker on to his back. A pair of arms began squeezing him from behind and he rammed his elbow backwards, driving it into his assailant's ribs. He heard a loud grunt and rotated so that he was sitting astride the enemy. A pink face stared back wildly beneath heavily ridged brows, and a long tongue darted out and wrapped around his throat and squeezed.

Kareem fell forward, one hand gripping the coil about his neck. His other hand landed beside the creature's head. He felt the rock beneath his hand and gripped it and swung it in a vicious arc against the struggling *Uaneac*, caving its skull inwards. The tongue fell limp, and it slithered from his neck.

He was still dazed from the first impact as he gazed about him. He saw a frenzy of flying bodies as everyone battled for survival.

Hawklight had launched himself sideways against the rock face on Kareem's cry, not a moment too soon. One of the *Uaneacs*, therefore, missed the target and slammed into the riverbed where Hawklight had just been standing. Another immediately landed on top of the first but rolled away unhurt. Not for long. Hawklight stepped out and hit him with a solid uppercut that snapped the jaw shut, cutting through the protruding tongue which fell to the ground and writhed like a snake with a broken back.

He glanced upwards, and saw knots of the lizard men clinging to the sides of the narrow gorge, dropping one by one into the fray.

"*Reicitor!*" Kate's command cut through the air and two of the falling *Uaneacs* above her head were catapulted backwards into the rock wall as if jerked by an invisible bungee cord.

"*Exstinguere!*"

This time the voice was Siobhan's, and the pulse of energy cut through another of the attackers and ricocheted off the wall, narrowly missing Hawklight's head. She was brandishing her weapon like a quarterstaff, felling opponents with dazzlingly quick blows and blasting others. The plasma noose had gone, and there was no sign of The Magician.

A long tongue snaked around Hawklight's wrist. He grabbed hold with both hands and pirouetted through three hundred and sixty degrees. The startled *Uaneac* was hauled off his feet in a tight arc and collided with the immovable object that was the side of the rock face.

Something hit Siobhan in the side of the head, and she dropped like a stone. Immediately three more *Uaneacs* fell on her.

"Mum!"

A tongue wrapped around Kate's forehead, covering one eye. She jabbed sideways with the blunt end of Rhyanon and caught the *Uaneac* in a choking lunge. She'd peeled the tongue off before he hit the ground.

"*Adnihilere!*" she screamed, and a red pulse that looked like a flying jellyfish with long trailing tentacles burst from her staff. It blew the three attackers away as though they were carried by a strong wind, and then slung them into the rock.

She felt the searing heat of another pulse above her head and spun to her left. A *Uaneac* holding a fist-sized rock was gazing uncomprehendingly at a hole that had just appeared in his chest as he'd been about to swing the rock into her head. His legs crumpled beneath him and he sank to his knees before toppling forward on to his face. Kate saw Kareem through the dust, his staff outstretched; he'd covered her back and kept her safe.

The tide had turned. Those few *Uaneacs* still clinging to the upper sides of the river gorge skittered back and disappeared beyond the top. Kareem flattened the last of them with a stiff-legged, sideways kick to the knee and another graceful circular kick to the bent head.

They were exhausted and had not escaped injury. They'd been choked and bitten and pelted with rocks and battered with branches. Hawklight was leaning against one wall, surrounded by bodies, some still moving and twitching. Kareem had dropped his staff and was bent over with his hands on his thighs, gasping for air. Kate sank to her knees and used Rhyanon for support to hold her up.

Which was why Charlie took them all by surprise.

Once Siobhan had severed the noose in order to defend herself with her staff, Charlie had scampered backwards on his hands and knees and found a space between a giant boulder and the side of the gully. He'd squeezed his bulk into the cavity and waited out the battle. It seemed like luck was on his side once more.

Kate's annihilate command had blasted the three *Uaneacs* backwards, and they had fallen each side of his boulder. He could still hear the sounds of the battle, so he risked a peek, using one of the unconscious bodies as cover.

Siobhan had been knocked unconscious and she lay sprawled in the sand nearby. Her bag had been torn from her, and Charlie saw where the talisman had spilled out and rolled away against a rock. At the same time, he heard the scuffling from above as the remaining *Uaneacs*, still clinging like leeches to the side of the steep cliff, began to retreat. He wondered if they'd spotted the talisman. Whatever! It didn't matter. The final few were being routed, and soon his opportunity would pass.

Siobhan was groggy, and had managed to raise herself up on to her elbows, cradling her head between her hands. He moved fast.

He slid from behind his cover and had grabbed Siobhan's staff before any of the others even realized he'd reappeared. He bent over Siobhan and hooked his left arm below her chin and hauled her roughly to her feet with her neck pressed into the crook of his arm as if held in a vice. He used her as a body shield and pressed the tip of her staff into her jaw.

"Oh, dear me," he said. *That got their attention!*

"Mum!"

"Uh-uh! Don't move!" he warned. Both Hawklight and Kate had levelled their staffs at him, though he was careful to ensure that neither had a clear shot at him. He jabbed Siobhan with the staff and her head snapped back.

"Mummy and I are going on a little date. I'm sorry you don't approve. Now, I'm going to need you all to drop your weapons."

"No!" Her voice was strangled and the word was clipped, but there was no mistaking the defiance in Siobhan's tone.

They kept their weapons trained on him. They had called Charlie's bluff. They knew he needed to keep her alive to use as a shield. They'd cut him down the moment he was exposed.

"Kill him!" Siobhan hissed. Charlie squeezed her throat using his forearm, and she began to choke. He loosened his grip again.

Kate caught a reflection out of the corner of her eye and glanced down. The talisman was lying on its side in the dirt. Slowly, so as not to alarm The Magician, she circled sideways and bent and picked up the statue. She lowered her staff.

"Let's make a deal," she said. "My mother in exchange for this."

"Kate, no!" her mother cried, horrified.

Kareem was standing to one side, without his staff in his hands. He began to shuffle unobtrusively towards Kate and the statue.

"We guarantee we'll let you go," Kate continued, "only, please don't hurt her."

Siobhan's eyes swivelled towards Hawklight.

"Shoot!" she croaked. Hawklight didn't react, just stood with his staff levelled at The Magician.

Charlie suddenly realized that he was being boxed in. When Kate had retrieved the statue, she had moved away from Hawklight, and he was now cornered; the soldier was to his left, and the girl and the young Arab were to his right. He needed a diversion and the golden skin on the girl's arms gave him an idea.

He turned to her and smiled. "I have a message for you—from Lord Varak."

He flicked the tip of his staff away from the woman's chin. In one smooth movement, he dropped his forearm like a salute and aimed at the girl.

"*Exstinguere!*"

"No!"

A blinding burst of energy flew from the tip. It caught Kareem squarely in the chest as he tried to deflect the shot by diving in front of Kate. The blast caught them both and blew them back against the rock where they collapsed in a crumpled, smoking heap.

Siobhan's scream had caught in her throat the moment she understood what The Magician had intended to do, but he was far too quick. The tip of the staff, still smouldering from the recent blast, was tucked neatly below her jaw again.

Charlie whirled her around so that they were both facing Hawklight. He held the advantage now. It was one-on-one, and he had the woman in front of him.

Hawklight's eyes narrowed, and he took one step towards them.

"Don't do it, soldier!" Charlie warned him. "I'll kill her, you know I will!"

Hawklight paused. Charlie took a step backwards, half dragging Siobhan with him. He took another. Hawklight smiled and lowered the tip of his staff fractionally. Charlie took another step back. He watched the tip of the staff dip slightly once more.

Kate slugged him from behind with the talisman, so hard she cracked his skull. He almost passed out as he let go of Siobhan and brought his left hand up to feel where she'd hit him. He felt the static fizz of sparks leaking from his head and his palm came away matted with a few black hairs. Lights were flashing behind his eyes as he staggered around and saw her standing, holding the statue in one hand. She'd made him truly angry. She shouldn't have done that! He raised the staff and pointed it towards her face.

"Exstinguere!"

The pulse of white-hot energy from Hawklight's staff passed through his chest and exploded against the opposite wall. The staff flew from his outstretched hand and clattered noisily on to the rocks littering the riverbed as Charlie staggered backwards from the impact, dropped to his knees, and then slithered all the way down to the dust and sand.

He managed to roll on to his back, felt the pain grow, and it suddenly occurred to him in a flash of déjà vu that he'd been in this same situation before. And, to remove any doubt whatsoever, the little voice began singing *Happy Deathday* to him once again. His vision grew dark and he saw dark, blurry shapes moving about beside him. He heard a young girl's voice cry out in an agonised wail, *He's dead! He's dead!* and he tried to sit up and reassure that he wasn't until he realized it wasn't him she was screaming about.

He tried to laugh, but the laugh turned into a grizzled, choking cough and a struggle to breathe. Then someone turned out the lights altogether, and all that was left behind was a dusty pile of torn clothing scattered in the dirt.

CHAPTER 18

"*He's dead! He's dead!*"

The insistent wailing, although distant, intruded on the serenity. Kareem was drifting, nestled in a bed of cotton wool, and he wanted to block out the sound so he could go back to sleep. He tried to work out where he was; nothing was familiar to him although it didn't really matter in the end. He put his hands over his ears to shut out the screaming, but it was just as loud so perhaps he'd just imagined he'd done so. He wished she'd shut up. She was beginning to annoy him!

She was crying now. He tried to scream, *Shut up!* but when he opened his mouth, no sound came out, and that just made him angrier still. He could feel the anger inside, burning in his chest—burning, burning!

He couldn't breathe for the rising pain, and lights flashed past him, tugging against his clothing. He was being drawn backwards, and he struggled to stay upright and in one place. From the distant horizon, a grey ball of light grew outwards, expanding, racing towards him and he turned to face it, determined not to shy away in fear.

It struck him like a giant fist and sent him tumbling backwards through the air, and he fought against it, couldn't breathe, and flailed like a drowning man desperate to reach the surface of the raging sea.

His eyes flew apart, and his head was spinning. Dim shapes hovered above him, and the noise of rushing water abated. Slowly his vision began to clear, and he looked up. His head was nestled in Kate's lap, and her face was looking down on him, streaming tears. He felt her fingers brushing through his hair and when he tried to move a sharp jolt of fierce pain shot through his chest.

He moaned, but he was lost in her embrace and he laid against her and felt her body heaving as she sobbed with relief. Suddenly, he didn't want the moment ever to end.

He heard Hawklight's voice.

"Let's get him sitting up."

Kate continued to cradle his head, and he felt someone lift him beneath his arms and drag him into a sitting position. He moaned with the pain.

Kate pulled away from him, and he was able to look down. His leather jacket was charred and smoking still, but there was no gaping wound in his chest. The pulse he'd intercepted had hit his bandolier of *shuriken* knives. One of the knives had melted, but it had absorbed almost all of the blast and had undoubtedly saved his life. He'd been blown into Kate, and the two of them had hit the rock wall. The blast had knocked him unconscious, but Kate had merely been stunned. The Magician had made the fatal mistake of turning his back on her.

She was wiping her nose and grinning at him, and she laid her hand on his arm and left it there.

"I honestly thought you were dead," she said. Her thoughts flashed back to another time when a courageous old *Chukkani* warrior had made the same sacrifice only then there had been no bandolier to prevent the killing blow. "Don't *ever* do that again!"

"I was trying to duck," he joked.

"Does it hurt?"

"Only when I breathe."

Kareem gazed about. The three of them were kneeling at his side. Siobhan wore a mask of relief where Hawklight was inscrutable, quietly assessing if there was any real damage done.

"What happened to The Magician?"

"He vanished."

Kate's answer made him laugh, but the pain around his chest pulled him up short. He grimaced and turned his head to one side, glimpsing the talisman lying in the dirt against a rock where Kate had dropped it. Both of the tiny arms had come loose, and it appeared as if the tiny figure were trying to do push-ups. A thin, wispy column of smoke appeared to be rising from a tiny hole in the back of its oversized head.

Something was seriously wrong!

"General—the *Toki-Moai!*"

Siobhan whipped her head around as if she had just caught someone in the act of stealing the statue. What she saw made the breath catch in her throat. She rushed to the statue and picked it up.

"It's the third lock!" she exclaimed. "It's open, but the whole thing appears to be broken!"

She dropped into the sand beside the others and held out the tiny statue. When Kate had crowned Charlie with it, she had slammed it against his force field with such rage that the object appeared to have imploded. The tiny arms swung uselessly at its side, and a sliding panel cunningly concealed in the back of its head had exposed a small circular hole the diameter of a peanut. A faint bluish vapour was slowly trickling out of it.

Only Siobhan grasped the full significance of it.

"The ancient ones are leaking away! We've got to close the hole again immediately!"

She scoured the talisman for a mechanism that would trigger the sliding panel, but she could find nothing that would work. Hawklight took the statue from her and covered the hole with his thumb, but no matter how hard he pressed, the misty film continued to leak away either side of his thumb.

"It's no use," he said.

"Can't we cake it in mud and bind it with a cloth?" Kate asked.

Siobhan shook her head.

"The ancients have no form that binds them together any longer," she explained. "The only way to contain them is to offer them a vessel that will hold them in one place. Without the vessel, we will lose them; we will lose everything, and it will all have been in vain."

"This is all my fault," Kate whispered.

Siobhan reached out and took her hand. "No, my darling, none of this is your fault. It was an accident, pure and simple. It's done, and that's all there is."

"Then we've failed," Kate replied.

Siobhan fell silent, and the four of them gazed at the leaking talisman.

"There is a way," Siobhan said at last. Kate looked at her and saw her eyes well with tears. Siobhan turned to Hawklight. "But I will need Captain Hawklight's help."

They stared at each other for a long moment. Siobhan knew Hawklight was the only one present with the strength of purpose not to turn away. She saw the flicker of recognition in his eyes and the fleeting despair as he understood the cost. He gave an almost imperceptible nod.

Siobhan turned back to Kate and took both of her hands in hers.

"The moment you were born, you were my pride and joy. I have loved you so, so very much, and it broke my heart to have to leave you. From that day to this, I have always thought about you, wondered about you; about what you could be doing, how you might turn out, and each night, I would wish you every happiness in your life."

"Mum—"

"Let me finish. I never thought I'd ever see you again, and now that I have, I can see you have become more beautiful, stronger, more passionate and caring than I could have imagined, could ever have hoped for you. That glorious golden skin of yours is no accident. It's a sign for everyone to see that you know to do the right thing. I am so proud of you. I love you—know that whatever else may happen, I will always love you, and I will always be with you."

"Mum—I don't understand what—"

Siobhan leaned forward and kissed her daughter on the forehead.

"Be strong—for me," she said.

She let go of Kate's hands and shuffled backwards. She stooped and picked up the talisman and gently cradled it in her hands. She looked longingly at Kate, and Kate realized she was saying goodbye.

"No—ooo!" she screamed and lurched forward but she felt Hawklight's iron grip about her arms as he held her back.

"Mum! No! Please don't!" she pleaded, and she struggled and tried to lash out at Hawklight with her boot. She caught him on the thigh, but he didn't react to the blow; instead, he gently but firmly lowered her on to her backside and continued to hold her tight.

Kate watched helplessly as her mother raised the talisman to her lips and covered the hole with her mouth. She closed her eyes and drew one long, deep breath. Strange sounds, like excited chatter, radiated out from the statue as Siobhan doubled over in pain and sank to her knees. Nevertheless, she exhaled through her nose then took another long draught of the contents of the talisman.

She began to age. Streaks of silver appeared in her long, auburn hair, and the skin around her eyes and mouth began to crease with wrinkles. Her arms turned brown, and their smooth bare skin hardened and cracked like parchment. Her hair continued to change colour until it was perfectly white and the full flesh of her face shrunk inwards until it resembled a grinning skull.

She shrunk in size with each new breath as Kate railed and swore and lashed out and sobbed as she watched her mother dissolve before her eyes. Kareem tried to move but was still too weak from the blast that had levelled him and could only lie against the rock and watch in disbelief.

When the last of the contents of the statue had been sucked dry, Siobhan let it fall from her hands. She was wizened and decrepit and bent with age, a shrunken hag robbed of her strength to stand. She struggled to raise her head, and when she looked at Kate, her bright green eyes, as strong and powerful as ever they had been, shone between the folds of skin. They were rimmed with tears, but there was no sign of remorse or regret in what she had just done. A tired smile turned the corners of her wasted mouth, and she lowered herself to the ground and closed her eyes.

Hawklight let go of Kate, and she turned and slapped him hard across the face with her open hand. He flinched with the blow, but he didn't look away, so she hit him again, and again—and again. She saw the hurt in his eyes, the cost of his betrayal, but she was wounded beyond caring.

She scrambled across to her mother and lifted her so that Siobhan was cradled in her arms. She was surprisingly light to hold. The old woman mouthed something, but it was too faint to hear, so Kate just sat and rocked her while tears streamed down her cheeks, but she wouldn't give the others the satisfaction of hearing her tear apart her soul in grief.

They camped for two days in the gulch, not moving from the scene of the battle with the *Uaneacs* and all that had followed. Kate sat with her mother, kept her shaded from the sun and covered during the cold nights, and refused to let anyone else touch her. She was openly hostile to Hawklight and refused even to speak to him, so he removed himself to one side and sat morosely keeping guard. He cut a lonely, stoic figure.

It had taken that long before Kareem was well enough to travel. They were all conscious of the fact that time was slipping by, and a war between the three factions involved in the siege at Cherath grew more likely with each new dawn. By the end of the second day, Kareem was strong enough to walk and insisted that they waste no further time waiting for him to recover.

They were still in hostile territory. The *Uaneacs* had backed away, and there had been no more sightings, although that meant nothing. If they didn't want you to see them, you wouldn't see them.

Kate had argued that they needed to build a litter to transport her mother, but it was an impractical suggestion and neither Kareem nor Hawklight reacted to it. They needed to be able to respond quickly in the event of another attack.

But on the third morning, when Hawklight moved towards Siobhan with his greatcoat beneath his arm, Kate stood between them and glowered at him.

"Don't you touch her!" she warned.

Hawklight easily held her gaze; he stopped and waited, but he didn't look away.

It was Kate who broke. She heard a wheezing noise behind her and glanced back at her mother. Siobhan's eyes were open, and she was glaring at her daughter. Her lips moved, but the words were whispered breathlessly, and Kate hurried to her side. She bent her ear to her mother's mouth.

Siobhan's bony arm reached across, and she gripped Kate's wrist with surprising strength.

"You will not punish that man!" she hissed. "You will leave him be and let him do what he has to do. This was my decision, not his! How dare you be so selfish!"

The effort seemed to drain her and the grip relaxed, but she kept staring up at Kate, locked inside her withered body. She willed Kate to step aside.

Hawklight brushed past her and bent over Siobhan. He carefully laid his coat flat on the ground, then gently lifted Siobhan and placed her on top, folding the edges around her to form a snug sling. He cut a strip of material from his blanket, and bound it around the bundle to secure the bottom He tied the sleeves together, looped them over his head, and then rose slowly to his feet. Siobhan looked like a baby swaddled and strapped to its mother's back. Only her head and shock of white hair poked out of the bundle.

Siobhan had slipped back to sleep, but Kate could hear the chatter and squeaks drifting out of her like a clutch of day-old chickens, muffled by the coat.

They had rescued the Hornshurst Talisman and were about to bring her home again.

They moved down the sloping plateau, headed for the vast lake once more. They were constantly surrounded by the familiar whistling calls of the *Uaneacs* throughout the journey, but not one of them showed its head above the bush.

Kate's eyes never strayed from the brush line. She ached for one of the creatures to attack so that she would have a target on which to vent all her anger and frustration. Rhyanon quivered in her hands, sensing her battle readiness, feeling the blood lust about to explode, but whenever the whistling drew near, a chorus of squeals would erupt from the greatcoat lashed to Hawklight's back and the intruders would back away.

Kareem led the way. Kate could see the effort it took him to keep walking hour after hot, dusty, dry hour. He moved hunched over with one arm across his chest, but he never stopped to rest, nor did he call out in pain. His forehead glistened with the effort, but his eyes remained focused on the ground ahead of him, leading them in a direct line back to the lakeshore where they hoped the boats would still be tethered.

Hawklight followed, carrying Siobhan on his back. He managed her weight with ease, and he moved with the grace of the agile hunter as if gliding through the air rather than bouncing along. Siobhan's head poked above the opening in the bundle and rested forward in the nape of his neck where she lay undisturbed in deep sleep as he marched. Not once did her head loll sideways or jerk upwards with a start, despite the treacherously rough terrain.

Kate brought up the rear. She was the first line of defence in an attack, although she felt relegated because she lacked the skill to do anything different. She felt the weight of the empty statue wrapped within the bundle across her back, and she was saddled with the guilt of knowing her desperate attempts to save her mother had, instead, resulted in her loss.

Each night when they rested, Kate would hurry to her mother's side and help ease her from the coat. She would sit with her back against a rock, nursing her mother on her knee and holding her, wrapped in a protective embrace.

Siobhan continued to waste away imperceptibly. Her skin looked grey and ashen in the evening light, but her eyes burned bright as if they were windows into the frail container she was trapped inside. Yet each night, she rose to its surface and spent the long dark hours whispering to her daughter, peeling the layers of pain from her and dabbing at the rawness beneath with words that sought to heal. And it would be Kate who first slipped into sleep.

Siobhan already knew that the bond between mother and daughter soon would be broken forever, and she needed to leave behind a legacy that would keep Kate strong against the world. Once Kate had fallen asleep, she would sing to her, and tell her stories of happier times that Kate had been too young to remember.

She told Kate of her arrival on Bexus and shared with her the events that had transformed her own life. She became an artist, scratching out a design on canvas, and filling it with a brilliant combination of textures, hues and colours, shapes and forms that became her own portrait and her gift to her daughter, to carry with her long after Siobhan had left.

Kate sat in the bow of the boat with Siobhan's head resting comfortably in her lap. The crunching of gravel beneath the keel gave way to the slopping of waves against the wooden hull as Hawklight and Kareem guided the boat into deeper water before hopping aboard. Kareem swung the tiller and the wind filled the sail and pushed the tiny craft out through the gap in the reef, past the wreck that once had transported The Magician, and out across the line of indigo that signalled the abruptly plunging depths where the shoreline fell away.

The air blowing off the lake was sweet and refreshing after the baking intensity of the high plateau, and Siobhan was revived. She lay staring up at the blue sky and smiled whenever Kate glanced down at her and stroked her head.

"That feels good," she whispered. "Don't stop."

"Do you want me to lift you up so you can see out?" Kate asked, but Siobhan shook her head as if the effort would tax her remaining strength.

"I'd rather look at you," she replied. Then she asked, "How are Captain Hawklight and young Kareem?"

"Kareem is mending well," Kate said. "I don't think he's in pain anymore. He led us straight to the boat, you know." She glanced at Kareem sitting in the stern, but he was preoccupied with maintaining trim and keeping the bow steered into the waves. Her eyes flicked beyond Hawklight, slumped low in the middle of the boat, watching the two of them. She couldn't hold his gaze and had been avoiding any contact with him wherever possible. She fell silent and stared out at the whitecaps as they drifted past the tossing smack.

She knew her mother was still looking up at her.

"What?" she asked.

"Sooner or later, you'll forgive him," Siobhan murmured. "Be gentle," she advised. "If you wait too long, you'll always regret the time you wasted, and you'll never get it back."

Kate heard the chatter like the voices of young children muffled inside her mother's gaunt frame.

"I have to go now," Siobhan smiled. "We can talk again later." She closed her eyes, and her breathing was steady and even. The corners of her mouth were still upturned, and she looked very much at peace with the world.

Kate gazed out over the horizon and thought about what her mother had said. Hawklight had been her rock for so long, perhaps the closest thing she had to a true friend since she'd arrived. They were so deep in mutual debt she had begun to think they were inseparable, which made his treachery at the end so hard to bear, and it had crushed her spirit utterly.

She would have saved her mother—she would have thought of *something!* But deep down, she understood only her mother and Kareem bore the Hornshurst mark that the ancients would have recognized. She understood they'd run out of time. Her own mother had known how she would react and had turned Hawklight against her. *What has he done to me?* she thought. *What have I done to him in return?*

Hawklight had increased the distance between them. He had retreated behind his inscrutable mask and was now as distant and aloof has he had been when they'd first met more than a year before. She had glimpsed the man behind the warrior, but he had gone again.

"Oh, Mama," she sighed. "What am I going to do?"

They were spotted entering the harbour at Goose Bay, and by the time Kareem had steered the smack back to its mooring alongside the jetty, its owner had organised a welcoming party with five of his friends, all brandishing Billy clubs and steel bars.

Kate was still itching for a fight. She had stepped over the gunwale before the boat stopped moving, clasping Rhyanon in front of her. She stood facing the six men with her feet apart, still experiencing the giddy, residual rocking motion from having spent so long in a pitching boat.

She felt someone alongside her. Kareem had joined her, holding his staff at a deceptively lazy angle. For some reason, she had expected Hawklight; had just assumed it would be him.

The chubby, bald-headed boat owner took a step towards them and stopped. None of his friends moved. They were all staring at something behind Kate. She heard the creak of a loose plank from a light footfall behind her and edged to one side.

Hawklight had stepped on to the jetty behind her. He towered above everybody and was cradling Siobhan's limp form in his arms. His staff was sheathed behind his back, but he showed no fear as he moved past Kate and Kareem. He didn't even appear to see the knot of street brawlers blocking his path as he walked towards them.

He stopped in front of the boat owner. The man broke his gaze and dropped his head, then meekly stepped aside. His friends peeled apart to either side and allowed him to pass through, gently holding Siobhan who was still fast asleep.

The prospect of a fight had ended before it had begun once again. Kate sheathed Rhyanon and followed Hawklight through the line of men and down the length of the pier. Kareem had picked up Hawklight's gear and also passed through, although not before one of the thugs regained some of his courage and pushed him as he moved by.

"Don't come back if you know what's good fer ya!" he called but the threat was lame and came too late.

Hawklight carried Siobhan in his arms all the way to the stable where he and Kate had discovered Siobhan's *Hon'chai* and they had tethered their own mounts. The stall owner was still sitting on his favourite bale of hay, half asleep from the drudgery of doing nothing.

He seemed to struggle with the memory of Hawklight as he pushed the large sliding door aside with the toe of his boot, but his eyes widened when he clapped eyes on Kareem.

"You!" he spat, edging off his seat and backing towards the wall. He hit the spot below the peg where Kareem had left him hanging last time and thought better of it, sliding away to his left. He eyed Hawklight and Kate craftily. "You got him then? Bring him here and string 'im up, see how he likes a taste of his own medicine, shall we?"

He stepped forward, emboldened by their presence until Kate stopped him by saying, "He's with us." That brought him up short, and he began to stutter, suddenly uncertain.

"Er . . . how, uh . . . how may I help?"

"We need our rides back," Kate replied.

"Well . . . er . . . you see, there's a bit of a problem. I've promised them to a gent who's dropping back in a day or two to pick them up."

"But they're ours!" Kate said. "We asked you to hold them, not sell them!"

"You said you weren't coming back," the little man complained.

"You misunderstood. We're back."

She waited. She watched the owner's eyes flit back and forth in panic. Either way he was going to make someone unhappy, and she'd already decided it wasn't going to be any of them. Kate had had enough.

"Kareem?"

Kareem dropped his staff and stepped forward to pick up the little man. He shouted in fear and darted back behind one of the stalls, slamming the gate behind him.

"Take them, curse you!" he cried, "and be gone! They're out the back".

"We need to borrow your cart too," Kate added.

The man wailed but quickly changed his mind when Kareem peered at him over the gate.

"Take it and get out!"

Kareem eased a gold ring from one of his fingers and dropped it in the hay beside the huddled, cursing owner.

"That should take care of it, and more," he said. He stayed long enough to watch the little man scrabble about in the hay to retrieve the ring—at least it shut him up—then hurried out back to join the others.

Hawklight had lowered Siobhan on to the tray of the cart, having first piled a soft bed of hay on it. Kate mounted the cart and sat beside her sleeping mother while Kareem and Hawklight hitched a pair of the *Hon'chai* to the cart. Kareem climbed on to the cart and gathered up the reins while Hawklight mounted the third animal.

As they left the yard, the grizzled owner spat at their feet and shook his fist at them, although Kate noted he kept hold of the ring he'd found. She had had enough of the good citizens of Goose Bay and was relieved to be heading away from the town once again.

The cart clattered against the uneven cobblestones and rolled from side to side, but Hawklight had packed it well with the hay, so Siobhan was insulated against the harsh jarring and was rocked gently in her sleep.

As they passed beneath the arching gates to the city, the sun was setting, and the clouds were ablaze in fiery orange hues that seemed to sweep across the sky in long, broad brushstrokes. Out to the east, the first of the moons had risen: a faint white orb against the pale blue backdrop of late afternoon.

The road had been compacted and worn smooth by years of countless feet and hooves trudging along it. Kate eased herself down alongside her mother and cuddled her. She felt drained and exhausted and as lonely as she'd ever been before. The people she cared about were gradually slipping away, one by one. She shut her eyes and silently and secretly cried herself into a fitful sleep.

Commander Elward Carter was peeved. He sat in the centre of a large U-shaped table. The contingent from Hornshurst sat to his right and, facing them, the contingent from Cherath glowered.

The arguments had swung back and forth between the opposing factions, to a point where Carter and his councillors were in danger of losing the battle to mediate between them. He was, in fact, equally scorned by both sides, who viewed the strategic position of Hogarth's army to keep them apart as a brazen attempt by Carter to seize the mantle of power from the vacuum created by Varak's defeat.

As far as Carter was concerned, they weren't that far from the truth. The ten-week window of truce was all but up, and the peacekeepers of Hogarth had already quelled outbreaks of violence. Some soldiers had been killed, and the ringleaders from both cities had been dragged away in chains, and Carter had had enough.

He'd attempted to convince his war council that a battle between the two principal cities was inevitable and that the sensible move would be to withdraw strategically to a safe distance and leave them to it. The ensuing carnage would weaken both and leave Hogarth as the last strong player to move in and pick up the pieces. That was the silver lining to this particular cloud; maybe he owed that favour to the girl who, by now, he hoped, had met a sad and untimely end.

His dreams were crushed after Mirayam had walked through the flap of his spacious tent. She was the constant thorn in his side at all the Council meetings; she had the gift of the gab and could talk her way past any obstacle, dragging the other councillors with her. He didn't have the numbers to put her out to pasture, no matter how graciously he tried to disguise the ploy.

"Don't be ridiculous, Elward," she'd scoffed. "You're inviting a blood bath and besides, we still have a few days before the deadline runs out. You have to go back and settle things down." She eyed him warily and added, "As the elder statesman, you must be the voice of reason." He squirmed, and she knew she'd hit the mark and earned another few days of maintaining the fragile peace.

The general in command of the city walls of Cherath was on his feet, shouting and pointing accusations at the elders of Hornshurst. Spittle flew from his mouth as he described the outrage when a group of citizens had been set upon and beaten by a vigilante mob of Hornshurst mercenaries. It seemed that everybody wanted a piece of the action when it came time to carve up Varak's imploding empire.

Carter wearily banged his gavel on the wooden desktop until the man fell silent and the shouts died away.

"Enough," he said. "General, you know the rules. Your citizens are to remain inside the city walls at all times—"

"But they were farmers who wanted to tend their animals—" the general interrupted.

"Rules are rules!" Carter insisted. "This was the consequence of breaking them." He turned to the Hornshurst elders. "You will find the men responsible and hand them over before nightfall. There will be no discussion!"

His head ached, and he massaged his temples.

"What's next?" he asked moodily.

Mirayam despaired. Hawklight and Kate had been their only hope, and once she'd heard the news of their departure, she'd left Hogarth and had made the long, slow journey to the encampment in the fields outside the massive black gates of Cherath.

This was the morning of the first day of the eleventh week since the pair had been gone. She was surrounded by her students who had all just returned from various points north of the city, searching for any news of the return of the talisman. All had come back empty-handed and despondent.

They could hear the clamouring and the shouts of men preparing for war coming from the Hornshurst camp. The rattle of armour and the clanging of metal echoed off the walls behind them, and the air was electrically charged with the sweet aroma of ozone as staffs were made ready for combat.

To the other side, the clanking of chains signalled the lowering of the portcullis across the main gates, and the stone parapet walks rang to the sounds of boots as defenders raced to take up position along the battlements.

In between, the soldiers of Hogarth formed a defensive ring facing outwards in both directions, but a nervous tension hung over them as they realized they were the bait between the steel jaws of a trap.

Elward Carter and a few of the senior council members had managed to retreat a safe distance so that some of the ruling integrity of Hogarth could be preserved should a battle ensue. Carter declared he was loath to volunteer to lead this group of city leaders but vowed to carry on in the event of an unfortunate massacre of many of Hogarth's citizens.

"It's time," said Mirayam. She had tried, in vain, to convince her students to leave with the others, but they would have none of it.

"You ought to know us better," Jackson chided gently.

"Besides, who's going to look after you?" Olivia added.

Sigrid nodded. "Varak couldn't separate us. This will be child's play compared to that."

Mirayam smiled at them. She was immensely proud of all of them and knew it would have been a waste of time and effort to try and convince them otherwise.

"Well then, what are we waiting for?" she asked. She threw aside her cloak to reveal a shining suit of finely woven chainmail. Her long white hair was tied back in a thick braid, and she stepped out tall and erect into the morning sun. Her group of loyal students trailed behind her, and she looked like a mother duck taking her family for a stroll as she strode down the lines of defenders, offering encouragement and support to the beleaguered troops.

The army of Hornshurst had re-formed the classic bull's head formation, with the mass of its troops in the middle facing the Hogarth peacekeepers and, beyond them, the city gates. Two flanks of horns fanned out either side ready to race inwards and smother the opposition. Cherath was already a sacked and looted city to them; the question was just in the timing.

The soldiers began beating their staffs against their shields and the racket built to a gigantic crescendo of fearless intimidation. An elder druid stepped out from the ranks and raised his arms, and the wall of noise disappeared. The ensuing silence was almost deafening by comparison.

"There is still time for you to leave," he called across the gap. "Our fight is not with Hogarth. You can leave peacefully, and we will guarantee your safety if you withdraw."

He waited.

"Stand your ground, Hogarth!" Mirayam commanded. No one moved.

"This will be your last chance!"

"Stand ready, Hogarth!" There was a unified snap as the soldiers' staffs were brought to bear on the opposing men of Hornshurst.

Something moved in the corner of Mirayam's vision, and she glanced upwards. She spied three smoking trails that were about to converge above their heads. They didn't come from the walls of Cherath.

"Cover!" she cried and slapped her palms across her ears just as the three pulses exploded in a single, terrific thunderbolt above the battlefield.

Everybody had flinched; some were still cowering, but the priest was recovering and about to release his troops in retaliation.

"Hold fast!" Mirayam screamed across the gap, her ears still ringing. "They're here! It's her signal, don't you see?" and she scanned the plains hoping to find what she expected to see.

"There!"

The priest had frozen, his arm still outstretched, holding his staff aloft, but his head had turned in that direction also.

She was aware of the buzz of general confusion as soldiers looked to each other to determine whether or not they were meant to attack, but she focused on the moving dots drifting out of the haze that hugged the desert floor.

The battlefield that, moments before, had hummed like a disturbed wasps' nest, fell silent as all eyes strained to make out the tiny figures. Seconds stretched out into minutes, and the factions continued to hold their collective breaths.

Sigrid's eyes were keenest. "It's Hawklight!"

Sure enough, his tall upright form was unmistakable. He rode stiffly in front of a cart with two people seated beside each other. The wind caught Kate's hair and blew it sideways, and it fanned outwards in the breeze.

"Stand down, Hogarth!" Mirayam cried, and the soldiers lowered their staffs. She heard a similar command across the gap, and the tension was deflated. Those lining the walls of Cherath began cheering, and people were laughing and grinning at each other.

Hawklight rode his mount into the gap between the armies of Hornshurst and Hogarth and dismounted. Behind him, Kareem swung the cart in a lazy arc and hauled back on the reins.

Kate stood on the bench seat and faced the priest as she rummaged around in her bag. She pulled out a small shiny object and tossed it in the air. It landed a few feet from the priest and rolled to a stop at his feet. He bent and picked it up.

Mirayam saw that he held a tiny metallic statue, although both arms appeared to be swinging loosely at its side.

The priest examined the back of its head, and then he let out a bellow of despair.

"Everything! All is gone! What have you done?"

The young man who had driven the cart moved to the back. Mirayam watched as Kate stepped back into the tray and bent and lifted a bundle of clothing in her arms, which she carefully handed to the young man.

Kate's voice rang with grief as the young man carried the bundle over and stood before the priest.

"Here is your *Toki-Moai!* Measure the cost carefully!"

She sank to her knees in the cart and buried her head wearily in her hands. The priest examined the bundle, and then signalled to the standing army. A path opened up between the ranks and he and the young man disappeared down it, gently cradling the bundle as the gap closed over like shifting quicksand and the army began to disperse.

Mirayam sought out Hawklight for an explanation, but all he did was shake his head sadly and led his mount from the field.

CHAPTER 19

Three months later.

The students ambled back across the training ground covered in dust and sweat. Mia was chatting animatedly with Olivia, and Jackson and Ethan were involved in a deep discussion over defensive tactics against a new move that Mirayam had just taught them. Sigrid walked alongside Kate, but neither spoke.

Since that day on the battlefield, Kate seemed to have lost her spark. Sometimes she was distant and apathetic, and yet equally she could explode in a fit of furious temper that would die away just as quickly and leave her startled and embarrassed by it all. Her friends had rallied around and excused her behaviour because they knew the cause though none could comprehend the sense of loss she had experienced—first Jaime, then her mother.

They had sought out Mirayam's advice, but for once their mentor was unable to help.

"She has to find closure in her own way, in her own good time," Mirayam would say. "But for now, just be there for her, be the way you have always been with her, and one day she will thank you for it."

But not today. Sigrid had been Kate's sparring partner and had surprised Kate with a new and unexpected move in the routine they had been practising. But Kate had reacted instinctively in a way none of the others had seen; she had easily parried the blow and had unleashed a killing shot that she had only just managed to pull at the last moment so that the blast had rocketed harmlessly above Sigrid's head.

Both had been unnerved by the incident: Kate more so, because she had nearly decapitated her friend while Sigrid had been alarmed at the raw savagery that continued to lurk just below the surface with Kate. Kate had apologised profusely and refused to take any further part in the training.

No one mentioned anything to Mirayam that evening. She had been caught up in another one of Elward Carter's interminable meetings. He had succeeded in the guise of elder statesman and had been nominated to broker a treaty between Hornshurst and Cherath. He had bitten off more than he could chew, and used the pretext of Council meetings to tap Mirayam's wisdom and insights and call them his own.

"I'm surprised he hasn't recalled Hawklight," said Jackson, while they were gathered in the courtyard, chatting and relaxing in the sultry warm air of early evening.

The mention of his name jolted Kate. She had been brooding and preoccupied and had tuned out of the conversation. She hadn't seen Hawklight since that day on the field when he'd walked his mount out of sight and out of her life. She discovered Elward Carter had selected him to lead an expedition to some distant part of the planet, and had been dispatched to organise the journey even before the army of Hogarth had left the field for home. No one had heard from him since, not even Mirayam.

Kate excused herself and headed up to her room. She no longer shared a room with Sigrid. She'd begun awakening in the night, tossing and moaning or screaming from nightmares that ripped the peace from her slumber. She'd lash out in her sleep or wake with a start to find Sigrid holding a cold towel to her forehead. It wasn't fair on either of them, so she'd asked Mirayam if she could move.

Her world had finally come apart at the seams.

Mirayam shook her gently awake early the following morning. Kate yawned and rubbed the sleep from her eyes. She'd had a better night but still felt shattered and drawn.

"There is someone downstairs to meet you," said Mirayam.

Kate collapsed back on her pillow. It was probably one of Carter's lackeys since he'd been trying to showcase her for the upcoming treaty signing.

"When you're ready," said Mirayam as she closed the door behind her.

Kate grumbled before throwing on a cloak and running her fingers through her hair in a half-hearted attempt to look presentable.

Kareem was waiting for her at the bottom of the stairs, and she squealed and leapt the final few steps and landed in his arms. She took him by surprise because he'd been the focus of Sigrid's and Olivia's attentions since he'd entered.

He laughed and twirled her off her feet in a circle, then stopped and held her at arms length, appraising her. She saw a momentary frown crease his forehead and then he smiled again and murmured, "It's great to see you again."

"Kate, where are your manners?" Sigrid laughed.

Kate beamed at them. "Captain Kareem El-Amin, these are my two nosy friends, Sigrid Rasmussen and Olivia Martin."

They shook hands. Olivia batted her eyelids at him, and Kate rolled her eyes.

There was an awkward moment before Kareem coughed and said to Kate, "Is there somewhere we can talk?"

The girls took the hint and excused themselves.

"Nice meeting you, Captain."

"Call again. We've heard so much about you."

Kareem smiled and looked sideways at Kate. "Don't mind them," she said as she took him by the arm, "they're always like that." She led him out into the courtyard, which was empty this time of the morning, and they sat on one of the seats.

"How's Mum?" she asked.

He looked away, stared at the ground and began to fidget.

"That's the reason I've come," he said. "The *Toki-Moai* has been repaired, and the priests are ready to move the ancients to their new home. Your mother has been holding out, but she only has a little time left. She will be joining the ancients, but she has asked to see you one more time before she leaves."

Kate faltered.

"I don't know if I have the strength to face her one more time," she said. "I've been trying to let her go for the last three months."

Kareem took her hand in his. "Is that really what you want me to tell her?" he asked.

Kate bit her lip. *I'm such a coward!* she thought. "Of course not," she replied. "Let me gather a few things together and say goodbye to the others."

Siobhan was propped up with pillows so that she could gaze out through the window to the garden outside her room. She had precious few reserves remaining and slept for long periods during the day to conserve her failing energy, but her mind was as clear and strong as ever. She longed to walk in the garden, to smell the fragrant scents and admire the rush of colour and vigour that bordered the pathways.

She had no regrets. She had been ready to lay her life on the line so many times before, and it need only have taken one well-aimed pulse from a staff to scatter her into oblivion. It was the way of the warrior: to live hard and die young.

She was about to join the exalted few whose knowledge and wisdom had made the city resplendent in its heyday. There were soldiers among them, and she had spent much of her time in their company lately. They were fine men and women, and they welcomed her with open arms into their ranks. She was ready, but there was one final task, so she had apologised to the ancients for the delay and had stubbornly refused to comply with the priests until she had met one final time with her daughter.

The door to her room opened, and a priest shuffled in and bowed.

"Your visitors have arrived," he said.

"Show them in, please."

Kareem entered first, leading Kate by the hand. He had hardly left Siobhan's side and knew how she had deteriorated over time, and so he knew to hold Kate close.

Kate saw her mother for the first time in months. She had shrunken to the size of a ten-year old child, and her skin was so translucent that Kate could almost see through to the pillows beyond. Kate almost toppled with the shock, and she leaned in to Kareem for support. He put his arm about her shoulder and led her across to the bedside.

Siobhan watched her daughter's face. Kate was shocked and horrified, naturally, but not repulsed, and she bravely fought back the tears so that she could be strong for her mother. She sat on the edge of the bed and reached across and took Siobhan's withered hand in hers.

"Mama," she whispered, and smiled. She saw the vivid green eyes, and she remembered her mother for the proud, strong, beautiful woman she had been.

"My darling, thank you for coming." Siobhan glanced towards Kareem who nodded and turned and left the two of them to be alone.

"How've you been?"

Siobhan lifted her frail hand and examined it. "What's to complain about?" she replied, and the absurdity caused both women to giggle aloud. Kate sniffed and fell silent, never taking her eyes off her mother.

"Seriously?" Siobhan continued. "It's a whole new journey for me, and I've already met some incredible people. There is so much to learn from them, and I'm honoured to be a part of it. Who'd have thought a housewife from Shepherd's Bush could come this far?

My life is not over, Kate. It has just changed. The saddest part is that I have only just met you and I have to leave you behind once more and I make no apologies for being that selfish."

"It's just not fair. I don't want you to go, and I'm not sorry for that either."

"Of course. But be happy for me, and you'll know where I am and that I will always be safe."

Kate bit down on her lip, but she squeezed her mother's hand gently in reply.

"How is Captain Hawklight these days?"

Kate shook her head, and this time, a tear trickled from the corner of her eye.

"I don't know. I haven't seen him. He's away . . . doing something . . ."

"Look at me, Katie. The time for pushing people aside is past, don't you understand? What's done is done. Would you rather it was Kareem lying here instead of me? Would you have preferred a war and countless, needless deaths because we failed? Hawklight would not have shot The Magician with me as a shield—he'd have let him escape rather than hurt me. You saved us all, Kate. *You saved us all!* Don't punish yourself because of it. Forgive yourself, please; let that be your gift to me.

I look at you, and I'm so proud of the woman you've become. But this world is such a hard place already without you making it harder. Take happiness where you can find it and *live* your life, promise me that. Make amends and get on with it."

Kate looked to the ceiling and took a deep breath and slowly exhaled. Siobhan watched her daughter, watched the way her words sunk in and took hold and knew that, despite the internal struggle, her words would win out in the end. Kate was too strong. Perhaps the road to recovery could begin here. All her daughter needed was a gentle guiding hand.

"You know," she said, "all the time I've been here, Kareem has sat by my side, and all he ever did was talk about you. I'm so pleased you're here because it might go some way towards just shutting him up finally."

Kate smiled.

"He likes you, you know that."

"He has his moments," Kate agreed.

Siobhan nodded and smiled. "I have something for you," she said. "There's a box in the drawer of the dresser. Fetch it for me, if you would."

Kate slid the drawer open. Inside was a small black box that fitted neatly in the palm of her hand. She held it out to Siobhan who waved it away and said, "Open it."

Kate prised the lid up. Inside was an unassuming golden ring, inset with three small, glistening gems.

"This is from me to you," Siobhan whispered. "Something to remember me by. Wear it, and know that I will always be with you.

Kate slipped the ring over her finger. It was warm to the touch.

"Thank you, Mama." She leaned forward and kissed away the tear that had trickled from her mother's eye.

"I'm very tired," Siobhan said at last, "but there is one thing left that you can do for me."

"Mama, anything!"

"Then lift me out of this damn bed and carry me out for one final walk through my beautiful garden."

The two old priests carried the *Toki-Moai* between them and stepped out on to the balcony. They raised the statue above their heads and were met by a tumultuous roar of approval from the crowd of citizens who had crammed the main square to catch a glimpse of it.

Kate stood proudly to one side, just inside the room. The talisman had squeaked at her as it had been carried past and she smiled. She felt Kareem's arm about her shoulder, and it no longer felt strained and unfamiliar.

The shouting and cheering continued long after the priests had left the balcony, reverently transporting the *Toki-Moai* to a new, secure wing of the Capitol building. Kate could still hear them celebrating as she sat with Kareem on a bench in her mother's garden.

"What now?" he asked her.

"I . . . I don't know. I need time to . . ." She faltered. Kareem pulled her close to him, and she rested her head on his shoulder.

"Stay. Take a week or so," he suggested. "Use your mother's room. There's no need to keep running. And then? Well, I guess you'll know when you're ready to make the next move."

So Kate stayed on. They battled her grief together until the sadness lifted and strength of purpose returned. It was time to move on once more.

She and Kareem were seated on the same bench. He smiled at her.

"It's time, then?"

She shrugged and returned his smile. "I guess I'll head back tomorrow morning. There are a few things that still need to be cleared up. How about you?"

"I don't know. I can't remember a time when I wasn't serving under your mother. I'm an unemployed bodyguard. Maybe I'll travel. I've said before that Hogarth seems like it would be an interesting place to visit."

She nailed him with those clear blue eyes.

"Maybe you could tag along with me," she suggested.

"Yeah," he replied. "That way I could get to meet Olivia again."

Kate burst out laughing.

EPILOGUE

The two mounted figures meandered down the path that led from the Great Forest, across the flat grassland and on to the arched stone bridge that spanned the ravine in front of the city.

Kate had returned home at the end of a slow, pleasant journey from Hornshurst where the healing had begun. Kareem rode alongside her, and the steel from the *shuriken* knives sheathed in his new bandolier glistened in the sunlight.

They made their way through the central part of the city and dismounted outside the gate to the home that she shared with Mirayam and the other students. She rapped the familiar pentangle-shaped code against the wood and the gate swung open.

"We're home," she announced. No one replied, which wasn't unusual. The house was mostly unoccupied during the day.

"They're probably up on the training field," she said to Kareem. "Drop your gear here and we'll go look for them."

They shut the gate behind them, and Kate turned down the side streets, using the familiar short cut which led along the inside of the city wall and eventually out on to the fields where the soldiers exercised.

The path took them past the disused stall that was the entry point to the empty cellar on the other side of the Great Chamber. Kate noticed the rusted padlock had been removed, and the door of the stall hung slightly ajar. That could mean only one thing: the students were tucked inside and eavesdropping on the affairs of state once again.

"Come on," she whispered to Kareem, "they must be inside. I've got to show you this!"

She took his hand and ducked beneath the low door. In the dim light, they could just make out the shadowed form of Ethan and Mia, waiting at the base of the shaft of the old freight elevator that was raised by a chain and pulley system and used to haul armaments up into the cellar.

She turned and placed a finger over her mouth, signalling to Kareem that noise echoed down here, and they needed to move quietly.

Ethan crept towards them and met them halfway.

"What's up?" she whispered excitedly.

Ethan was deadly serious which wasn't like him at all. Kate suddenly experienced an uneasy feeling of dread.

"What?" she demanded.

"Carter has convened the Great War Council again," said Ethan. "They're talking with a couple of soldiers, debriefing them."

"What happened?"

"All we know so far is that they were part of a platoon escorting an expedition up in the mountains way south of here. Something happened—they were ambushed! They were blown off the path into the bush, so they don't remember anything.

When they came to, all that was left were smoking uniforms lying along the path. They managed to escape back down here to report, and have only just arrived ahead of you. Mirayam was called out to the meeting, so we all ducked away to hear what happened. The others are still upstairs, listening in."

Kate waited. Ethan hadn't finished. He shot her a look of alarm through the gloom of the dark stall.

"Kate, Hawklight was in command of the platoon. He's been killed, and we don't even know who did it or why!"

ACKNOWLEDGEMENTS

*J*ve discovered that writing a book is an intensive and individual pursuit, especially if the book is a self-published affair. There are no teams of editors to provide the finesse, no agents to market the product, and no publishers willing to take the risk of printing thousands of copies destined for bookshops around the globe. That's all still part of the dream, as is the movie franchise.

However, there are still a number of people I'm indebted to.

I want to thank Jan Sintes—my sister—for selflessly spending time proofreading the original draft. She is, in the words of her daughter, 'lethal' when it comes to picking up typographical errors, commenting when a description makes no sense whatsoever, or noting I have used the same sentence on pages 46, 67 and 132. As a result, I'm certain this second book in the trilogy will read more fluently and have markedly fewer mistakes than the first by the time it is published.

I want to thank *all* the friends who purchased the first book in the series to stave off the embarrassment of no initial sales on release—Wendy, Pennie, Julie S and Jeff spring to mind—and whose positive words of encouragement were enough to spur me on to consider extending the story of Kate into a trilogy.

ALAN CUMMING

I want to thank the people at Trafford Publishing for the package of support they provide for self-publishing authors. The quality of the product and the cover design are a part of the fantastic deal, and I would recommend them to others who also have a story to tell and are in search of a vehicle to convey it.

Finally, I want to thank my wonderful wife, Sue Skye, who has always been unfailingly supportive of all my writing ambitions, however large or small. Without her, Kate would just be a faded figment tucked away in my subconscious, never to have seen the light of day.

Alan Cumming
March 2013